"MOTHER!"

For a moment I felt dizzy. I was confused, disoriented. I closed my eyes and steadied myself on a table.

When the pain lessened, I opened my eyes again. I took a few steps forward, stepping right in front of the woman. She looked up and dropped her book.

"Elizabeth," she said in a shocked whisper. She backed away. Then she started to run.

When I followed, she stopped and turned toward me, tormented. "No, no, no!" she said, with tears in her eyes. "Don't follow me, I beg you! *I beg you!*"

Other Avon Books by
Susan Berman

Fly Away Home

SUSAN BERMAN

SPIDERWEB

AVON BOOKS ◆ NEW YORK

AVON BOOKS
A division of
The Hearst Corporation
1350 Avenue of the Americas
New York, New York 10019

Copyright © 1997 by Susan Berman
Published by arrangement with the author
Visit our website at **http://AvonBooks.com**
Library of Congress Catalog Card Number: 96-94950
ISBN: 0-380-78180-8

First Avon Books Printing: April 1997

AVON TRADEMARK REG. U.S. PAT. OFF. AND IN OTHER COUNTRIES, MARCA REGISTRADA, HECHO EN U.S.A.

Printed in the U.S.A.

RA 10 9 8 7 6 5 4 3 2 1

In memory of my beautiful mother, Gladys Berman,
born Elizabeth Lynell Ewald
September 7, 1919–February 12, 1958

Our time together was much too short.

ACKNOWLEDGMENTS

In loving memory also of my mother's lovely cousin and dancing partner, Lorelei Hjermstad, who always kept my mother's flame alive by sharing all her stories with me of the years they danced together as The Evans Sisters in Minneapolis. I'd like to thank my cousins Tom Padden and Raleigh Padveen for all their kind words about my mother over the years.

Thanks to my fabulous agents, Charlotte Sheedy and Neeti Madan, without whom none of my books could happen. And special appreciation to my wonderful editor, Carrie Feron—an editor and also a mother, the best of both worlds. Special thanks to Ann McKay Thoroman.

1

When I was nine, I went to my mother's funeral. But she wasn't dead. I knew it then, I know it now. Twenty-six years later, I'm still positive my mother is alive. She's out there, somewhere . . . and she's looking for me.

We were a Mob family. After my father died, his partners didn't want to give his widow and child his estate, the twenty million dollars that was our fair share. They offered to settle with my mother for a penny on the dollar. In return, she threatened to turn them in to the authorities, for crimes she knew they had committed. They warned her that if she didn't sign off on the will, they'd settle all right, not in money, but in blood.

Her death certificate read "suicide by barbiturate overdose." Most people thought she had been murdered. At the funeral, they told me I was too young to see her body; her coffin was closed. The funeral consisted of my uncle Charles, my best friend Donna Mason, also eleven, her parents and me. The rabbi said my mother "was with my father now."

They placed her coffin in a drawer in the mortuary. The funeral director told me that when the nameplate came back, it would say, "Lorelei Stein, September 7, 1937–February 23, 1970. Beloved wife and mother." I still vividly remember the last time I saw her. She was pale, her long fragile hands shook. She was a beauty even without makeup, with lush, black curly hair, naturally red lips.

"Elizabeth," my gentle mother said, stroking my long, straight black hair, "you're a big girl now, I'm very proud of you. I know how much you miss Daddy. I do, too." She stopped to wipe the tears out of her cloudy, dark brown eyes.

"Now listen to me very carefully. You're going to visit your uncle Charles for a couple of weeks. I will never leave you. So we won't say good-bye." I threw my arms around her, kissed her creamy white cheek. I never saw her again.

On the way to her funeral, Uncle Charles said, "She's not in that box, honey. You're going to see her again."

The day after her funeral, my father's faithful bodyguard, Lou Baskin, came to see me. He told me that instead of killing my mother, as he had been ordered by his new Mob bosses, he got her out of the country. He told me never to tell anyone or he would be killed. I didn't.

Two weeks later, Lou's body was found. The death certificate said, "suicide by barbiturate overdose." Uncle Charles died a year later, I never got to ask him what he really meant that day. I told all this only to Donna, my closest friend. She interprets it all as mere attempts to comfort a child, not proof that my mother is alive.

Mob crimes against widows are usually covered up. There was, of course, no investigation, no charges. I was raised by distant cousins in Los Angeles. They told me she was dead, but I didn't believe it.

I haven't stopped looking for my mother, fantasizing about her every minute. She's the phantom who haunts me constantly. Her shadow shades the bright sky every sunrise; her visage nestles in the clouds in the afternoon; her profile sleeps in the moon at night.

I'm thinking of her more than ever, now that I've moved back to Los Angeles after living in Rome for many years. My father was a mobster in Chicago for most of his life, but he met my mother when he was older, semiretired, living in L.A. This is where I was raised.

I lived abroad, in Italy, until recently, when my entire life changed. My adored husband, Paolo Manganaro, died of a heart attack. We met as students at UCLA. My friends were scandalized that I entered into a serious romance with a foreigner, but that was one of the attractions. It was never one of my conscious goals to marry an Italian, and move to Italy. But when the opportunity presented itself, it seemed like the perfect solution to so many problems.

By then, I had grown sad, waiting so long for my mother to find me. That became my obsession. Donna even sent me to a therapist to discuss it. I went once, never went back. I graduated from college, and had every intention of becoming an art history professor.

But I never took an easy breath. Memories of my mother and my father were everywhere—they tore me apart. I still missed them in a raw, searing pain without end way. Periodically, rude former associates of my father's contacted me to sign various papers. I assumed I was signing off investments that should have been mine. But I never questioned them. These meetings were always sinister, brief.

A check came for me in a plain envelope each month, signed by a bank. There was no return address, no one to contact. I was told I would get a thousand dollars a month for the rest of my life. When I died, the annuity would end.

The underworld my father had lived in, although I did not know it as a child, now seemed black, murky, infinite, most of all, threatening. I was costing someone a thousand dollars a month, someone who could find a better use for that cash. I felt that at any moment the Mob might swallow me with its huge, pernicious, anonymous mouth.

It's not that life in Italy as a wife and mother totally fulfilled me. In some ways, it was like going back in history, but I figured it was already much, much more than I deserved. I was responsible for what had happened to my mother.

She was not a materialist; money meant nothing to her, even though my father had so much of it. In fact, she wanted him to get out of his business, but he was in a business that you didn't just leave at will. She wanted my father's estate only for me.

My mother wouldn't have known what to spend such a great sum of money on anyway; she wasn't a consumer if she wasn't buying me clothes. Her greatest joy was watching robins take a bath in the white, stucco birdbath in front of our house.

Her little Yorkshire terrier, Brenda, meant more to her than the expensive diamond jewelry that my father bought her. She always thanked him, tried it on, then quickly put it in the safety deposit box. She never wore his gifts of a mink coat or sable stole. I don't know if she was an early animal rights activist or just embarrassed, but they hung in the storage closet in mothballs.

It was because she loved me that she was marked for death, that she had to live out her days alone. I could never repay her, return her life to her as it should have been lived.

I gave birth to Jane Lorelei ten years ago. I'm trying to raise my daughter the same way my mother raised me, selfless, loving, honest. I read her the same stories, sing her the same songs. I pay homage to my mother in this way.

Paolo was a loving family man, devoted to me, to Jane. He was from a very wealthy family. This, at first, was a shock to me. He never wore anything but black jeans and old sweaters on campus, lived austerely. He was studying for his M.B.A., so that he could run his family's business, which turned out to be an empire.

I knew none of this until we got engaged, then I went home with him to meet his family. They were traditional aristocrats; Paolo never would have accepted me working outside the home. My life revolved around his. Any dreams I had of being a university professor became unrealistic.

I settled in some ways, but still felt the victor since I have that shroud of guilt always on me. Yet something was always missing. Was it a piece of me forever rendered mute by my decision to hide behind matrimony? Or was it the part of me that only my mother could bring to life? I'll never know.

Time does have a way of distancing you

from emotion. Since I've been back, I see my childhood more in terms of filmy reverie than of bad dreams. I bought a small house with an attached garage in Westwood on Wellworth, near the house I had lived in with my parents. Jane is in fifth grade at Fairburn Avenue Elementary School, where I went. I walk her there every day, after I pack her lunch box, just as my mother did.

Money solves a lot of problems, but it doesn't solve all of them. Paolo left me several million dollars; believe me, I'm very grateful. At this time in America, I would be happy just to have a house. I have so much, I plan to live simply, leave most of the money to Jane someday.

And I'll help Donna, if she ever needs it. She's the reason I had the courage to come back to L.A. She's been more like a sister to me than a best friend. I've been fascinated by her since the first time we met, when we were five years old.

It was at the Beverly Wilshire Hotel, as it was known then, in the sixties. Our fathers knew each other. The Masons were visiting from Canada, staying there, as we were, while renovations were done on our house.

I loved that hotel. It was so grand, sparkling with huge floral arrangements of orange and green birds of paradise everywhere. The large mirrored elevators had operators named Inez and Phoebe, who wore maroon suits. I spent all my time riding up and down.

On that day, we were eating lunch in the hotel coffee shop. My father was eating his usual, a small steak well-done with tomato slices, always watching his weight. My mother never ordered anything but a club sandwich, which she fingered with long, red-manicured Revlon's Fire and Ice fingernails but didn't eat. All she did was smoke, drink black coffee.

I hungrily consumed a cheeseburger drowned in big globs of catsup, drank a chocolate malt. Then I climbed down, ran over to the drugstore part of the restaurant, where they had a plethora of fancy perfume and nail kits. I liked to smell the perfumes, especially Joy, which my mother wore, and Zizane, which my father favored. Joy came in big, cut crystal bottles.

I asked the salesgirl to take down the large sample bottle for me. Then I grabbed it with both hands, held it up high, toward the chandelier, so I could see the light refracted. Finally, I smelled it, then dabbed it behind my ears while the salesgirl patiently smiled. She sighed with relief when I handed it back.

Next, I went to the glass case containing the nail kits; some were open. My mother laid down the rules, I could handle the new cases but not open them. I loved the smell of soft leather. And I could look at the sample case, use the silver nail file, but not the scissors or clippers.

My mission completed, I grabbed two packs of butterscotch lifesavers, told the salesgirl to "charge it to our room." It wasn't till years later that I realized that every time I did this, my father later bought some Joy or a nail kit as a way of apologizing to the salesgirl.

I raced back to the table. It was then that I saw Donna for the first time. She was a perfect little lady in a matching red coat and hat. She had on black patent Mary Janes, was delicately eating one scoop of vanilla ice cream. Her hair was black, curled in a bob. I was wearing jeans, a Western shirt, cowboy boots. My long black hair was braided in pigtails, tied with striped satin ribbons. I was a rambunctious tomboy.

"Elizabeth, this is Donna Mason. She's your age, she's from Canada. And these are her parents, Fred and Elaine," my mother said.

"How do you do?" Donna inquired, in a Canadian accent. I was intrigued. She looked like one of my many elegant, feminine Madame Alexander dolls that I never played with, preferring loud cap guns and wood building blocks instead.

Later, my parents let me go up to her room. She welcomed me into the living room of the suite. Her parents were in the bedroom.

"Hello. I'm mad at my father," she said, as I walked in.

"Well, tell him," I said. My mother encouraged me to be forthright.

"Oh no," she said. "I have a better way." She quickly took off her underpants, lifted her leg like a dog, peed on the coffee table. My mouth fell open. Then Donna put her underwear back on.

"They're having friends over, and they'll have to smell it," she said.

"You're going to get in trouble."

"No, I'm not. They'd never believe that I did it, they'll just call the maid and yell at her," she said, smiling a malicious grin. A few minutes later, her parents walked in.

"Fred, do you smell something?" her mother asked. Fred took a cigar out of his mouth, inhaled.

"Smells like piss. I'm calling the goddamn maid!" he shouted. Donna looked down primly as her father grabbed the telephone, bellowing loudly into it.

"Why don't you girls go into Donna's room? The maid has to clean up here," Elaine said.

"Yes, Mommy," Donna said. We went into her room, where she showed me all her beautiful clothes. She said she was going to be very rich someday, live in a mansion and have her own little girl.

The next time I saw Donna, we were seven. She was no longer rich, we still were. The Masons had lost all their money, moved to L.A.

They lived in a small, dark Spanish house, south of Sunset. North of Sunset is the more desirable area in Beverly Hills.

The house had thick old curtains in it, not much light at all. The living room smelled like cigars. My parents brought a huge basket of cheese and crackers that day. Elaine seemed embarrassed about the plates and knives that she handed us.

"We had to sell the silverware and the china," Donna whispered to me. Later in her room, she told me that this wasn't really their house, it was "rented," they would be moving soon. When we were leaving, Elaine thanked us for coming.

"It's been hard on Donna," she said. "She'll have to go to a public school for the first time, I hope she likes it." My mother, who loved all children, looked at Donna.

"Donna, I'm taking Elizabeth to get some clothes for school, would you like to come?"

"Oh, no, thank you," Donna said, airily.

"Donna, be polite!" Elaine said, then by way of explanation to my mother, "We couldn't afford to get her any new clothes this year, she's very upset."

"Donna," my mother said, "I saw a couple of dresses at Pixie Town in Beverly Hills that would look wonderful on you. Let me take you shopping with Elizabeth." Donna looked as if a miracle had occurred.

She went everywhere with us for the next

two years. Her family never moved out of that house. By the time we got to UCLA she was always fighting with her parents, couldn't wait to get away from them. She was estranged from her parents halfway through college. They refused to pay for her college tuition and dorm, so I paid for it. We were roommates, anyway.

As I grew older, I became withdrawn. Maybe it was the loss of my parents, or maybe it is who I would have become anyway. But Donna had enough spirit and connection to life for both of us. When I called her from Italy, told her of Paolo's death, she flew over immediately. I was dazed with grief. She took charge.

"Elizabeth, you have to come back to Los Angeles to raise Jane. Italy is beautiful, but it's a foreign country; you'll be lost here. Who will you meet?" Donna asked.

"I don't want to meet anyone. I'm not interested in remarrying; I just want to be with Jane," I said.

"Fine," she said, patting my shoulder. "Then come home and let her see what it's like to be an American. I want you both to get to know my son, Valentine, better, especially since you're his godmother; he's fourteen now. And you'll get to know my husband Randall, too. We're your only family now, Elizabeth."

She was right. Los Angeles called to me

with her siren song. I wanted to go home. I missed the order of the streets, my familiarity with them, the fact that I could get anywhere on Sunset Boulevard, Wilshire, Olympic or Pico, the parallel streets that traversed the city. And I missed living in a city full of the memories of my mother, proof that we had once had a life together.

So two months ago, I moved back home. I hoped my life here would be restful. I had memories, so much to think about, sort out, a constant internal dialogue between the past and the present. The time would be filled with motherhood. I asked of the future only that it be tranquil and safe. How different it all turned out.

Things began to go wrong very soon. The first incident seemed like a small annoyance at the time, but it started a deadly chain of events. If only I had known then, maybe it all could have been averted. It was on a day that classes had started late for Jane.

I returned home after walking her to school. I stress education to her so that someday she can support herself. Who knows how much our estate will be worth in twenty years? Or even if it will still be there? If anyone knows that inherited wealth is a dangerous illusion, it's me.

I looked at a picture of my mother that was on my mantel. She was holding me when I was a baby. I was losing myself in memories of the past, when Donna knocked.

I looked out the window. Her black Mercedes was parked at the curb. I opened the door. There she was, strikingly pretty as usual, her back ramrod straight, her attire stylish. Her black hair curled at her shoulders, she was in black designer pants, a black turtleneck cashmere sweater, matching blazer.

"Hi, Donna, I'm almost ready for lunch," I said, letting her in. She walked past me with her usual brisk efficiency.

"Elizabeth, we've got a twelve-thirty at a new place in Malibu. Hurry up, they don't hold reservations."

"I'm ready, I just have to grab my purse and a jacket," I said. We walked into my bedroom. Donna looked around.

"You know," she said, "I wish you had bought a house in Bel Air near me, or Brentwood."

"I love this house," I said. "Anything with two stories gives me a sense of my childhood. It's like the one we lived in over on Ashton when I was little."

"You've never known how to live grand, and you can afford it. Randall and I are going to sell Bel Air and get a bigger house," she said.

"We figure with the terrible real estate market, it should be the time to get a bargain. Randall is working on a big deal."

"What's wrong with the house in Bel Air?"
I asked.

"It's too small. I want a house I can entertain
in," she said. I took a thick, gold braid bracelet
that had belonged to my mother out of my
jewelry box and put it on.

"You're wearing that?"

"Yes, why?" I asked. Donna gave a sigh of
displeasure, sat down, lit up a filtered cigarette, took a drag.

"First of all, all good jewelry goes into a
safety deposit box. L.A. isn't safe anymore.
Our house in Bel Air has been broken into
twice. Thank God for the security system. Sec-
ondly, whenever you wear something of your
mother's, you wind up staring dreamily at it,
and you don't eat."

"You're right, but I won't stare at it today,
I promise."

"You shouldn't wear good jewelry. I don't
anymore, just my diamond earrings. Look,
I've just got them and a cheap watch on.
Everybody I know has been mugged," she
said.

"In broad daylight in Malibu? We're just
getting out of the car and going into the restaurant."

"Nowhere in L.A. is safe now. Times have
changed."

"Well, I'm scared of other things, not mug-
gers. Besides, I have my gun in my purse," I
said.

"You know, kidnapping really isn't a threat like it was in Italy. Who even knows you were married to Paolo here?"

"A lot of people. Italian kidnappers have been targeting families abroad. Paolo's aunt was kidnapped in London five years ago, and the family had to pay five million dollars in ransom to get her back. His family is very well known. You know that I had my lawyer get me a gun when I came back," I said, grabbing my purse.

"I know," Donna said, shivering. "Just keep the gun in your purse and don't let me see it. It scares me."

The restaurant was packed. People looked important, well connected. Several men and women had cellular phones. I noticed a man with a dark complexion in an expensive green silk suit, staring at me from a corner table. It made me uneasy.

"What's wrong?" Donna asked.

"It's probably just my imagination, but that man looks Italian, and he's looking at me," I whispered.

"Calm down. The chance of an Italian kidnapping you in Malibu is remote," Donna said, sarcastically. The fear wasn't realistic to her, but it was to me. I tried not to stare at him.

"This place is smoke free. I need my nicotine fix," she said.

"How long till we can be seated? We had a

twelve-thirty," she asked the good-looking all-American waiter/aspiring actor. He broke into a toothpaste smile.

"Five minutes max. They're clearing the table now," he said.

"I'm going to go outside for two minutes, have a cigarette. Want to come?" Donna asked me.

"No, I want to look at the view. It's been a while since I saw the Pacific Ocean," I said. As Donna walked outside, I went over to the window, unconsciously stroking my mother's gold bracelet as I stared at the waves.

My parents had friends in Malibu Colony when I was growing up. Then, it was a sun-drenched pocket of elegance, the whitish brown sand clean, soft, the water pure, fragrant, invigorating. I remembered my mother, smiling, tan, in a trim one-piece black bathing suit, holding my hand, walking me down the beach.

"Walking is good for our thighs, Elizabeth," she told me. I was about seven. We'd walk at least a mile before I'd ask her to do it. I would be exploding with anticipation.

"Mommy, skip rocks, please!" I finally begged. She'd search for a flat thin rock, then jump backward a few steps before she ran up to the surf, artfully tossing the rock. There it would go, once, twice, three times, wow! It skipped four times. No matter how patiently she showed me how to do it, I never mastered it.

I imagined her sitting in the sand with me building sand castles, finding shells to decorate my structures. Our arms were exactly the same color of tan, but she had dark hair on her forearms, just a little. She hated it. I was drowsy from the pungent memories of the smells that day, her Coppertone, the salty sea, a little hint of her Joy perfume, some Prince Matchabelli cologne that she let me wear.

"Elizabeth," Donna said. I swung around, hurried to her side.

"Our table's ready; it's over there," she said, leading the way. We sat down, and the waiter handed us menus.

"I can't wait till Randall gets back tomorrow. He's been gone a week," she said. The waiter brought wine.

"I ordered it before we sat down," Donna said, raising her glass.

"Let's toast our friendship. Thirty years and going strong," she said, smiling. I raised my glass, grateful to have her companionship in life's difficult journey.

"To us, Donna," I said, as we both drank a sip. She smiled, patted my hand, then pulled it away.

"I'm going to have the crab salad," she said.

"Could you order the same for me? I have to go to the bathroom," I said. As I walked across the restaurant, nostalgic thoughts of my mother threatened to overwhelm me again. I was drawn again toward the window, but resisted the spell.

When I got back to the table, the waiter brought our elaborate lunch plates. I reached down to make sure my purse was near my chair; I didn't feel it. I looked down.

"Donna, do you see my purse?"

"Oh no, did you leave it when you went to the bathroom? I went to make a call," she said, as she scooted her chair back to look for it.

"It was so stupid of me . . ." I said.

"Elizabeth, I hope you didn't have a lot of cash in it. Because someone stole it!"

2

I didn't care about the cash, but that black leather purse had belonged to my mother! I had so very few of her things. A friend of hers was kind enough to send me a box of her clothes after her funeral. There were two evening purses, one white satin, beaded, another a black velvet clutch. And there was the black leather purse. I had carried it for years, already had it restored twice.

"Don't worry, you can cancel the cards, you won't be charged for them," Donna said.

"No, it's not that . . . the purse was my mother's," I said.

"We can get another one like it," Donna said. Another one like it. I nodded. No one ever understood. I was seized with a terrible feeling of vulnerability. I pictured the purse being emptied quickly, tossed in a filthy trash bin.

My mother had touched that purse, used it! I shivered. It was almost as if her body was defiled. Skin was being torn off her arms. I couldn't protect my mother; now I hadn't even protected her purse.

"Let's just go. I'm not hungry anymore, Donna," I said. I looked around for the staring dark man, but he was gone. There was probably no connection. What would he want with my purse?

"Are you sure you want to go?"

"Yes, lunch is spoiled for me. Besides, I have to call the credit card company—I just carry one."

"I understand," Donna said, motioning for the waiter, then handing him her credit card.

"I guess I should report it to the police," I said.

"How much cash did you have?"

"About fifty dollars, and my car and house keys."

"Take my advice, forget the police. Just call the credit card company. The police department is an incredible hassle for fifty bucks, and nobody is going to rob your house. They probably already threw away the old purse. It's worthless," she said.

Worthless. Every inch of it was of priceless value because my mother carried it. I felt sick.

"I'm going to report it to the manager, just in case someone takes the cash, tosses the purse in a trash can here," I said. Donna shrugged. I reported the theft, gave the manager my phone number. We got into Donna's car just as her car phone rang. It was her son, Valentine.

"Again? Valentine, what happened? Fine, I'll be right there," she said, sounding upset as she handed me the phone.

"Call the credit card company. I have to stop at Valentine's school—he's in trouble again. He asked me to pick him up in the principal's office."

"What happened?"

"He told a teacher off. I never bothered you with this, but there have been constant problems," she said, lighting a cigarette, taking a long puff.

"That's why I haven't wanted you to see him yet. I hoped he would straighten out a little. Well, he probably won't, and you've already been home two months. This is the third time I've been called to the school. I just hope they don't kick him out."

"What do you think his problem is?"

"Being a fourteen-year-old boy, for one thing, and he has issues with Randall. He doesn't feel he's reliable. Randall is under a lot of financial pressure from his investors, and Valentine is too young to understand why he can't do all the father-son things. I can't seem to talk any sense into him; he even quit therapy."

Donna started the car. I called the credit

card company, reported the loss. Out of the corner of my eye, I thought I saw the Italian from the restaurant in a car near us. I whipped around, it was him in a silver car!

"Donna, it's the same man!" I said. She turned to look when we got to a stoplight, but he was gone.

"I swear it was him," I said.

"So what? Other people have a right to drive, it doesn't mean they're after you, Elizabeth, calm down." Maybe she was right; I was on edge.

We got to Valentine's school. A security guard checked Donna's identification before he let her into the exclusive private school in Brentwood.

"I'll go to the principal's office and send Valentine out to the car. I want to talk to his advisor alone. Do you mind?"

"No. I'm looking forward to seeing him. I haven't seen him for years," I said. Donna nodded, gave me a worried look, walked toward the school. I remembered Valentine as a tall kid. He was sensitive, introspective, used to like to be by himself. Although I saw him seldom, just when Donna brought him to Italy, I felt some rapport with him.

I hardly recognized the scowling adolescent who approached the car. He bore just a faint resemblance to the Valentine I had seen several years before.

"Valentine?" I asked.

"Hi, Elizabeth," he said, softly, almost defeated. He was still a good-looking kid, brown hair hanging gracefully over his eyes, taller, still lean, with pouty lips. His expression, though, was hostile, tormented. He opened the back door of the car, got in, slammed it, turned his face to the window.

"Bad day?" I asked, softly. He just looked down, miserable. There was a long silence.

"Can I do anything to help, Valentine?"

"Nobody understands. I just feel angry all the time."

"About everything?"

"Yeah, mostly about Dad. I know this is going to sound weird," he said, hesitated, then went on, "but I almost figured out how I could kill my father, but I couldn't get away with it."

"Kill him? You don't mean that?"

"Yes, I do. He keeps these barbells in his room, at the foot of the bed. I'd go in there in the middle of the night, bludgeon him to death, pretend it was a burglar," he said, seething with anger.

"But you're not going to do that."

"No, because I can't figure out how to do it without getting caught. He always leaves the security system on, so if there was a burglar, it would go off. He'd notice if I turned it off."

"That doesn't sound right, Valentine," I said, gently. "You've got to talk to someone about these feelings." At that moment, Donna got in the car, furious.

"That's it, Valentine!" she screamed. "This is the second school you've gotten kicked out of. I've had it." Valentine smashed his fist into the top of the car.

"I can't stand this. I have to drop you off and take him home," Donna said. I nodded, turned to look at Valentine, who had his eyes closed. His face was taut.

"Donna," I whispered, "should I try to talk to him?"

"No, just let me handle this," she said. "Wait, I forgot you're locked out. You'll have to come home with me."

"No, I have an extra key hidden in a Hide-A-Key under the seat in my car. And I have extra car keys inside the house. I'll be fine. I have to pick Jane up at school."

"Be sure to have the locks changed on your house, just in case," Donna insisted.

"That's a good idea," I answered. Not a single word was exchanged between Valentine and Donna on the way home. Her face was white as she skidded to the curb in front of my house.

"What are you going to do now?" she asked.

"Get Jane, then come right home, I guess."

"Good, I'll call you, I may have to talk to you about . . ." she said, nodding her head back toward Valentine. I gave her a quick kiss good-bye, got out; she sped away. I grabbed my house key from my car, went into the house.

Then I remembered the gun. It had been in my purse. Now it was gone. I'd have to get a new one. I took off my mother's treasured gold braid bracelet, put it in a safe place, glanced at the clock. It was almost three. I rushed out the door. Jane didn't like me to pick her up in the car. She liked to walk the few blocks home with me.

I felt a little shaky, it was the first time in years I had gone anywhere without my gun. I always felt more vulnerable when I was with Jane. I had to protect her. Paolo had had bodyguards for us. Here, I wanted Jane to grow up as normal as possible. I remembered how stifled I felt as a child, always surrounded by my father's "friends."

Did I have any Mace? No. Well, I'd get another gun. I started to walk toward the school, past the peaceful Spanish houses with the red tile roofs. This had always been a family neighborhood. Each street brought back warm memories of my childhood.

There it was—the big house with the huge expanse of lawn in the corner. When I was little, my mother got me a dog, Blackie, at the pound. He was part cocker spaniel, part everything else, full of energy. We used to run him on that very corner.

There was the brown ranch-style house that my mother's friend, Mickey, used to live in

She had danced with her in Hollywood, when they were young. I saw all the photos of them in their Carmen Miranda costumes and hats, ruffles upon ruffles. They were tap dancers. Mickey had a daughter, Sonia, a year older than I.

Sometimes after school we'd stop at their house. Both Sonia and I wanted to be dancers. My mother taught us the Bill Robinson time step on Mickey's hardwood floor. I still remember it; shuffle, stomp, shuffle, stomp, shuffle, stomp, stomp, shuffle, stomp.

I looked up at Mickey's former house. It had those graceful curved windows in the front that echoed the sloping arches of the house. It was a light cream color, like many of the Spanish houses. Two Iranian children played in the front yard; a white Mercedes was parked in the driveway. Mickey had moved away long, long ago. I allowed myself to enjoy a brief fantasy as I continued walking.

Mickey still lived there. My mother and I brought Jane over to meet her. My mother was now a proud grandmother, she held Jane's hand. When Mickey opened the door, she commented on how much the three of us looked alike. She noticed how Jane had my mother's smile.

"Mom, Mom, the teacher wants to talk to you," Jane yelled at me, dispelling my daydreams. She was the only person better in reality than in my fantasies. Wearing big pants and an oversize shirt with black Doc Martens boots, she already had her own style. She looked more like my mother than me, with that same black curly hair and creamy skin. I hoped she'd have Paolo's height, his slim build. So far, she did.

"Mom, hurry," Jane said, standing just inside the school fence, not venturing one inch beyond. I had trained her well.

"I'm coming, honey. What does she want to see me about?"

"Field trip," she said, taking my hand, leading me toward a classroom. We walked in. The walls were covered with student compositions, artwork. Jane's teacher, Ms. McKirdie, smiled at us.

"Hello, Mrs. Manganaro," she said.

"Hi, I hear there's a field trip pending?"

"Yes," she said.

"I volunteered you," Jane said.

"The parent who was supposed to help me went out of town," she said. "We're going to the County Art Museum in about three weeks, and the Simon Wiesenthal Museum of Tolerance the following week. Could I persuade you?"

"Of course—I can drive. I'd love to. My mother was the room mother here when I was in the fifth grade. I'm happy to help in any way. Come on, Jane, we have to go home."

"Thank you. Jane is doing beautifully, by the way," Ms. McKirdie said. I smiled, took

Jane's hand, led her down the hall.

"Which room was your homeroom?" she asked.

"Right over there. It was Mrs. Richler's room in those days," I said. Jane smiled, gave a quick skip. She liked the fact that we attended the same school.

As we exited the school, I saw a silver car parked across the street. I tried not to tense up when I saw the two men in it look at us. One resembled that man in the restaurant. As soon as they saw me, they drove away. I held Jane back for a minute to make sure the car was gone. Was I paranoid?

I took a deep breath, tried to stay calm, so as not to upset Jane. We walked slowly up and down the gentle hills on the way home. The car did not reappear.

"Mom, look at that lemon tree," Jane said, pointing to one that was completely covered with the oval yellow fruits. I thought of Uncle Bernie's lemonade tree, an imitation lemon tree in Uncle Bernie's Toy Menagerie in Beverly Hills when I was growing up. My mother used to take me shopping there. First we'd go in the back of the store, get a paper cup of lemonade from the fake tree. How I wished it was still there, so I could share it with Jane.

We turned the corner, started to walk to our house. A van was parked in front. Just as we got to our small wrought-iron gate, a tall man got out of the van.

"Mrs. Manganaro?" he asked. Who knew me here?

"Yes?"

"I'm Blue Calloway; you called me?" he asked. I called him? Who was this six-foot, thirtysomething man in paint-spattered overalls with thick blond hair hanging to his shoulders?

"From The Recycler? About painting your kitchen?"

"Oh, yes. I'm sorry, I blanked for a minute," I said, relaxing. I had answered his ad for a house painter, left my phone number, address.

"I expected you to call first," I said.

"Sorry. I was in the neighborhood, so it was just easier to stop by. Is this a good time?"

"I guess so. This is my daughter Jane. Jane, this is Blue," I said.

"Your name is a color," Jane said.

"That's right. It worked out because I'm an artist. I'm just glad my folks didn't name me Black or White," he said, smiling at Jane. We walked into the house. Jane skipped toward her room.

"Where's the kitchen?" Blue asked. I led him to it through the dining room.

"Congratulations," he said, looking around.

"For what?"

"This is the only kitchen I've seen lately that hasn't been redone in modern Italian for three hundred thousand dollars," he said. "Where are the shining copper pots, where's the old-fashioned-but-new oven?"

"Oh, I like it plain and homey, like our kitchen was when I was growing up."

"You grew up around here?" he asked. I nodded quickly, dismissively, then looked away. I didn't want to get too friendly. I couldn't help but notice how personable and warm he was. He was rangy, attractive in a loose, comfortable way. The sleeves of the blue wool crew neck sweater, under his overalls, covered his biceps like tight skin. He waited for me to say something.

"Oh, I get it, I overstepped my bounds?" he asked, laughing, like it was an amusing joke. He could have said it in a hostile way, but he didn't.

"I'm sorry, I don't mean to be rude. I'm just in a hurry."

"Should I come back another time?"

"No, no, I'm just flustered today. My purse was stolen this morning. I've been living in Europe. I guess I didn't realize things had changed here; there's more crime than when I left."

"My wallet was stolen last year," he said, with empathy. "Can I give you a ride somewhere? To get new car keys made up? To the bank?"

"No, that's taken care of, but I do have to go now and get some new house keys made," I said.

"Look," he said, with a twinkle in his eye, "I didn't mean to come on strong before. I wasn't coming on to you or anything. I have kind of a whimsical streak; I was just teasing. No hard feelings?" he asked.

"No, no problem," I said. Why did he make me nervous? There was just so much of him. Paolo and my father had both been medium-sized, compact men.

"Good," he said. "What do you want to pay me to paint this kitchen?"

"How much will it cost?"

"Whatever feels right to you."

"Don't you have a set price?"

"No. Whatever is fair. I do this to support myself, so I can do my art. It's not like I'm a professional kitchen painter."

"But you advertised in the paper. . . ."

"Relax, I can do it. I just mean I'm not a member of the house painters' union or anything. When do you need it done?"

"As soon as possible."

"No problem, I'll start immediately. Nice to meet you," he said, extending his hand. I shook it.

"See you," he said, as he walked through the living room, out the door. He didn't even wait for me to see him out. I forgot how casual things were in America.

I felt flustered. Was I attracted to him? How could I be? He was so different from Paolo. Maybe that was why. No one could compete with Paolo in the ways that he was manly. Blue was almost a different species. No, I wasn't interested in dating, so that couldn't be it. I had no desire to meet anyone. Paolo was my only love, and he was dead.

It was odd to ruminate about things that ordinary people thought about. Love, the possibility of meeting someone new, a daughter's homework. I felt carefree as I went upstairs to check on Jane. I was going to be able to handle life here. The following half hour was the last time I would ever feel that way.

I took Jane with me when I went to the locksmith to get new keys made. When we got home, she went up to her room. I went up to check on her after about fifteen minutes. She was watching television, her history book in her lap.

"Hungry? Want a snack?"

"Do we still have any pizza from last night?"

"Sure, but you have to eat an apple and drink some milk with it."

"OK," she said, hopping off the bed. I ran my hand through her wild hair, then she hurried ahead of me toward the stairs.

"Honey, you want to go to the movies this weekend with Donna and her son Valentine?"

"Which movie?" she asked, sitting down.

"I don't know, we'll look through the paper. When I was your age, my mother took me to see *Fantasia* at the Fine Arts Theater in Beverly Hills."

"You took me to see that movie back home, with the dancing ostriches?"

"That's right," I said, taking out the pizza. I opened the microwave, stuck it in, handed it to her when it was warm.

"Now what kind of homework do we have tonight?"

"Math, and I have to write an essay."

"Good, do what you can. I'll help you after dinner."

"OK, Mom," Jane said, walking out of the kitchen. It was 7:00 P.M. by the time I thought about dinner. The doorbell rang. I looked through the peephole; two men were on the porch.

"What is it?" I yelled through the door.

"I'm Detective Ralph Karowisc, homicide, Pacific area. I'm looking for Mrs. Elizabeth Manganaro," one of the men said. I opened the door immediately.

"Yes?"

"Please get your things and accompany us to the police station. We need to question you in connection with the investigation of a crime."

I was stunned.

"May we come in?" the detective asked. They walked in. He showed me his identification and introduced me to his partner, Detective George Fernandez.

"But what's this about? What crime?" I asked.

"We can't discuss that here. Once we get to the station, we can reveal that," he said. Jane had come out of her room. She looked scared.

"I can't leave my daughter here alone."

"Is there someone you can call?" Karowisc asked.

"Yes, my friend Donna Mason," I said, rushing to the phone, dialing her number. No answer.

"She's not home."

"Then we have two options. We can either take your daughter with us, or Detective Fernandez can stay with her here." Those were the options? Jane moved to my side, took my hand. I didn't want her at the police station.

"Can't you tell me what this is about? I'm sure you have the wrong person," I said.

"A gun registered to you appears to have been used in the commission of a homicide," Detective Fernandez said.

"What?" Then, I remembered. "My gun was stolen this afternoon. It was in my purse, which was stolen at a restaurant." They looked at each other.

"If that's true, then I'm sure we can eliminate you as a suspect. But you have to come with us," Karowisc said.

"Jane, will you stay with the policeman until I get home? It shouldn't be long."

"Yes," she said, in a small voice.

"Thank you, honey. Donna's number is in the Rolodex if you need to call her for anything." The ride to the police station was unnerving. Karowisc didn't talk to me. Once we got there, he took me into a small room in the Culver Boulevard station.

"Where were you today at approximately 4:00 P.M.?" Detective Karowisc asked.

"Today? I was at my daughter Jane's school, Fairburn Avenue Elementary School, picking her up."

"Where was your gun stolen?"

"At a restaurant in Malibu. I don't remember the name but I can call my friend later and get it for you."

"Did you file a police report?"

"No. I didn't have much cash in it, just my gun and a credit card. But I reported it to the restaurant's manager, in case the purse was found there. Who was murdered with the gun?"

"A woman was murdered in Venice with your gun."

"How horrible!"

"The victim is an unidentified Jane Doe at this point. Do you have any idea who stole your purse?"

"No, but it happened at about one-thirty."

"And someone saw you at your daughter's school?"

"Yes, her teacher, Ms. McKirdie, she teaches fifth grade at Fairburn School. And, of course, my daughter," I said. He wrote that down.

"Can you get me the name of the restaurant now?"

"No, my friend Donna will know, she's the one I just called for Jane; she isn't home. I'm sure I can reach her later."

"I want to describe the victim to see if you know her. She was shot in the face, so her features are not perfectly known to us," Karowisc said.

"She appeared to be around forty years old, Caucasian, about five-foot-five," he continued, "130 pounds, gray-and-black long hair. She was dressed in a torn black skirt, old dirty sneakers and a green sweater. She had no identification on her. Her purse, if she had one, was missing. We have to wait for the fingerprinting. She appeared to be one of Venice's homeless persons. Does any of this ring a bell?" A homeless woman?

"No, I'm sure I've never met her," I said. Karowisc nodded.

"Excuse me for a moment. Do you want some coffee?" he asked.

"No thank you. Do I . . . do I need a lawyer?"

"Not at this time. You're not a suspect. If you become a suspect, we will notify you of your rights," he said, as he went out of the room. For what? To check my alibi? What if the school was closed, what if the teacher had an unlisted phone number?

My gun had been used to murder a poor, unfortunate homeless woman. How many times it had pained me to see homeless people since I had gotten back to L.A., especially homeless women. Could it have happened to me if I hadn't married Paolo and the Mob didn't send me that $1000 a month? You never know. You're never truly safe from need. Things can change at any moment.

Murder! Was this my karma? Was I to hear that horrible word, murder, again and again? Was I always going to be recoiling from violence connected with me? Was I ever going to be allowed to enjoy the softness of life?

I remembered the feel of the smooth steel of the gun in my hand. I counted on it for protection, to preserve the sanctity of life. Now it had been used to destroy life, the life of a woman I didn't even know. I felt betrayed.

Was it part of a mugging? But who would mug a homeless woman? I was unnerved. The detective came back in.

"We're going to let you go now while we check your story. An officer will take you home. If you think of anything helpful, please call me," he said, handing me a card. "We will be keeping your gun since it was used in a crime."

I trembled visibly on the ride home. When we got there, I rushed in, grabbed Jane, hugged her and thanked Detective Fernandez as he left. I immediately called Donna to tell her what happened.

"How frightening!" she screamed into the phone. "What did I tell you about L.A.? It's as bad as New York City now."

"God, why did it have to be my gun? It's like I'm doomed or cursed or something. Not only was my purse stolen, but my gun was used to commit a murder. It's too weird."

"Nonsense. It's just your alienation thing acting up again. Your purse was stolen because we were stupid enough to leave it unguarded, in full view. And there are muggings and random shootings all the time here. It was just coincidence."

"Well, maybe, but I'm not convinced. What was the name of the restaurant again?"

"Pacifica. Look, I've got to go, I have some errands to do for Randall before I pick him up at the airport tomorrow."

I called Karowisc, gave him the name of the restaurant. Suddenly, I was exhausted. It seemed like there was no way I had the energy to go to the grocery store, shop for dinner. I didn't want to have servants like we had in Italy, but this was one time I questioned that decision.

"Jane? We have to go to the grocery store," I said. She came to the head of the stairs.

"Mom, I'm ten. I can stay home alone. All my friends' mothers leave them home alone during the day."

"Honey, I don't have the energy to argue. Just come on, it won't take long." She gave me an exasperated look and went to get her jacket.

I drove to the local supermarket. Jane and I walked up and down the aisles. Nothing sounded good to her. She finally said she'd eat roast chicken and mashed potatoes with canned peas, the small ones. We carried the bags to our car, drove home.

While I made dinner, I thought about the Italian man in the restaurant. Should I have told Detective Karowisc? But would my story about Paolo's family in Italy and the frequent kidnappings there sound farfetched? What to do? And it could have been the same car when I picked Jane up from school.

Life seemed overwhelming. I had to get on track again. At 2:00 A.M., I was fighting my constant hostile companion, insomnia. I always used this time to go over in my mind all the details of my mother's disappearance.

Was there anything I heard, when I was younger, that could tell me where she had gone? Was there some clue buried in my subconscious? Had she given me a hint the last time I saw her?

I went over every detail of our last days together in microscopic detail. But I came up with nothing. This agonizing replay was a weekly routine. I had tried hypnosis, every New Age "getting in touch with the past" technique, employed psychics in an attempt to remember anything meaningful about my mother's whereabouts. Nothing worked.

I fell into a fitful sleep. I dreamt that I saw my mother walking down the street in front of me. I followed her, calling softly, then louder. She didn't turn around, I started running after her, she ran faster. I finally got close enough to grab her. I clutched her shoulder, but my hand went through her! It was just an illusion. I woke up shaken, then stayed in bed until my alarm went off.

After I walked Jane to school, I drove to Donna's house, turned into Bel Air's west gate. When we were at UCLA, she used to drive me up these roads, saying that someday she wanted to live up here. She'd stop her car by the edge of a mountain, make me get out to look at the view with her.

"Imagine how powerful you'd feel if you lived on top of the world here," she'd say. I'd look at the smoggy view, get dizzy. She thought she had reached her goal when she married Randall and he bought the house in Bel Air. Only it was in the west gate, the newer section, rather than the east gate, where all the huge estates were.

And she certainly didn't live on top of the world, I thought, pulling up before a modest ranch house on a flat plateau. Her car was in the driveway. So was a black Jaguar, probably Randall's car.

I had met Randall Scott in college when

Donna met him, but I didn't know him well. She had brought him to Italy to visit, and I'd seen him a few times since I moved home. It was hard to form an opinion about him; he was elusive. To Donna, a husband was an absolute necessity; life was impossible without one.

While I was looking for love, she was looking for a practical match with financial support. She never wanted to be self-supporting, although she had the ability. She couldn't understand why I wanted a career. She was confused when I said I was happy with Paolo but felt unfulfilled, that I wanted to experience the world through my own reality, rather than through a man. She didn't empathize with these feelings. I knocked. Leticia, her El Salvadoran maid, answered the door.

"Is Donna home?"

"Elizabeth, is that you?" Donna yelled from upstairs.

"Yes. I'm sorry to just drop over, but it's important. Is this a bad time?"

"No, I'll be right down," she said. Randall walked into the entry hall. He was tall, handsome, with a determined look. He wore an Armani suit, carried a bulging briefcase.

"Hi, Elizabeth, everything OK?" he asked.

"Fine, I just wanted to ask Donna something."

"She'll be right down. We want to take you

to dinner, soon. Are you completely booked for the entire week already?''

"No," I said, smiling. The concept was ludicrous. I had every night free.

"I don't have any plans. I may never have any again."

"I doubt that," Randall said, smiling. "I'll have Donna arrange something. I've got to get to work," he said as he left.

I walked into Donna's living room, sat down before a blazing fire. There was new furniture—large overstuffed white brocade couches. She walked in, sank down into a big chair.

"Do you like the couches? We just got them."

"I do. Donna, you look completely stressed-out. I haven't seen you with that ponytail on your head since high school," I said.

"My hair frizzed when I picked Randall up at the airport. But that's not why I'm hysterical—it's Valentine. I'm trying to get him to agree to go to a new therapist."

"Is there anything I can help you with?"

"No, just go to lunch with us Saturday. Maybe you can talk to him. I don't know if I can drag him to a movie. What's up? Do you want Leticia to get you some tea?"

"No, I have to get back, a painter is coming over. I need to ask you what to do about something," I said.

"I wonder if I should have told the detective

about the Italian and the silver car? I think I saw the same car following us, remember? And I think I saw it again at Jane's school when I picked her up. It could be kidnappers from Italy, or it could be the Mob following me.

"You know I still get that check for $1000 every month. I don't even need it, but I don't know how to get rid of it. What do you think I should do about the car?"

"Well," Donna said seriously, "it could be someone from the Mob connected with your mother's death, somebody who thinks you will make trouble about the will," Donna said.

"My mother's disappearance, Donna. You know I think she's still alive."

"Yes, I know, dear," she said, as if saddened that I just couldn't accept that my mother was dead.

"If you want," she said, "I'll ask Randall. He knows law enforcement types. Let's get his opinion."

"Thanks, Donna, I'm worried about kidnappers and Jane," I said, getting up to leave. I kissed her good-bye.

3

I got home just as Blue pulled up in his van. He jumped out, carrying paint cans, brushes. He moved in a secure manner, comfortable in his skin. Was he comfortable in the world? I wasn't. I don't know why.

"Sorry to be a little late. I had to call my mother, it's her birthday. You know how mothers are, you can't get them off the phone," he said.

I felt sad. Who was calling my mother on her birthday? I always spent that day, September 7, wondering what she was doing. When I was a child I made her birthday cards and a host of childhood gifts; my handprint in clay, finger paintings that said "Mommy," lanyards, waxed paper with leaves pressed between them, to use as place mats.

She was always delighted, made me feel as f my little gifts were rare, valuable items.

Whenever I see a bottle of new, elegant perfume, I imagine that I have sent it to her as a birthday gift. I try to visualize her delight when she opens the gift, sniffs the scent.

"Did I say something wrong?" Blue asked.

"No, no, sorry. I was thinking of something, that's all."

"You looked so unhappy for a moment."

"I was just thinking of my mother's birthday."

"Forgot to call?" Blue asked.

"You might say that," I said, knowing I had to change the subject.

"Were you able to match the color in the kitchen? I'd like to see."

"I have everything right here," he said, cheerfully. I opened the door for him, followed him to the kitchen. He held up a swatch of paint to the wall—it matched.

"That's perfect. Go ahead, start, the kitchen is yours. We're planning to eat out for the next few days," I said. Later, when I went to get some water, he was sitting on the stairs, eating his lunch.

"Want part of my sandwich?" he offered, as if we were children at snack time. It was peanut butter and jelly.

"No, I'm going to take Jane out for some food later."

"Your daughter is cool, really alive."

"Thank you. Do you have children?"

"No," he said, looking down. Was he uncomfortable? "No, I don't. I was married once, but we didn't have kids."

"I didn't mean to ask something so personal," I said, suddenly shy.

"That's all right. Marriage, divorce, L.A. is the town of multiple marriages, it isn't personal. What about you? Are you married?"

"Widowed. My husband died six months ago," I said, feeling embarrassed. How did the conversation get so intimate? There was a silence.

"So . . ." he said, finally, "it shouldn't take me more than a few days."

"What?"

"The paint job."

"Oh, right. Can I get you a soda?"

"That would be great," he said, taking the last bite of his sandwich. I was happy to turn away from him, walk to the refrigerator. I felt myself blushing when I talked to him. When I came back with the soda, he was staring at the floor.

"You know, I find you interesting. There's something very feminine about you," he said, grabbing the soda from me. I didn't know what to say, compliments always made me uneasy. Should I be annoyed? I was flattered but anxious.

"You going to fire me for insubordination?" he asked, with a smile. "Better not. It's hard to find a good house painter. I guess I'm just trying to make a connection. I've been pretty isolated lately. You probably have better things to do than to talk to me."

I found his honesty charming, appealing, if it was honesty, not just a line. But why would he use a line on me? Surely he could do better than a thirty-five-year-old widow with a child to raise. When I was growing up in L.A., twenty-four was considered old for a woman.

"Why have you been isolated?"

"I've been working on a painting. It's all-consuming. It takes over and suddenly you realize you haven't seen anyone for weeks, except the people in the grocery store. It's the feeling that life everywhere is going on without you, since you are only living in your mind. Does that make sense?" he asked.

"I understand what you're saying," I said. He gave a quick nod, wiped his hands on a rag, started painting again. Was the conversation over? I waited a few moments to see if he would turn back around, continue talking, but he didn't.

Later, I walked past him on my way to the door. I had to pick up Jane.

"I have to leave at three-thirty today. I'll probably be able to work tomorrow," he said.

"Fine. I'm up early," I said. He started to wipe his paintbrushes.

"Do you have a lot of friends in Los Angeles?" he asked, as I opened the door.

"No, no I don't. I've been away a long time."

"Well, if you ever want to come over with Jane and see my studio, that would be great. I live in a guesthouse in Santa Monica."

"That might be nice. Thank you for inviting us," I said, quickly hurrying out the door. The fresh air felt good on my face. I couldn't deny that I was interested in Blue, however inappropriate it was. I hoped the feeling of attraction would go away. How long did it take to paint the kitchen? Once he left, it would probably be a case of out of sight, out of mind.

Since the kitchen was covered with a tarp, I took Jane out to dinner at a popular pizza kitchen in Beverly Hills. As we drove down Wilshire Boulevard, I remembered all the stores that my mother used to shop in on that street, long since gone.

Haggerty's and I. Magnin's had been two of her favorites. I pointed out to Jane the location of a restaurant where my mother used to take me, the famous Beverly Hills Brown Derby. It had a big plaster brown derby on the roof.

"There was an ice-cream parlor on that corner there, on Beverly Drive, Jane, called Wil Wright's. They gave you a single scoop of ice cream in a silver dish. It came with a macaroon and a white paper napkin that had the face of a smiling angel with a halo in red."

"Can we go there?" Jane asked.

"I wish it was still there, but it isn't," I said.

The pizza place was crowded, so we waited for a table. My attention was drawn to a woman standing by the door. Sometimes women reminded me of my mother; not because of the way they looked, but because of an attitude, a stance, a lifestyle.

This woman was an attractive sixty-five-year-old, refined, still glamorous. Her clothes, jewelry, makeup were perfect, selected with care. She wore her ash blond hair in a bun, was dressed in beautifully tailored silk pants, a white silk shirt, a white cashmere cardigan. She carried a straw basket purse decorated with red cherries; my mother had had that very purse.

She looked like she had been an actress or a model when she was young, then married well and devoted herself to homemaking. There was something traditionally feminine, passive, loving about her. She was holding a baby—no doubt her granddaughter. A younger woman, probably her daughter, inquired about a table.

The delicate grandmother stood with an attitude of innocent acceptance. She looked as helpless as a fawn, ill equipped to deal with the world. Once a man had taken care of her, made all her decisions; now her daughter probably did. That trusting quality reminded me of my mother. I missed her so much that tears came to my eyes. I quickly wiped them away, before Jane saw.

Later that night, as I searched for sleep, I found my thoughts drifting back to Blue. Did

I like him because he was a distraction from my constant thoughts of my mother? Maybe.

I dreamt I was visiting him in his art studio. He was helping me climb up a small ladder so I could see some pictures that he painted, hung above the bookcase. My foot slipped, he grabbed me. The next thing I knew, he was kissing me. I woke up in a panic. Was this my unconscious desire? I had to avoid him tomorrow.

Saturday morning, I was dressed, waiting for Donna, when she arrived.

"Let's go to the Farmer's Market for lunch. Remember when we were children, and your mother used to take us?" Donna asked.

"Oh, I love that place. I didn't realize it was still there. I'd love to show it to Jane," I said, excited at the prospect.

"They were going to tear it down, but they didn't," Donna said.

"Valentine likes it, and he's going with us. He's in the car. I have to check my contact for a minute, there's a speck of dirt on it. It's killing me," she said, walking toward the bathroom. The phone rang, it was Blue, asking if he could come to work today at noon. I agreed.

"Who was that?" Donna inquired, walking out.

"Oh, just the painter, Blue."

"Blue?"

"That's his name, Blue, Blue Calloway."

"Blue Calloway?" she asked, astonished. "Blue Calloway is the man who murdered his wife!"

4

"*What are you* talking about?" I asked. Donna sat down, lit a cigarette, took a long puff. Jane walked in.

"Jane, can you leave us alone for a moment?" she asked.

"Why?"

"Just for a minute, honey, go back up to your room," I said.

"All right, I'll leave my sweater here," she said, hanging it on the chair, then going toward the hall. Donna got up, shut the door.

"It was all over the papers about four years ago," she said.

"I lived in Italy then. What are you talking about?"

"Blue Calloway's wife disappeared under mysterious circumstances. Her family accused him of murdering her. He had some phony story about what happened the day she disappeared."

"Did they arrest him?"

"No."

"So then he wasn't charged. Maybe he didn't do it," I said, finding it impossible to picture Blue as a murderer.

"Elizabeth, don't be naive. Where there's smoke, there's fire. He just didn't get caught."

"Did he deny it?"

"Of course. Did you expect him to confess?"

"I don't know, he could be innocent," I said. Donna put her cigarette out with a flourish, stood up.

"And there's really a Santa Claus. He's just a house painter, what's the big deal? Fire him, get another one. How hard is it to paint a kitchen? I wouldn't want a murderer in my house," she said, opening the door.

"Jane, come on," she yelled.

Was he just a house painter? Or was he more? Could he have murdered his wife? Donna pushed us out the door before I had time to really think about it.

"Valentine, get out. Let Elizabeth sit in the front," Donna said. Valentine turned his atonal music down two levels, got out of the car, sullen.

"Hi, Valentine, this is Jane. You met her when she was much younger," I said.

"Yeah, whatever," he said, angrily. Jane looked at me for an explanation.

"Valentine, could you show some courtesy?" Donna said.

"Fuck you! I didn't want to come anyway," he said, slamming the door, rushing down the driveway.

"Wait, where are you going? Come back!" Donna shouted, running down the street.

"What's wrong with him?" Jane asked.

"He's very upset, honey; it's not because of us," I said. Donna stood in the driveway, staring after him. Finally she turned around.

"Do you want to go after him? We can catch him in the car," I said.

"I don't know what to do," Donna said, in a small voice. "I guess we should just let him go. Maybe he'll be in a better mood later."

"What does he want to have lunch with us for anyway, Donna? It would bore him to death."

"Right," she said, as she got into the car. During the drive, she was a million miles away. After many attempts at conversation, I gave up and turned on a radio station that I knew Jane enjoyed.

As soon as we turned onto Fairfax, I saw the familiar Farmer's Market. It still looked inviting, down home in the midst of urban Los Angeles. There were the white wood buildings trimmed in dark green, the clock on the brick tower with FARMER'S MARKET in white letters.

Dozens of warm memories overwhelmed me. My mother and I came here often to eat

Chinese or Mexican food in one of the outdoor food stands. The smells were tantalizing. There were so many interesting shops, including one where you could buy autographed black-and-white glossy pictures of movie stars, entertainers. I got one of Elvis Presley there.

My favorite shop in the casual, folksy, single-story complex had been the pet store. It sold tiny turtles that had FARMER'S MARKET painted in white on their green shells. We bought two turtles there with an oval turtle bowl, complete with a plastic palm tree in it, special pink and blue gravel and a box of turtle food. I had those turtles, Irma and Smokey, for years.

In the middle of the pet store was a glass booth that always had four energetic puppies in it, frolicking on shredded newspaper. Sometimes they were cocker spaniels, sometimes black poodles, once, brown Pomeranians. The clerk let customers hold the puppies, but only if they were thinking about buying one.

I begged my mother to say we were considering a purchase, but she wouldn't. She said too much handling upset the puppies. I'd spend at least fifteen minutes staring at them, longing to pet them.

There was a gigantic magazine stand across one wall, near an exit. My mother would glance through movie magazines, I'd buy comic books. We'd spend the whole afternoon in this open-air jackpot of adventure, end up buying takeout food for dinner, including either chocolate cupcakes or a bag of nuts and dried fruit for dessert.

On the way out, we'd stop by the Mexican handicrafts store that sold big appliquéd sombreros, and handmade colorful wool jackets with Mexico and Tijuana written on them. At the entrance, there was a big, green parrot named Polly, inside an ornate wrought-iron cage. I'd stick my hand in the cage. Polly jumped on my finger with her dry light claws, while my mother handed me a cracker. The parrot squawked happily as she ate it. Then she'd stare me in the eye, yell, "Polly want a cracker! Polly want a cracker!"

Finally, later, I had to be dragged away, desperately trying to find an excuse to stay a little longer. Life seemed so happy and natural there. We pulled in the same parking lot today; it was almost full. People were bustling about with shopping bags. There was now a preponderance of old people.

"Usually after my mother brought me here for lunch we'd go for a pony ride at the Beverly Kiddie Park across the street," I said, as we got out of the car.

"I remember that place. It's been gone for years," Donna said.

"Are there pony rides anywhere?" Jane asked.

"Griffith Park. We'll take you. I don't know if they have ponies, but I know they rent horses," Donna said, as we got out, walked in. So much was the same, I felt joyous. There were the open-air counters full of different food. The benches and tables were still in the middle.

"What do you want, Jane?"

"A hot dog," she said.

"They have those over there," Donna said, pointing to a stand. We started to walk toward it.

"I'm getting some seafood," Donna said, going in the opposite direction, "I'll meet you at that table near the stand." After I got Jane her hot dog, we went to the Chinese food stand. It was in the exact place that it had been. I ordered chop suey, fried rice, green tea, began to get lost in a fantasy that my mother was standing next to me, ordering her chicken chow mein.

"Lady, lady," the man behind the counter said, breaking into my fantasy.

"Sorry," I said, paying him.

"What were you thinking about, Mommy?" Jane asked, as we sat down at the table.

"I don't know," I said. I didn't want to depress Jane with my obsession with my mother. As it was, I talked too much about the past in connection with her father. But I wanted her to know how much he had loved her. Now, I needed to give her more room for a present and a future.

Donna found us, put down her scrumptious seafood platter.

"This place never changes. It always had a lot of elderly Jews from the Fairfax area because it's right here in the middle of the old Jewish section. Now it has more. It's too funky for me," she said. Two Chasidic Jews walked by, followed by two metalheads. After them, a blond, sunny family straight out of Orange County walked toward a fruit stand.

"Can I have dessert? A chocolate ice-cream cone?" Jane asked.

"Sure," I said, digging out some money. "The stand is right there. Be careful, I'll watch you."

Jane took the money, got in line. I ate more of my Chinese food—it was delicious. Donna finished her crab.

"I'm going over there to get a cup of cappuccino," Donna said, pointing to a coffee bar. I watched her walk away, then turned my attention back to Jane.

That's when it happened. I experienced a vague, uneasy feeling. I felt jarred. Was there danger? I quickly looked toward Jane, but saw no one threatening or odd near her. I got up anyway, stood with her as she purchased her ice-cream cone, then walked her back. I relaxed, it was probably just a panic attack. I had had major ones when I was a child, but they had abated.

I glanced in the direction Donna had gone.

She was nowhere in sight. I looked back at Jane across the table. She smiled at me. Once again, something bothered me. This time, I felt a surge of familiarity. Was someone wearing perfume I smelled often?

"What's wrong, Mommy?" Jane asked.

"Nothing, honey, why?"

"You look weird, you're so pale," she said. I smiled at her reassuringly, when suddenly I froze. I know what I saw. I had just seen my mother! I spun around. She was sitting at a table near the Chinese food, the very table we used to sit at when I was a child.

I looked more closely, could it be? The last time I saw my mother she was thirty-three, now she would be fifty-nine. The woman looked about that age. My mother's hair was jet black, this woman had black hair streaked with silver, the same hairstyle but shorter. Jane pulled on my hand.

"Mom, Mommy, you look like you've seen · a ghost!" she said.

"I . . . I'm sorry, honey," I said, frantically looking for Donna. I had to get a closer look at the woman, but I couldn't leave Jane alone. I stared at her from afar. She was self-contained, eating her lunch, reading a paperback. If this wasn't my mother, then the resemblance was remarkable. She wore a belted cotton jacket of large red-and-white plaid. I remembered my mother wearing a similar jacket. How could that be? Could she still have it? Maybe it was new, but she still had the same taste. At last, I saw Donna headed toward us.

"Honey, here's Donna, stay with her a few minutes. I have to go to the bathroom," I said to Jane, jumping up as soon as Donna got back. I mouthed "bathroom" to her. She nodded.

I rushed off in the direction of the bathroom, so they wouldn't see where I was going. If I was wrong, I didn't want to be embarrassed. Then I circled back, behind a line of tables and umbrellas, until I was standing close to the woman. She couldn't see me, I was obscured.

I studied the woman's face. She had the same-shaped brown eyes as my mother, but she didn't look exactly as I remembered. Yet it had been twenty-six years, age would have taken its toll. My glance drifted to her hand— she was wearing a diamond wedding ring, a diamond watch. It looked like the same jewelry that my mother wore.

I started to tremble, moved a little closer. I smelled Joy, my mother's scent. I wanted to approach her but was paralyzed. She was eating chicken chow mein, drinking her coffee black, just like my mother did.

I took a deep breath, prepared to take a step toward her. But my legs were numb. I opened my mouth, no words came out.

Wait! This couldn't be my mother, she wasn't smoking. My mother always smoked with her coffee. That habit was as much a part of her as flesh and bone. Tears of disappointment came to my eyes. It wasn't my mother, there would be no joyous reunion here. I felt the blood return to my limbs, my breathing normalized.

False alarm. Was my mother dead, after all? Were her bones rotten, turned to dust in her catacomb in the mausoleum?

Every inch of my body hurt. It was visceral. My beautiful mother, her flesh eaten away, her graceful head now a hollow skull. I couldn't even picture what she was wearing in her coffin since it had been closed.

I turned away from the woman, started to walk away. All of a sudden, I poked my eye on the edge of an outdoor umbrella. I backed up in shock, my eye watering, stinging furiously. For a moment, I felt dizzy. I was confused, disoriented. I closed my eyes, steadied myself on a table.

When the pain lessened, I opened my eyes, took a few steps forward. Somehow, I had gotten turned around, I stepped right in front of the woman. She looked up, dropped her book.

"Elizabeth!" she said, in a shocked whisper. It was my mother! I felt warm all over. I moved to embrace her, she backed away.

"No, no, no," she said, frightened. She started to run, I followed. She turned toward me, tormented.

"Don't follow me, I beg you," she said, with

tears in her eyes. I stopped in shock, allowed her to rush away. Everything started whirling around me. I sat down fast. Then I saw the sign. NO SMOKING. Of course, smoking wasn't allowed in Los Angeles restaurants anymore. She couldn't smoke, even if she wanted to.

My mother was alive! A second after that realization, my joy was tempered by grief. She didn't want to see me. I put my face in my hands, cried and cried. All these years, I imagined she missed me as much as I missed her, but I was wrong. She fled from me.

The truth was harder to bear than the pain of constantly missing her. My worst fear was that she was dead. I never imagined that she didn't want to be with me.

Part of me now just wanted to succumb to the past, where it was safer. If this was to be my present, this horrible truth that she was alive but didn't love me, then I couldn't face it. All my life I had lived as a skeleton, a partial outline of a being, waiting to see my mother again, so that the substance could fill in the holes of my body and spirit. Now, I would live forever as translucent ectoplasm. I put my head on my knees, felt small, insignificant. I was in agony. Then, I felt nothing.

"Elizabeth! What happened?" Donna asked, finding me. She put her arms around me. I rested my head on her shoulder, sobbed.

"Don't let Jane see me like this," I pleaded, between cries.

"What is it, Elizabeth? Tell me! Don't worry about Jane, she's with a friend of mine I ran into. What happened, what's wrong?"

"Donna, Donna, the saddest thing, my mother doesn't want to know me!" I said, sobbing.

"What are you talking about, Elizabeth?" Donna asked, holding both my arms with her hands, staring into my face.

"My mother, she's alive! She was sitting right here. I walked up to her, but she ran away! She asked me not to follow her."

"What? You saw your mother?" Donna asked, looking very worried. She probably thought I had lost my mind or that some drifter had dropped acid in my coffee.

"Donna," I said, very calmly, "I saw my mother. I know it sounds fantastic, but it happened. When I went up to her, she recognized me and said, 'Elizabeth.' "

"She knew you?"

"She's my mother. I was right all these years, she's alive. But," I said, tears running down my face again, "she wants nothing to do with me."

Donna was silent. I knew she didn't believe me. She seemed to be trying to figure out what to say. Finally, she spoke.

"Honey, you've been under a lot of pressure lately, just take it easy. Let's go home," she said. I had to get away from her before she talked me out of what I had seen. I jumped up.

"Just watch Jane for me," I said. Donna looked as if I'd had a psychotic break.

"Elizabeth, just come on. I've got to be home soon."

"It's just two o'clock," I said, "I'll meet you at your car at three." Before she had a chance to say "no," I was gone.

Maybe my mother hadn't meant to run away. Had it been a fear response? Did she think I was dead? If she hadn't left the premises, I could find her. First, I went into the bathroom. Would she be there redoing her makeup? No one was at the sinks. I looked under the stalls—no legs. I started down the row of stores. I popped my head into each one, searched thoroughly.

Before I went into each store, I looked up and down the walkways, praying for a glimpse of her. Nothing. She wasn't in any of the shops. She wouldn't have gone back to the eating areas. All that was left was an auto shop in front. I dragged myself into that. Of course, she wasn't there.

I was fooling myself. She left, she left me. I would never know why. The abandonment made me feel more hollow than usual. All was lost.

I knew no one that knew her or even if she was using her real name. I could hire a private investigator, but he'd come up empty. She probably had no paper trail to trace, possessed no credit cards, owned nothing. If only I had told her that I loved her. Now she'd die, without ever knowing how much I longed for her.

I had an idea. I'd come here every day for the rest of my life at exactly 1:00 P.M. Maybe in a year or two, for whatever reason, she'd decide she wanted to see me, and she'd come here, too. I was standing outside the auto shop on Fairfax. I looked up at the white hands of the clock; it was already five to three.

Depressed, I walked toward the parking lot. There was Donna opening the car door for Jane. She saw me approach.

"Are you all right?" she asked, worriedly. I nodded. The disappointment was brutal. Could I survive it?

As I reached the car, I stared at Jane through the window. Usually all I had to do was look at her, and I felt invested in life. Now I was numb. I shuddered, hoped my ability to feel would return. I couldn't adequately love and mother Jane if I was just a shell.

I started to get into the car, when I felt a tap on my shoulder. I turned around—it was my mother! She grabbed me, hugged me, crying, then shoved an envelope in my hand, and fled.

She rushed to a brown car, got in, drove away. It happened so fast, I almost thought I'd imagined it. But it was real.

5

"Oh my God, it's your mother!" Donna said. She took a step toward me, then staggered.

"I feel like I'm going to faint," she said, just before she fell to the ground.

"Mom, what's wrong with her?" Jane asked, climbing out of the car. Alarmed, I bent over Donna, raised her head.

"Donna, Donna," I said, shaking her. She slowly opened her eyes, shook her head from side to side.

"I've ... I've never passed out before," she whispered, weakly. "Now I feel nauseous."

"Here, I'll get you into the car, lean on me, just lie down in the backseat," I said, helping her stand up, then climb into the car.

"I'll drive your car. You're in no condition to drive," I said.

"Mom, Donna said that woman was your mother. Was she?" Jane asked.

"Yes, yes she was. I want to tell you about it, Jane, but let's wait until after we take Donna home," I said, starting the car. Donna rested in the back. She never did well with emotional upheavals. Arguments with her parents used to force her to take to her bed for days in college.

My mother was alive! Thoughts of her engulfed me. There had to be information in the note about how to contact her. What else could it be? I had an unusual feeling of well-being, a sensation of soaring.

I put my hand in my jacket pocket, felt the envelope. I wanted to read it, but restrained myself. I had to explain the situation to Jane. She had been told my mother lived far away, that I hoped someday she would meet her. I would have to create a plausible story about the past; the truth would probably be too hard for Jane to understand, whatever the truth might be.

"Was I dreaming or was that really your mother?" Donna asked, when she sat up.

"It was, it was!" I said, finding myself laughing. This was more than going to make up for all the birthdays of my mother's I missed, all the holidays I cried through. I wouldn't be able to normalize all those years, but at least now I could see a future.

Donna reached up to the front seat, squeezed my arm. I glanced back. There were tears in her eyes. She knew how much this meant to me.

"She's still beautiful, isn't she, Donna?"

"She is. I still can't believe the whole thing. Did she say . . . ?"

"Later, we'll discuss it later," I said, interrupting her, pulling up to her house.

"Do you need me to help you?" I asked her.

"No, I just want to go in, lie down. You take the car. I'll have Leticia run me down later to pick it up. Just park it in front of your house, put the keys under the seat. Will you call me?"

"Tonight," I said, waving good-bye. I could almost feel heat emanating from the letter. I had to get home fast. I was tempted to pull over to the side of the road, but I wanted to be alone when I read it.

"Does your mother know about me?" Jane asked.

"I don't know, honey, but when she meets you, she's going to be so delighted." The fifteen minutes it took to go from Bel Air to Westwood seemed like hours. I rushed into the house past Blue (I had totally forgotten about him), told Jane I needed a few moments alone, went into my room.

I closed the door. Shaking with anticipation, I sat down in the print armchair by the window. As if I could change the words that were already on the page, I fantasized that my mother said she missed me, as I missed her.

I tried to keep my expectations low. If all

that came of today was that I had seen my mother alive and knew that her life hadn't been cut tragically short, then that would have to suffice.

I carefully took the envelope out of my pocket. I stared at it for a moment, trying to intuit what was in it. It was a thin business envelope, the cheap kind. She probably couldn't afford anything better. My heart stung at the thought that she was going without when I had so much. There was no name on the envelope because she knew she was going to hand it to me.

I pulled the single sheet of typing paper out of the envelope. She had written the note with a ballpoint pen.

My dearest Elizabeth,

Please meet me Monday at 2 p.m. at 1740 Yale St., Apt. 215, in Santa Monica. I'll be waiting. Keep this confidential.

I love you,
Mother

My heart raced. How many hours until then? I checked my watch. The time seemed endless. I touched the writing to feel her vibrations. Her script was linear, measured, that of a balanced person.

She wanted to see me, how could I have doubted her? "I'll be waiting." I had waited over twenty-five years. "Keep this confidential." Why? Was she in danger? Would I be, once I connected with her?

I went over a hundred possible scenarios, as if I were an out-of-focus camera. I kept trying to bring each of them into sharp focus, but I couldn't. I'd have to wait to make sense of all this. I held the note to my heart, then secreted it in my jewel box.

"Mom, you said you'd take me for art supplies," Jane yelled up at me.

"I forgot. I'll be right down," I said, coming out, nodding to Jane to follow me. Blue turned toward us as we reached the door.

"Does it look all right so far? The wall?"

"Yes," I said, trying to avoid conversation with him. "We have to get to the art supply store before it closes." I pulled Jane by the hand, out the door, slammed it. I had to devote some thought soon to the problem of Blue. It was difficult to think of him as a murderer. Besides, I had more important things on my mind.

We got in the car. There was no sign of the silver car. I kept up a conversation, but I was thinking of my mother. I'd have to make arrangements for Jane after school Monday, when I went to my mother's apartment. I'd ask Donna. I'm sure "Keep this confidential" didn't extend to her.

I looked at Jane. Would she exist if my mother had not disappeared? Would I have married Paolo, given birth to her? Would I have married at all?

What would my life have been like? Where would my mother have chosen to raise me? I assumed that the reason my mother didn't take me with her was that she wanted everyone to think she was dead. Soon, I would know the truth about everything.

We picked up drawing tablets and pastel chalk for Jane at the Art Store. Then we drove to Donna's house. She had revived.

"Sit down, let's talk about it," Donna said, pouring coffee in her modern kitchen when I told her why I had come. She had a view of the Bel Air hills; they looked greener than usual, we just had rain. Jane went into Valentine's room to play with his video games.

"Talk about what? All I'm asking you to do is pick Jane up from school, bring her up here. I'll pick her up at five," I said.

"I don't know about this," she said, inexplicably.

"Know about what? I can't take her to my mother's, not this first time."

"Not that. I'm not sure you should go alone. What if it's dangerous? How do you know what her situation is?"

"I don't. She wouldn't put me in danger. There's no other way I can contact her, I don't have her phone number."

"You could send an overnight letter, ask her

to meet you at your house, a public place, even here. It would be safer."

"Donna, you know nothing in the world can keep me from my mother. There may be an element of danger, but I'm going."

"I wish you wouldn't. I'm worried about Jane."

"She'll be fine here."

"Don't go," Donna said, raising her voice. "I mean, what if something happens to you? What about Jane? You're a single parent now."

"Nothing is going to happen to me. Besides, if it does, you're her guardian, remember?" I asked.

"The Mob might be after your mother," Donna practically yelled.

"Donna, calm down. You're overreacting. Really, you are," I said, giving her a hug.

"Maybe you're right. I feel a little unhinged," she said. The front door slammed.

"Don't say anything to Randall," I said. She nodded.

"Donna?" Randall called. He came into the room, threw down his briefcase, gave her a quick kiss. He was dressed in an Italian suit, like the ones Paolo used to wear.

"Elizabeth, this is perfect timing," he said. "We were going to call you, how about having dinner with us next week?"

"That would be great," I said. "I'm late, I've got to get Jane." I couldn't really concentrate on anything but my mother. We got home, walked up the path to the house. I opened the door. Did I smell dinner?

"Who cooked?" Jane asked, as we walked in. My sentiments, exactly. In the kitchen, Blue stood at the stove, stirring a big pot. He had taken some of the tarp down so he could cook.

"Is vegetable soup too prosaic?" Blue asked, his voice a comforting baritone.

"What's prosaic, Mommy?" Jane asked.

"I just meant, do you like vegetable soup?" Blue said.

"Yeah, with carrots?" Jane asked.

"Yes. I had all the ingredients in my car to make soup, at my house. I thought I'd make it for you," he said. I didn't know what to say. Jane sat down at the table, more than ready to eat.

"Really, Blue, you shouldn't have done this. You've gone to all this trouble," I said, worried about what he might expect in return for this culinary effort.

"I know I took liberties," he said, grinning, "but there's plenty of food if you want to invite a date over."

"It's not a matter of inviting a date," I said, angry at his aggressiveness. Then I looked at Jane, didn't want to make a scene.

"I promise to eat and leave quickly," he said. "Or I could brown bag it and take my dinner home. I don't want to make you uncomfortable." He looked chastened, unhappy. Maybe I was making a big deal out of nothing.

Maybe Blue's friendliness was not so unusual. But, it was my house he was being so friendly in. Oh well, no harm done. I smiled, took off my coat, sat down. He looked relieved, spooned soup into our bowls with my big soup ladle. The soup had big chunks of potato, carrots, zucchini, onions, even peas floating in it.

"This tastes good," Jane said, enthusiastically, happily looking up at him. It was the first time she had been around a man since her father died. I shook away any thoughts of Blue as a potential stepfather; it was so unlikely. It wasn't as if I didn't have a complicated past, not to mention the cloud he had hanging over his head.

It was impossible for me to think of anything but my mother. I watched Blue and Jane talk, but didn't hear them. I thought only of my mother's face, a face I would see again on Monday.

All my photographs of her were frayed, falling apart, because I had fingered them so many times, looking for any bits of visual information that I might have missed. I went over every detail of her appearance in my mind.

"Dreamer girl, do you want apple pie?" Blue asked.

"Dreamer girl?"

"He asked you three times, and you didn't hear him, Mom," Jane said.

"I'm sorry to be so...preoccupied. You made apple pie?"

"The very same," Blue said, jumping up, taking a pie out of the oven. He cut it, served us each a piece.

"Are you always like this at dinner?" he asked.

"No, she usually talks all the time," Jane said, stuffing apple pie in her mouth.

"It's true, I do," I said, nervously. "There's just a lot going on right now. I have some important things to take care of Monday."

"Reentry issues?" Blue asked.

"Not really, it's too involved to go into," I said. Blue smiled, got up, grabbed his coat.

"Wasn't watching the time," he said. "I've got to get home."

"Thanks so much for dinner, Blue."

"Sure," he said, smiling as he left.

It was while I was helping Jane with her homework, that it hit me. What if something did happen to me? What if there was mortal danger? I stared at Jane, writing her essay. What if this was the last time I would ever get to help with her English composition?

I fastened on her small, lovely face. I had assumed that I would watch her grow into maturity, see her gracefully embrace womanhood. I would be there every minute, every second, guiding her journey into adulthood.

Adolescence would be a challenge, but we would meet it, somehow, together. Then she'd go to college, have romances, hopefully, later a career and marriage.

How many times had I tried to figure out what she would look like as an adult? What her style would be, her attitude? What would be her biggest difficulties? Her greatest assets?

"Mom, how do you spell monsoon?" she asked.

"M-o-n-s-o-o-n," I spelled it for her. Then I stroked her hair.

"What?" she asked, as if something were wrong.

"Nothing, sweetheart, I was just thinking how much I love you."

"I love you, too, Mom," she said, smiling her too-sweet smile. Fear flowed through me. What if I never saw her again? How dangerous was it really to visit my mother? She was obviously not free to see me in public. Why? What if someone did see me go into her apartment?

What would the punishment be? Would it be death? For my mother? For me? I was nine when my mother disappeared; Jane was now ten. Would history repeat itself? It was too terrifying to contemplate.

No, my mother wouldn't knowingly put me in danger. But what if there was something she didn't know? Hysteria was winning. I fought for control.

Nothing was going to happen to me. I would see my mother, then come home. Or would I? I had to take the chance.

6

Monday morning, I packed Jane's lunch carefully, put in an extra chocolate chip cookie. I walked her to school more slowly than usual. I lingered when I kissed her good-bye at the school gate, watched her go into the main building. I kept staring at the door long after she went in, seeing the last corner of her skirt frozen forever in my mind.

On the way home, I touched my cheek where she had kissed me. I could almost feel the imprint of her tiny, perfectly formed rosebud mouth. I went into the house, tried not to think that I might never see her again.

I put on three or four different outfits because I wanted to look my best for my mother. Mothers are supposed to feel unconditional love for their children. Would she?

I wanted her to be proud of what I was. When I told her about my life, would she be happy that she was my mother? I felt that I should have become more, accomplished more. At least I had done nothing that I was ashamed to tell her.

I wondered if she would be angry that I hadn't looked for her. How could I explain that I was convinced she was alive, yet I had done nothing to find her? The truth is, I thought a search would put her at risk. Even though I knew she was alive, I feared I couldn't convince anyone else, that they'd react to me like Donna had, think my obsession had pushed me over the edge.

I was almost unable to contain my anticipation as it got nearer to one-thirty. Finally, it was time to leave. I drove down Ashton to Beverly Glen, took a right to Santa Monica Boulevard. It was then that I saw the silver car. It must have been parked on a side street because it wasn't in front of my house.

I had to lose the car; I couldn't put my mother in more danger. I drove down Santa Monica a few blocks before I turned right. The car was on my tail. When the coast was clear, I made a treacherous U-turn, zoomed toward the Veteran's Administration grounds in Westwood. I moved too quickly for the silver car to follow. I knew a short cut through the VA, took it. The whole routine was like something out of a bad cop movie, but it worked.

I drove around a couple of the college-named streets in Santa Monica—Princeton,

Harvard, before finally turning onto Yale. I found my mother's small, bland, tan stucco apartment building immediately but parked my car two streets away, in case the silver car was still looking for me.

I kept looking over my shoulder as I hurried toward the apartment. No one followed me. I glanced at the second-floor balconies, wondering which was her apartment. I pressed number 215 on the intercom. There was no name typed in place next to it.

No one answered. Had she left? Did I have the wrong apartment? My mind flooded with despair. Maybe she was waiting for me to say my name. I pressed the intercom again, whispered, "It's Elizabeth." The door opened. I rushed up the flight of stairs, found number 215, knocked softly.

"Are you alone?" my mother whispered through the door.

"Yes, I am." The door opened soundlessly, I rushed in, closed it behind me. She hovered near the door, I threw my arms around her. When I had hugged her good-bye at nine, she was so much taller. Now she came up to my nose, was trembling.

"Mom." The word sounded odd coming from my lips. "Sit down, take it easy," I said, easing her into a chair. I sat on the couch. The apartment was a one-room studio, small, shabby, barely furnished. There were no personal effects decorating it, no pictures, no candles. There was no TV, not even a phone. The curtains were tightly drawn.

"I was so worried . . ." we said simultaneously, then smiled with relief.

"You're here, you're alive, Elizabeth. Not a day went by when I didn't think of you," she said, beginning to weep. She took out a white, lace hankerchief with the initials "LS" in the corner. She used to leave similar hankies all over the house. I put my arms around her, held her till she stopped crying.

"I know you were thinking of me. I thought of you constantly, too, Mother. I never gave up hope that I would see you again," I said, my voice quivering.

"I didn't know if I would see you again," she said, looking down. She took a cigarette out of her purse, lit it with her sterling silver lighter with Lorelei written on it. I remembered it. I wanted to ask her so many questions but didn't want to upset her. We gazed at each other tentatively, lovingly.

"You want to ask me about the past," she said, quietly, reading my mind.

"We have time," I said. Then, I thought about it.

"Do we? Have time, I mean?" I asked, quickly.

"I don't know, Elizabeth, I hope so. I don't want to put you in harm's way. I hope I haven't," she said.

"You want to know why I didn't take you

when I disappeared," she said. I nodded.

"It was like this," she said, slowly, as she got up and started to pace.

"I was fighting your dad's partners for what was rightfully yours. I know that's what he would have wanted me to do. He never thought they'd deny you your rightful inheritance.

"They threatened to kill me; I thought they were bluffing. These were the men that had been in the hospital with your dad when you were born. I had known them my whole married life. Your uncle Charles kept telling me I didn't know what I was dealing with, that I was playing with fire," she said, then stopped, the emotion too much for her.

"Oh, Elizabeth, I'm so sorry," she said, walking to me. I put my arms around her, sat her back on the couch.

"You thought you were doing what's best for me, that's all I can do for Jane," I said. She looked at me with rapt attention.

"Jane? Was that your little girl in the car?"

"Yes, that's your granddaughter. Jane Lorelei," I said. She looked down again, her eyes welled up with tears.

"This is too much for you. Let's save it for another time," I said. She looked fearfully toward the window.

"No, I want to say everything, tell you all about it, in case . . . in case—"

"In case what?" I asked, interrupting. "This

isn't going to be the only time I see you. It can't be!"

"I hope not, oh, I hope not, Elizabeth," she said. I froze. Would she go away again? Was she to be killed for this transgression? She was remembering now. I didn't want to interrupt her recitation of history just to quiet my fears.

"The day before I disappeared, Uncle Charles came to visit me. He said that your dad's partners weren't kidding, if I didn't sign off on the will, they'd kill me. Maybe I just wasn't realistic. Or maybe it was just too hard for me to accept that our supposed 'friends' would kill me over money. It seemed such a lack of respect for your dad. He started them out—they were his protégés. Once again, I refused.

"As you remember, I sent you away two weeks before this, so I knew you would not be hurt. The next morning Lou knocked on my door at 6 A.M.," she said, staring at the wall in front of her rather than at me. It was too hard for her to tell her story directly to me, the person it impacted the most.

"He rushed into the house and told me to pack anything I wanted to take in one small suitcase. 'What do you mean? I'm not going anywhere,' " I said.

"Lorelei, listen to me," he said. "I accepted a contract to murder you, so I could save you. I'm supposed to kill you by midnight tonight. I'm risking my life to do this. Get your things together, fast. If you refuse, I'm going to knock you out and get you out of here," she said, gasping for breath from the memory of Lou's words.

"Mom, take it easy. Let me make you some tea," I said, getting up, opening a cabinet in the tiny kitchen alcove. I took down a tea bag, looked for a teapot to make tea in. There was only a hot plate.

"No, Elizabeth, I'm fine now, honey. It's just so hard to talk about all this. Please sit down," she said. I obliged. She continued, now looking at me. Her cigarette lay ignored in the ashtray. She had forgotten about it.

"I didn't know I'd be going away for the rest of my life. I threw a change of clothes and makeup into a suitcase. At the last second, I put in some baby pictures of you, and I took my jewelry. Lou said he'd send the rest of my things, everything, eventually.

"The next couple of weeks were a blur. I stayed with friends of Lou's in Las Vegas. They gave me tranquilizers every day and didn't let me go outside. Then one day Lou came. He drove me here, to LAX, put me on a plane for Buenos Aires.

"He made arrangements for me to stay with friends of his in Argentina. He told me that a small check, $300, would come every month until he could work things out. He said he'd take care of you in the meantime.

"Oh God, Elizabeth, I'm so sorry, I didn't

know I'd be saying good-bye to you forever. I didn't mean to make you an orphan," she said, sobbing.

"Stop," I said. "You did what you had to. Just tell me what you need to. The only thing that matters is that I have you back now." She closed her eyes to gain control, took a deep breath, then proceeded.

"After about a month, a man came to see me. His name doesn't matter. He's dead now, thank God. He told me that he knew Lou had killed a vagrant, put her in my coffin and sent me out of the country. He said that Lou had been killed for it.

"Even though I was supposedly dead, this man asked me to sign off on the will. My statement was predated.

"He said that he and two other partners had decided that if I would sign off on the will, I could live. Some higher-up had granted me my life, because your father once saved his life. But I had to promise never to come back home. I did what they asked. I never looked for you because I didn't want to endanger you in any way.

"A couple of months ago, I found out that two of the men who I made the agreement with were now dead. The third, Sam Mazzelli, is old and ill. He lives in New York.

"I'd been gone over twenty-five years. I wanted to come back to L.A. It seemed the danger was minimal. I didn't think I'd ever see you again. I was told you were in Europe. I planned to live here, retracing all the paths you and I had walked together in your childhood."

"Was that why you were at the Farmer's Market yesterday?" I asked.

"Yes."

"I've been doing the same things, going to places that we had visited, sharing the memories with Jane," I said.

Suddenly, the buzzer rang, we looked at each other in surprise. My mother rushed toward the bathroom, motioning me to do the same. I went to the window instead, drew the curtain back an inch, looked out.

"It's just a Jehovah's Witness," I said. My mother walked back in, exhausted.

"You look so tired, maybe we should stop for now," I said. She nodded sadly.

"I got so scared. Now I feel drained," she said.

"But there's no real danger, right?"

"I don't know; Mazzelli has friends. And with the Mob, well, you never know who your enemies are. Besides hating me for giving them problems, I might know something that is dangerous to someone, something I don't even realize."

"I don't think there's anything to worry about—it all happened so long ago. Don't you think everyone's forgotten by now?" I asked. My mother shook her head "no."

"The Mob never forgets, that's what Lou told me. They remember vendettas for decades. If the parents die, the sons carry on. I'll never really be safe, and if we continue to see each other, neither will you."

"Even if it's true, I'll take the chance. I can't lose you again."

"I'm still your mother, and I know best, Elizabeth. If we continue meeting, you must be very, very careful. You must never bring Jane. Tell me you promise," she said, looking at me intensely.

"I promise," I said, realizing sadly that this meant my mother might never get to know her only granddaughter.

"Thank you for understanding," she said, carefully sitting down in the chair farthest from the window, even though the curtains were still drawn. She had lived her life on this precipice of fear and uncertainty. She looked older, paler than when I arrived. All these memories had taken their toll.

"Mother?" It took her a moment to raise her head, she seemed dazed.

"What, honey?"

"I think it's time for me to go. But I'm coming back tomorrow."

"No," she said, fearfully. "Tomorrow is too soon. Just in case someone is watching. Come Wednesday at noon."

"That's too long. What do you do every day all alone here?"

"The same thing I've done all my life. Read, walk, and remember. Now I will have something new to remember—your visit."

"Do you need anything? Money? Can I get you a television?"

"No, I'm fine. Just promise me you'll come back."

"You know I will. Here, let me give you my address and phone number in case you need anything before then," I said, scribbling it on a piece of paper, handing it to her.

I bent down, kissed her cheek. She looked at me, squeezed my hand. She squeezed hard once. I waited for that second squeeze, it didn't come. That was strange. When I was little she always gave my hand two quick squeezes. She probably forgot, it had been such a long time.

"Good-bye, I love you," I said, tearing myself away, walking toward the door.

"I love you, too," she said, as I left.

"You have no idea what it was like, to be there, in the same room with her after all these years," I said to Donna, in her living room.

"It's a miracle. I still can't believe Lorelei's alive. I guess this means I can never disagree with you again," Donna said, laughing.

"No, you can't," I said.

"So what's the story?"

"I can't tell you, it's so complicated. I can't

even see her again until Wednesday. I can't ever take Jane over there."

"You mean your mother is in danger?"

"That's what she says."

"But it's been over twenty-five years," Donna said, emphatically. I shrugged. That was true.

"Maybe she's just imagining it," Donna suggested.

"But even if she is, it's real to her. I wouldn't want to raise the issue with her, she's been under so much stress her whole life."

"So you're going to meet with her in secret for the rest of her life?"

"I'm just taking it one day at a time," I said, getting up. "Where's Jane?"

"Up in Valentine's room." I walked up the stairs, the door was open. Valentine was on his bed listening to music. He had headphones on. Jane was playing one of his video games.

"C'mon, honey, let's go."

"Just a minute, Mom," she said, not quite finished with her game. I waved at Valentine because he couldn't hear me. He took off his earphones. His eyes looked glazed, and I wondered if he was stoned on pot or worse.

"Thanks for letting Jane play with your games," I said.

"That's cool. I don't play with them anymore."

I grabbed Jane's hand, walked out of Valentine's room, more worried about him than before. I didn't want to upset Donna by mentioning it. I hoped she was in touch with Valentine's alienation and torment.

We stopped by Donna's bedroom to say good-bye. Jane was always fascinated by her floor-to-ceiling closet across one wall. Donna was at her cosmetics table, putting on eye makeup.

"Thanks for picking up Jane," I said.

"We had fun, didn't we, Jane? She tried on several pairs of my shoes."

"She has tons of shoes, and eight pairs of boots," Jane said, enthusiastically.

"Jane's bored with my practical four pairs of shoes, one pair each of dress heels, flats, tennis shoes and boots. Paolo was always trying to buy me shoes in Italy—they use such gorgeous leather there," I observed.

"Plenty always made you nervous. You're nuts," Donna said. "The more I have, the more secure and grounded I feel."

"Not me," I replied. "Possessions cause me anxiety. I have to worry about each one, give it emotional weight." Donna shook her head in puzzlement, something she did often around me.

"I hope everything works out," she said.

"Me, too," I said, as we left.

"Mom," Jane said, right after the door closed, "you said you'd tell me about your mother."

"I will, honey, on the way home," I said,

searching for a way to explain the situation to her.

"Well, what do you want to know?" I asked, starting to drive home.

"Is she like Teresa?" Jane asked. Teresa was Paolo's mother, aristocratic, haughty, anything but the usual Italian grandmother. She didn't even like to be called one. Paolo's father, Papa Luca, as he liked to be called, was the opposite—warm, loving, all about family. Jane adored him; it was mutual. Papa Luca had already been on the phone begging us to come back to Rome for Christmas.

"No, she's not like Teresa."

"What's she like?"

"You'll find out, honey."

"Did she know Daddy?"

"No," I said, sadly, "she didn't. She lived in a foreign country very far from Italy."

"What will I call her?"

"Grandma, I guess."

"What's her name?"

"Lorelei."

"My middle name. Was I named after her?"

"Yes."

"Why didn't you ever tell me I was named after her?" she asked.

"I don't know, I guess it made me sad to talk about her because she lived so far away."

"Do you like her?" Jane asked.

"Like her?" What an understatement. "Jane, I love her very much. For all the years I didn't see her, I thought of her every single day."

"If you ever go away from me, I'll think of you every day, Mom," Jane said.

"Oh honey, I hope not. It's such a heavy load," I replied, remembering all those sad daydreams, the longing, the hoping, the lack of connection to anything immediate.

Two hours after I left my mother, I still felt elated, had the "in love with the whole, wide world" feeling. Jane said I was acting silly when I fed her dinner, but everything struck me as humorous. I put two maraschino cherries for eyes on a scoop of cottage cheese, an orange slice for a smile.

"What's that, Mom?"

"Just call him Smiley. Now I'll eat him," I said, wolfing down a cherry.

"You're in such a good mood, Mom."

"I guess I am."

After dinner, I had more energy than I'd had since Paolo died. I answered a bunch of letters, sent everyone back in Italy my new address.

The next day, after I came home from walking Jane to school, I decided to call Detective Karowisc about the silver car. Maybe there was a connection between the occupants of the car and the murder in Venice.

"Did you find out who the victim was?" I asked.

"No. No one has reported a similar woman

missing. She had no ID on her. We're just holding her body in the morgue, hoping for a break."

"Did you find out who stole the gun? Weren't there fingerprints on it?"

"Only yours. We checked."

"Only mine? How could that be?"

"Well, since your alibi checked out, it means that the murderer either wore gloves or wiped his prints off the gun."

"This whole thing gives me the shivers. Do you have any leads?"

"I'm sorry, Mrs. Manganaro, I'm not at liberty to discuss the case further with you."

"Detective Karowisc, there's something else. Who could I talk to about a suspicious car following me?"

"A car? Do you think it has a connection to the theft of your purse?"

"I don't know, it could have been a random event or there could be a connection," I said as I told him of my suspicions.

"Did you get the license plate?"

"No. Maybe I'm mistaken, maybe there isn't a connection. I'm not really sure," I said.

"We'll work on it. If you see it again, try to get a plate identification."

"Thank you, Detective, I will."

I sang while washing the breakfast dishes; it was very unlike me. Just to know my mother was alive took such a weight off. And now to have her back with me. I was on an emotional flight. I looked in the mirror, hardly recognized myself. My face had lightened, gravity was not as evident, all the sadness and depression were gone.

What was my mother doing now, at nine-thirty in the morning? She had always been an early riser. Did she eat breakfast in her apartment or did she walk to a local coffee shop? Did she read the newspaper with her morning coffee or did she read a book? Or did she simply think, remember?

How I wanted to be with her. If only she could live with us, we'd have the newly popular three generations under one roof, endless time to catch up. Although nothing could make up for the years of togetherness stolen from us, it would be wonderful to be able to live out my mother's remaining years with her.

Blue knocked on the window. I threw open the door, feeling in every way that I could finally let life in. I was complete. I no longer had a truncated past; I was whole.

"You're one happy woman today," Blue said. His overalls were splattered with light green paint. I smiled as I shut the door.

"Coffee? I was just cleaning up from breakfast."

"Sure, strong?"

"Espresso," I said, pouring him a mug. He sat down, I slid it to him. He put in sugar and Half & Half.

"What's gotten into you? Wait, I know. You met someone," he said. I thought about that. It was true in a way.

"It's not what you think," I answered.

"What, he's not Italian?" he asked. Presumptuous was the word for him, but nothing bothered me today.

"Blue, I appreciate the attention, but you wouldn't want to be involved in my life right now. It's very complicated."

"Living is complicated," he replied.

Was it? Was all living complicated? I thought it was only my life. He drank his coffee in two long gulps, got off the kitchen stool.

"I better get started. Thanks for the coffee," he said, as he got his painting materials together. I went back to washing the dishes, gazing outside.

A car pulled up in front of the house, a woman got out. For a moment, I fantasized that it was my mother. Then I looked closer— it was my mother! She was upset. She looked up and down the street, then ran toward my porch. I went toward the front door, almost knocking Blue's ladder over in my quick transit.

"Hey, easy," he said, as I reached the hall, opened the door. My mother rushed in, terrified, slammed the door shut. She looked over my shoulder, saw Blue.

"He's the painter. Come with me," I said, leading her into the living room.

"Oh, Elizabeth," she said, in a trembling voice.

"What is it, Mom?" I asked her, putting my arm around her frail body.

"He found me."

"Who?"

"Mazzelli."

"What? How?" I asked, incredulous.

"I don't know," she said, nervously sitting down on the couch. Her purse hung lifeless from her wrist, an afterthought. She looked confused.

"Don't worry, we'll work this out. Now tell me what happened," I said softly, in what I hoped was a comforting tone. She looked tense. Repeating it made it truer than she wanted it to be. She jumped to her feet.

"Why did I come here? What if they followed me? Now they'll know where you live," she said, starting for the door. She looked like an animal about to be ambushed. I grabbed her hand.

"Wait. Just tell me what happened. You don't have to leave. I'm not afraid," I insisted.

"But they could be on their way to kill me. Better my place than here."

"Don't even talk like that," I said. She sat down again, opened her purse, lit a cigarette, inhaled.

"I can't stay here long . . . just in case . . . anyway, I was walking to the coffee shop I go to for breakfast. I saw a man coming at me from the opposite direction," she said, starting to shake.

"I smiled and stepped to the left, the sidewalk is narrow there. But he stepped right in front of me, blocking my way. Then he said . . ." she told me, starting to cry, "he said, 'Mrs. Stein?' I said, 'yes?' He said, 'I have a message for you from Sam Mazzelli, here' and he handed me this," she said, putting a piece of paper in my hand.

I opened it. The message was written in letters cut from a newspaper. "Be at the pay phone at the corner of Montana and Sixteenth in Santa Monica tomorrow at noon. Answer it when it rings." I was chilled.

"I don't know how they found out I was here," my mother said. "I've talked to almost no one. I took the apartment under my name, but how would they know to look in that building? The utilities are included in the rent.

"I bought the car for cash, don't have a driver's license. I don't have a bank account. I just don't know, Elizabeth, I don't know."

"Look, calm down. He has something to say to you. You have to be there tomorrow to find out what he wants. The only other option is the police."

"No," she screamed, then covered her mouth. "Not the police, I can't trust them. And Lou told me if I ever did, I would be killed."

"All right. I'll pick you up tomorrow, go with you."

"Elizabeth," my mother said, jumping up again, "I've got to get out of here. I'm putting you in danger."

"No, wait . . ." I said, but she ran out the front door. I yelled at her to stop. But she got into her car and quickly sped away.

I stood by the door, staring up the street for a moment in her direction. Then, wracking sobs shook my body as the truth set in. I could lose my mother, again.

"What is it?" Blue asked, rushing to me. He steered me into the living room, eased me onto the couch. I was crying so hard that I couldn't breathe, started to gasp for breath.

"Stop, calm down, let me get you a glass of water," he said, rushing toward the kitchen. I felt like I was losing control. Someone could arbitrarily end my mother's life. The tyranny of it, the oppression, the injustice. I had to do something.

"Here, take a sip of water, Mrs. Manganaro," Blue said, handing me the glass.

"Call me Elizabeth," I choked out, gulping down some water.

"Elizabeth, what happened?" he asked, genuine concern on his face.

"I, I, can't tell you. You'd never believe it anyway. I can't trust anyone; I'm all alone in this," I said, frightened.

"You hardly know me, but I assure you, you can trust me. Tell me, sometimes it helps to share a burden," he said. I was too wary to respond.

"Hey, listen to this for a qualification," he continued. "I have a B.A. in philosophy from UC Berkeley. I'm very philosophical. Does that help?"

I laughed ruefully. What a qualification for an ally to defeat a potential murderer. An absurd thought crossed my mind. A thug was holding a gun on my mother and me and I was able to grab it because Blue distracted him for a moment with a discussion of Descartes's Ontological Proof for the Existence of God.

"You're smiling," he said, triumphantly.

"Yes, don't make me do it again, the situation is far too serious," I said, annoyed. He looked pensive for a moment, then took my hand.

"Tell me, I really do want to help," he said. I struggled not to, knew I shouldn't, but the temptation was strong. Whom could he tell, anyway? Maybe the urge to unburden myself was so great that I fooled myself into thinking someone could help me. I felt so alone. The weight of being solely responsible for my mother's life was too difficult.

"You have to promise never, never to tell anyone, Blue. It's a matter of life and death," I said.

"I can tell it's serious from your reaction. You don't have to worry about my ability to keep secrets, I keep a lot of them," he said, with more than a hint of mystery.

"This is going to sound strange, I mean, the whole story, but for people coming from my background it's understandable," I began.

"I'm from a Mob family, although I never knew it, because I was still a child when my father died. Mob families live in the shadows. We do things in our own way," I said.

"Say no more, just tell me what happened today," he said, sitting down across from me. I told it from beginning to end. I even told him about the silver car that I was sure was following me.

He didn't say a word, but occasionally looked at me with empathy. After I finished, the whole story made me sad. It seemed like I was powerless again to help my mother. There was a long silence. Would he withdraw?

Instead, Blue took my face in his hands, tilted it toward him. I knew he was going to kiss me, did nothing to stop him. He did it, did it well. Then, Blue pulled me toward him, kissed me again, holding me in his strong arms. His touch, his caring, his kisses gave me comfort. But I had to pull back.

"Thank you, Blue ... for ... being so kind ... but I've got to figure out what to do," I said.

"Do you want me to go and check on your mother?"

"I couldn't ask you to do that. I wouldn't want to involve you in—"

"Don't worry about me," he said, interrupting. "Very little scares me."

"But, you know about the Mob, you know they kill. You could be in danger."

"I can't imagine that they would harm her before they contact her tomorrow. I'd go over there to make sure she's OK, but she might be terrified if I buzzed her apartment," he said.

"You're right. She could have a heart attack from fright."

"The truth is, she's probably safer than she's ever been, until noon tomorrow. They have something they want to tell her. If they didn't, then the man who handed her the message, could have killed her this morning," Blue said.

It made sense. "I've got to go, I want to discuss this with my friend. Could I ask you a huge favor, Blue?"

"Of course."

"How long do you think you'll be painting today?"

"Maybe until five."

"Would you pick up Jane with me after school today? I just don't want to do it alone."

"I'll be waiting," he said. I grabbed my coat and purse, started for the door, when he stopped me.

"Wait here a minute, I want to get you something," he said, walking out the front door to his truck. He opened the door, took out a leather pouch, which he brought to me. It looked like a traveling case.

"Take this, just in case they followed your mother here, and you're at risk." It was a gun.

"Why do you carry a gun?" I asked him. Why did a painter need a weapon?

"Hey, it's L.A. Riots, gangs, muggings, you never know. I keep it locked in my glove compartment," he said.

"But you need it. I had one, but it was in a purse that was stolen. I'm going to get another one."

"So you carry one, too," he said, looking at me strangely.

"Yes," I said, feeling like I was suspect.

"But it's not just L.A. for me. I told you my mother's story, but I didn't tell you mine," I said, softly, embarrassed by what I was about to reveal.

"I was married to a very wealthy man in Italy. Kidnapping is a way of life over there. Paolo made me carry one. Jane and I never went out without a bodyguard and a driver. That's one of the reasons I moved home, to give her a more normal life. Unfortunately, since his family is quite well-known, we're not completely safe anywhere. I think the men in the silver car might be Italian kidnappers."

"Boy, you live dangerously," he said, seeming amazed at what I'd told him.

"Not intentionally," I said. "Sometimes, I wonder if the theory of karma could be true.

Did I terrorize people in a previous lifetime? Is this my payback? Will I always have to worry about my loved ones? Will they never be safe?"

"It sounds more like you followed the pattern that you were born into."

"What do you mean, 'the pattern'?"

"Well, you were born into a powerful, wealthy family even though it was part of a subculture, the underworld, the Mob. People who are wealthy have a certain sense of entitlement. Then you married into an influential, wealthy family."

"But I didn't know about my husband's family when I fell in love with him. He was very discreet," I said.

"No, but you probably felt comfortable with things about him, his ease in the world, his sense of self-esteem, the same things you had been raised with. You related to him effortlessly. Based on unconscious cues, being with him felt familiar, natural," Blue said.

"I never looked at it like that."

"So you were born into a powerful family, then you married into another one. And great wealth always brings problems."

"You really are a philosopher."

"That may have been Psych I or maybe Psych II," he said, smiling and sticking the traveling case with the gun in it into my big Sportsac purse.

"As long as you're not afraid of guns, you, of all people, should carry one."

"All right. I'll give it back to you as soon as I get a new one."

I knew Donna was going to a luncheon, she never answered her phone when she was getting dressed. I had a better chance of catching her by going to her home. What she called "being social," I called social climbing. She kept lists of people who invited her to functions, those that didn't, and she never forgot a snub. She had to be validated by others to feel self-worth.

That was not, obviously, the side of her I treasured. She had never been concerned with my lack of regard for social status. No, we had a real connection, not a superficial one.

We were always in opposite moods. If she was down, I'd pull her up. If I was morose, she'd grab me like a rubber band, pull me by force out of the doldrums. We could always make each other regain the balance of life.

Paolo could never understand my fondness for her. She seemed arch to him, a stereotypical American. Her strength and dry sense of humor were lost on him. And Randall never evidenced much interest in getting to know me. Donna's car was still parked in her garage.

It often seemed like she was the only resident that was home this time of day. On her cul-de-sac, in this newer section of Bel Air, most of the other garages were empty by 10

A.M. The hills and canyons seemed populated only by South American maids, going in and out of the homes silently, invisibly.

I rang the doorbell. Leticia let me in. Upstairs, Donna was dressed, just finishing doing her hair. She wore a tan Calvin Klein silk dress, looked spectacular. With her slender grace she could have posed for the cover of *Vogue*. She was surprised to see me.

"Hi, Donna."

"Hi, sweetie, what's up?" she said, sitting down on a forest green, velvet love seat. I put my coat and purse down between us, sat next to her. I told her quickly about my mother's visit this morning.

"This is a nightmare, Elizabeth," Donna said, sorrowfully. "It should be one of those long-lost relative reunion stories with a happy ending."

"It has to be, this is my only chance for a happy ending."

"I know you won't let me ask Randall to get you a bodyguard. And I know you'll be at that phone booth tomorrow. So, since that's a given, go through with it, be careful and then come right over here. I'll be waiting. Bring your mother if you want."

"Will you help me figure out what is the right thing to do? I'm afraid I'll blow it, and lose my mother again," I said.

"Of course I will. I wish I could talk to you more about this now, but I've got to go. I have to get to the country club for lunch. Do you want me to cancel, because I will?'' she asked.

"No, of course not."

"Barbara is sponsoring Randall and me for membership at the club. You know how much I've always wanted to belong."

"Because?"

"Just because. Because my parents didn't have money, doesn't mean I'm not as good as all the women who belong. These are some of the same women who wouldn't let me into the sorority at UCLA. Remember, I almost got into Kappa?'' Donna asked.

"Whatever makes you happy, it's bewildering to me. You got straight A's in college, you could have had any career you wanted. You're already so much better than any of them."

"Thank you, Elizabeth," she said, gratefully. "But you say those things because you love me. You never needed any measuring stick but your own. Keeping up with the Joneses never meant anything to you."

"You're right," I said, getting up. She got up, hugged me, accidentally knocked my coat and purse to the ground.

"Boy, your purse is heavy. You have bricks in there?'' she asked.

"Oh, it's Blue's gun. He loaned it to me," I said.

"His gun?'' she asked, frozen. "You didn't fire him? You don't have enough problems? You have Bluebeard's gun with you? The gun he used to kill his wife? Are you crazy?"

"I can't believe he killed his wife. He's a very gentle guy."

"So he killed her gently, what's the difference? Will you get rid of him?"

"I . . . I don't know, I'll think about it."

"Elizabeth, I'm not kidding. Go to the University Research Library at UCLA on your way home and check the *Los Angeles Times* microfilm. It was in the headlines for weeks."

"Well, that will be easy enough to do. I think I'll go to the library now," I said.

As I drove away, I was relieved to be able to think about something else, anything else, besides my mother. I hoped I could concentrate long enough to go through the clips. Should I just ask him what the story was? But, how could I say, "Did you kill your wife?" And how would I know he was telling the truth?

Every time I thought about the phone call tomorrow, I thought I'd explode. Any distraction was welcome. Maybe it would be comforting to walk on the campus again.

The university seemed even more crowded than when I went there seventeen years ago. The ethnicity had changed. There were a lot of Asian students now. The grounds had a casual, sunny, spacious feel—very California. No one rushed, everyone seemed wholesome, collegiate, focused. It was very much an urban campus without the urban grit.

I remember, when I was there, wishing that I had gone to a secluded, small liberal arts college in the middle of a forest somewhere. There, I thought, everyone would be without their family. I wouldn't be different. UCLA was a commuter campus. Although it had dorms, most kids were from L.A. and lived off campus. But, even back then, I knew I couldn't voluntarily leave the city I had shared with my mother, without a very good reason. That reason turned out to be Paolo.

As I walked around the sculpture garden, I thought of life in Dykstra Hall, the dorm, with Donna. We lived harmoniously in a room the size of a closet, with the de rigueur bathroom down the hall. She decorated her side of the room with posters of music heroes, fashion-magazine covers, a garage sale fifties white chenille bedspread.

My side of the room was bare. I never had much sense of place since my parents had died. In my fantasy, someday I would again live in a two-story house from my childhood, as I now do. Nothing else mattered. The dorm was noisy, but Donna and I lived in our own sea of turmoil unrelated to collegiate life.

When I was on my bed, supposedly studying sociology, I was usually thinking about my mother, hoping for a future when I could be with her. I was almost never in the present. I was lucky that my attraction for Paolo was so

strong that it galvanized me out of my daydreams and into his life.

Donna was embroiled in daily conflict with
her parents, rivalries with her siblings. Her
priority was the search for a man to serve as
her anchor and to support her.

We confided only in each other. Her parents
were of no more daily use to her than mine
were to me. Suffice it to say, neither of us had
a "home" to call on Sunday nights.

The glass monolith that was the University
Research Library was unchanged from the
outside. I walked inside. It was now comput-
erized. I picked up the directions that explained the coding system for the computer,
punched in "Blue Calloway." A long list of
articles appeared. I took down the notations,
went to the microfilm room.

Most of the articles were from the "Metro"
section of the *L.A. Times*, city news. "Heiress'
Family Accuses Husband of Murder," was the
first headlined story. Many followed. The facts
were that Blue's wife, Alexandra Wellington,
29, had disappeared in 1992.

They had met earlier at the Pasadena Design
Center, when they were students. She was a
sculptress and an offspring of a wealthy California family, recipient of a large trust since
her father had died five years earlier.

According to her mother and sister, the marriage had been unhappy. They had always
been suspicious that Blue was a fortune

hunter; now they accused him of murdering her. He denied it. Her family hired private detectives, but they didn't turn up anything. Most of the articles described Blue as "silent" and "mysterious." He refused all interviews.

She left her money to Blue. The family sued and prevented him from getting it, saying that the inheritance was his motive for murder. There were no articles after 1993. She had not been found, dead or alive.

"Dead or alive." The words jumped before my eyes. So much had happened in such a short time, I was on a roller coaster careening out of control. Any moment it would jump the track and I'd be lost forever.

I had to stay calm. Right now, I had to go home, get Blue, steer clear of any future romantic moments, and go pick up Jane. Then I had to get through the rest of the afternoon and evening without rushing over to my mother's to make sure she was alive. Tomorrow, I had to meet her at the pay phone at noon. After the phone call, I had to do whatever was necessary to save her life.

Just as I turned the corner before my house, I saw the silver car in back of me. He drove away before I could see the plate. Had he followed me all the way from UCLA? I must think rationally.

He, if it was just one person, had ample opportunity to kill me. I was unprotected. So that wasn't his mission. Had he had an opportunity to kidnap me or Jane? I wasn't sure. Were they after my mother? Not likely, since whoever wanted to find my mother found her yesterday.

But I didn't want to think about the car now. I couldn't do anything about it. It was a low priority now. Blue was just finishing painting the wall when I walked in. He stopped immediately, prepared to go with me.

"Thanks in advance, I really appreciate this, Blue," I said, holding the door open for him. One look at how appealing he was, the jeopardy surrounding me, and I entertained the thought that my mother, Jane, and I might be better off living almost anywhere but Los Angeles.

"You look pale," Blue said, as we got into my car.

"It's been a long day," I replied. After today, I planned never to be with Blue again socially. I was surrounded by enough problems without another one. If Blue's wife wasn't dead, where was she? And he didn't seem too broken up about her unresolved fate.

"It's just a few blocks to Fairburn," I said, as we drove. "It's probably silly of me to ask you to come, but I feel unusually nervous."

"You've been through a lot already, today," he said, in too intimate a way. I should never have kissed him. He thought we were at the beginning of a relationship. I wished it had never happened. I allowed it in a weak, vulnerable moment.

"Do you want to double-park, and I'll run in for her?" Blue asked, seeing all the cars lined up on the street after school.

"No, she would never leave with you, even though she knows you. I've trained her only to go with me, or with someone she knows if she sees me parked here."

"That's smart. You live defensively," he said, as I zoomed into a parking place right in front of the gate. Jane saw me. Live defensively? I guess I did, always had, didn't know how else to live.

"Hi, Blue," she said, as if it were the most natural thing in the world to see him walk to the gate for her. He put his arm on her shoulder, steering her through the kids. She didn't seem to mind, maybe she didn't notice.

"You hungry?" Blue asked her, when they got into the car.

"Yeah. I played handball during lunch," she said.

"Been to the Apple Pan?"

"Have we, Mom?"

"I don't think so. Is that place still there on Pico? I used to go there when I was in college," I said.

"Best apple pie in town. I'll treat," Blue said.

"We can even get a couple burgers to go, so you won't have to make dinner," he said to me. I yielded. It was now less than twenty-four hours until the phone call. I didn't know if I'd be calm enough to make dinner.

The Apple Pan seemed like a relic left from a former civilization. It was a small, white, wooden building completely dwarfed by the modern Westside Pavilion, which had sprawled outward and upward across the street. The tiny place was packed; there wasn't even a seat at the counter. Customers knew the waiters by name. I noticed a couple of television actors waiting for seats.

Blue made sure we were next in line. He told Jane and me to take two counter seats that opened up, he stood behind us, ordered for us. A seat opened up next to Jane. He took it, engaged her in a discussion about school.

I was surprised at how easily she responded to him. Blue had such a charm about him, like a big, genial bear. I couldn't imagine him angry enough to commit murder. But, maybe it wasn't an act of anger. Was it a cold calculation, for financial gain?

Why was I even thinking about this? Just as I was about to cut in on their conversation, the food came. I was famished and hadn't realized it until I tasted the cheeseburger. I took another ravenous bite. Blue was amused at my appetite. We all started to laugh; life was fun for a moment.

Two hours later, the three of us were watching television, or rather, one of Jane's videos on television. Blue looked as nervous as I felt.

We were sitting in chairs next to each other, I could feel the heat coming off his body. He glanced at me every few minutes. I pretended not to notice.

"Do I have to do homework now?" Jane asked, when the movie ended.

"Yes, honey. I'll help you," I said, expecting Blue to take his cue and leave. Instead, he opened a magazine. I went upstairs with Jane, knowing he'd still be there when I came back down. When I did, Blue was in the kitchen. He was gathering his paint cans together. I started to make coffee.

"Are you nervous about tomorrow?" he asked.

"Petrified. I just hope I'm able to do whatever it takes to . . . you know."

"You will be. You seem to have awfully good judgment. You've been in a lot of difficult situations, and you've never broken down."

"I think about that all the time," I said. "Why haven't I just had a complete nervous breakdown? It must be in my biochemistry— my nervous system doesn't know how to break down."

"There's probably something to that. I was in a very stressful situation a few years ago, I thought I'd crack, but I didn't," he said. I sat down at the kitchen table, hoping he would go on. He didn't. Since I was never going to see him again, I risked an inquiry.

"What was the situation that was so upsetting?" I asked, softly. He jumped, as if shocked by an electrical current, then looked down. He stood there, pondering the question. Finally, he turned his impossibly blue eyes to mine, shrugged, sat down across from me.

"You'd find out anyway, so I might as well tell you," he said, resigned.

"My wife disappeared in 1992. We had been married three years, the last two unhappily. And . . . and . . . that's the story," he said, evasively.

"What happened to her?" I asked. He stared at the wall, then looked at the coffeemaker; the coffee wasn't done.

"It's hard to tell you."

"Try it," I said, with a sinking feeling. There was no denying that I was involved with Blue. I was hanging on his every word. Maybe finding my mother had released such feelings of intimacy that I was just looking for an outlet for them. I wanted to find any excuse to discount my attraction to Blue.

"I wish it didn't matter what you think," he said, slowly. "It doesn't matter to me what others think, never has. Well, here goes, I hope this comes out all right.

"Most people think I murdered my wife," he said. I opened my eyes wide, didn't want to trust my voice. It might betray that I wasn't surprised.

"Her family hated me from the start of our

romance, and she hated them. I like to think she married me because she loved me, but she may have married me to get away from her family. They were society types. They wanted her to make a San Marino match, some blue blood like herself, from the same neighborhood.

"My family is white-bread, middle-class all the way. I grew up in the most boring Bay Area suburb, Foster City, ticky tacky little houses, all the same. It was anticreative, but my mother wanted to be an artist before she did the homemaker trip, so she named me Blue." He stopped, lost in thought for a moment. Then he continued.

"Anyway, Alex, that was her name, had a very unhappy childhood. I didn't know it when I married her, but she had used drugs since she was a teenager. The first year we were married it wasn't so bad.

"Then she started using heavily, hard drugs. She hid it from her family; so did I. They still don't know.

"I begged her to get help. The last year we were together, she would be gone for days at a time. Then one day, she was gone, forever. I didn't even know which day it was, because it was her habit, by then, not to be home regularly. After a week I called her family, thought maybe she had moved home. They hadn't heard from her.

"I called her friends—no one had seen her," he said, taking a deep breath.

"Later, when the police questioned me, I figured out that the last day I saw her was September 27, 1992. It was the last day anyone saw her. When she didn't turn up, her family accused me of murdering her. She had made a will leaving me her money. I didn't know.

"I couldn't account for my 'whereabouts,' as they say, on the day she disappeared, because I was home painting. My life is usually solitary when I'm painting. I only go out if I need something. I didn't that day.

"Her body has never been found. I assume she's dead. I didn't kill her," he said, his voice now a whisper of despair, pleading with me.

How could I not believe him? Hadn't I tried to convince everyone for years that my mother was alive? And no one ever believed me. Pretty soon, your internal filtering system tells you to keep the truth to yourself. If it goes against popular sentiment, nobody wants to hear it.

I grew tired of pitying, patronizing friends telling me how 'anything was possible' while they shook their heads. Would I tell them I had been abducted by a UFO next?

It was brutal being a self-appointed bearer of the truth. I knew the unbearable loneliness of such a journey well. There was nothing I could ever say to convince even Donna, my closest friend, that I was right. She accused me of obsession, and, at times, dementia.

Without a body, how could Blue prove his innocence? If Alex came back alive, he would be cleared. If her body were found, and there was no evidence that she had been murdered or been murdered by him, then his innocence would be established. Now he was in limbo.

"Can they convict someone of a murder if no one is found dead?"

"I understand that they can. They call it a 'no body' case, but they have to have enough evidence. They didn't, in my case," he said. Oddly enough, I didn't question whether he murdered her. I wanted to believe. But did he still love her?

He sighed, turned his palms upward in an expression of exasperation, shook his head. His big blond visage seemed alien to my world, which was inhabited by lean, dark people. Didn't the blood of Nordic hunters flow through his arteries? Somehow he had wandered beyond his ancestral land, his primordial territories, and gotten involved in an incomprehensible nightmare.

I had the same feeling about my life. I had picked up the wrong guidebook along the way. I felt that we were the only two people in the world that shared a secret, our lives somehow had gone wildly out of control. Would the rest of the world forever regard him as a killer? Dark shadows would cling to him for the rest of his days.

I had the urge to comfort him, so I put my hand on top of his. He was surprised, slowly turned his hand over and folded mine into it, a gesture of solidarity.

"I loved her when I married her, but by the end of our marriage, that love had been destroyed," he said, answering my unspoken question.

"Sometimes, I still hope they'll find her alive. Maybe she ran off with some guy. But in my heart, I know she's dead," he said. He remained motionless, our hands intertwined.

I guess I wanted to seduce him from the first moment I saw him, but I resisted, even after he made the advances. My friends all talk about their ability to be seduced. That is foreign to me. I have to be the seducer.

Because of my childhood, the emotional losses I sustained, I don't trust easily. I've always made the decision on sexual partners. Not that there have been many. I was looking for the soul mate, the person to fall in love with, and Paolo, my third affair, turned out to be it.

As I tried to combat my fiery attraction to Blue, I realized that part of the reason I wanted to sleep with him were the upcoming events. I was apprehensive that tomorrow might be the last day of my life. Who knew what lengths I would go to to defend my mother if need be?

I wanted the security of Blue's arms around

me, if just for a short time. I wanted to feel his breath on my cheek. Making love would center, calm me, give me some emotional resources with which to face the unknown.

Jane was asleep, my bedroom was on this floor, she would never hear. I took my hand away, moved to him, sat down in his big lap, leaned toward him. He stared at me for a moment, wanting reassurance that I believed his story, I gave it to him with my eyes.

He knew that my invitation went all the way. He grabbed me, kissed me hard, then softly, covering my face with kisses like white dandelion breath. I could tell he had fierce energy for lovemaking. I was glad. My aggression was in a holding pattern, waiting to be tapped tomorrow. All I was capable of now was sweet acceptance.

He held my head with his big, square hands as he kissed me. It was strange to feel immobile. I was used to being a free agent. I was anchored to earth for just a moment. He started to remove my sweater. I stopped him, ed him to my bedroom.

Give me love and strength, I begged silently. will need it for tomorrow. It was easy, natral to respond to him as we lay naked on the ed, as if we were born making love to each ther, after experiencing it in the womb.

When we were done, I had drained his sap. e lay next to me, exhausted, one big paw on the top of my head. But he looked happy, so I had given as well as received.

He pulled my body into the spoon position, hugged me, fell asleep. I looked at him in repose, he was sculpted big, too big, for this small bedroom. I tried to fall asleep.

But a thought at the back of my mind would give me no peace. Had I just made love to a murderer?

7

Blue woke up at 5 A.M.—it was still dark out. I had been staring at him for hours, sleep eluded me. He kissed me on the forehead.

"I always wake up early. I like to paint by the first light," he said.

"Go ahead, go paint," I said, smiling.

"I'm not leaving you today," he said, tracing my lips with his finger.

"Absolutely not," I said, "it'll be fine. Just come over later, in case I fall apart."

"It's the last hurdle," he said, reassuringly. "You'll liberate her for good at noon."

"I hope so," I said. He pulled me to him, kissed me again, lovingly. I looked at him, studied him. Was this the last time I would ever see him? I hoped there would be a later." He lumbered into his clothes, grabbed my hand, turned my palm over, kissed it.

"Bye, good luck," he said as he left.

I tried to get some sleep. Every time I started to drift off, faceless, willowy, black silk figures tried to strangle me. They flew over my head like dervishes. Just as they swooped down and grasped my neck with their long, black, gossamer fingers, I woke up.

I had to keep busy or I would go crazy. I was never up this early. Now that I had the kitchen back, I decided to make Jane a big breakfast rather than her usual juice and oatmeal.

As I baked blueberry muffins and scrambled eggs, I refused to give in to fear. This would not be the last breakfast I cooked for my daughter.

Jane smelled the food, came down in her Lanz flannel nightgown. "What's the occasion? Is it a holiday?" she asked, sitting down, starting to eat.

"No, honey, I was up early," I said. I didn't say, if this is the last breakfast I ever make you, I want it to be a good one that expresses how much I love you. When I walked Jane to school, I hugged her very hard. Later, I called Donna to tell her what time to pick up Jane if I ran into trouble.

"I won't rest until you get up here," she said. I promised I'd come immediately. I decided to go to my mother's apartment early to help allay her anxiety.

I rang her apartment intercom; she buzzed me up. She opened her door cautiously. Sh was dressed in a lovely gray suit of a popular style from the seventies and was wearing a small pearl-and-gold pineapple on a chain around her neck. It looked familiar.

"Elizabeth," she said, kissing me quickly on the cheek, "maybe you shouldn't come."

"Don't be silly. I'm coming. Mother, didn't you have that pineapple locket when I was a little girl?"

"Why yes," she said, looking very pleased. "What a memory you have. Do you remember what was in the locket?"

"No," I said. She walked over, stood next to me, opened the locket. Inside were pictures of my father and me. I was about four. I had the same picture of my father in my home.

"I remember when I took you to the photographer. You wouldn't let go of that little white lamb with the pink skirt. You can see it, you're holding it in your hands." I stared at it. A tiny animal was barely visible in the corner of the photograph.

"I used to have your picture professionally taken every year. Come here, I'll show you," she said. She walked to a drawer, opened it, took out a small leather album. Inside were several pictures of me, one every year until I was nine. I was always posed against a floral backdrop; the years were marked by my different hairstyles and missing teeth.

"This album was one of the few things I grabbed that night I had to leave," she said, putting it carefully back in the drawer. She took out an envelope before she closed it. She handed it to me.

"What's this?"

"The keys to my safety deposit box and its location are in there. The box contains the few pieces of jewelry from your father that I took with me. Just in case anything happens to me today, I want you to have those," she said, her voice low. I grabbed her, hugged her.

"Don't even say that, put that envelope back," I said. She pulled away.

"Please, Elizabeth, I don't mean to be maudlin, but I'm realistic. There's also a key to this apartment in there and my final wishes, if you should have to dispose of my body."

"Mom, please. I'll put it in my purse just to placate you. But I'll give it back to you after the phone call. Everything is going to work out, I know it." I opened my purse, quickly stuck it in.

"What are you doing with a gun in there?" she asked, backing away from me.

"Oh, I borrowed it from a friend until I get one. It's a long story, but basically it's for protection."

"Why?"

"I didn't get a chance to tell you," I said unsure how to broach the subject, "but my husband, Paolo, was from one of Italy's richest families, and he left me around twenty million dollars." My mother was stunned. "You know," I added, "there's a lot of kidnapping for ransom there. Recently the gangs have been targeting people outside Italy."

"Your husband left you all that money? That's wonderful, Elizabeth. I'm thrilled for you," she said. "What will you do with it?"

"Do with it? Just live, save it for Jane."

"You could take some wonderful trips, you could go anywhere for as long as you want," she said, enthusiastically.

"Trips? What for?"

"I just mean take vacations, or educational trips. It would be so good for Jane."

"That's true. Well, if we can, we'll all go somewhere exciting together," I said. "Now, do you have a coat? It's chilly for L.A. today." She opened her small closet, took out an old black cloth coat. I saw her shiver as she put it on.

"Are you getting sick?"

"No, it's just anxiety. You don't think someone will drive by the phone booth and just gun me down, do you?"

"No, no, they could have done that yesterday."

"Maybe we shouldn't go to the phone booth."

"What do you mean?"

"I could go to the airport, disappear again. How many years do I have left anyway? Ten? Only," she said, starting to cry, "I'd hate to leave you again, now that I've found you."

"I'm not going to lose you again, Mother. I can't! If we have to make you disappear, we can always do it after the phone call. Let's at least see what they want," I said. She took a deep breath, agreed, walked toward the door. She seemed taller for a moment.

She got into my car with a stoic attitude. Is this the cloak she had worn all those years in Argentina? Her face was masklike, devoid of expression. This must be how she handled fear.

"Do you know where it is?" she asked.

"Sixteenth and Montana? Sure, it's just a few blocks from your apartment, Montana? You know Montana?"

"Montana?"

"You know the street, above Wilshire, with all the stores and restaurants?"

"Oh yes, of course," she said with uncertainty. How could she not know Montana? How small her world must be, since she came back to L.A. How small it's always been since my father died. She hasn't had a home, a sense of place since, I thought with sadness.

I parked down the block from the phone booth. My mother seemed almost not to breathe, closed down, became a nonperson, taking up very little air and space.

"Whatever it takes, we'll do it. This is just a phone call, nothing more," I said. She nodded silently, got out of the car like a soldier marching to her doom.

We walked to the phone booth, the door was ajar. I checked my watch—it was noon. The phone rang. We looked at one another, then she stepped into the booth, answered the phone.

"Hello?" she asked, tentatively, then, "Yes, this is Lorelei Stein." That was the last thing she said for a couple of minutes. If possible, she got even paler. Then she said, "Yes, I understand. I'll be here tomorrow at noon." She listened for a moment, looked puzzled, replaced the receiver.

"He didn't say good-bye," she said, stepping unsteadily outside the phone booth. She looked down, as if she were trying to center herself. I put my arm through hers, walked her toward the car. She had a distant look in her eyes.

Mazzelli must have plunged her into a strange memory space. How long since she had heard that threatening voice? Over twenty-five years.

She seemed to have forgotten where she was. I stopped her when we reached the car, opened the door for her. She finally looked at me sadly, got in. I locked both car doors for the feeling of security.

"Mom, tell me what he said."

"I should never have asked you to meet me. This is going to end very badly. For so many years we've escaped our fate—now it's caught us. We can't run fast enough, there's nowhere left to run," she said, as if in a trance.

"Mom, first things first. What did Mazzelli say?"

"It doesn't matter, it's not possible."

"Just tell me what he said," I insisted. She turned hopeless eyes on me.

"He said he doesn't bear a grudge anymore. He won't ever bother me again if I gave him a million dollars. He said he's old and ill, that he needs the money. But if I can't come up with it, then he'll, he'll . . ." she said, couldn't finish the horrible threat.

"Mom," I said, relieved, "we can put this all behind us by buying your freedom. That's great. I've got money. I've got the million dollars. You're worth a lot more than that to me."

"No," she said, seriously. "Your husband left that money for you and Jane, you can't spend it like this."

"Mom, are you kidding? Who's more important than you? You're the only mother I have, the only grandmother Jane has. I have more money than that and nothing to spend it on. If all it takes to spring you from the Mob is money, I'm thrilled."

"I can't let you, Elizabeth. Just take me back to my apartment. Please, honey. I'm exhausted, I want to lie down."

"How did you leave it with Mazzelli?"

"He told me to be at the phone booth tomorrow at noon with my answer. He'd call me."

"Mom," I said, "please let me do this for you. It's for me, too. I don't want to live the rest of my life without you. You stood up to the Mob for me. Now I can do this for you. Please let me. It's all I'm living for," I said, as I put my arm around her. She looked old. A thief had robbed her of so many years of her prime.

"Oh, I don't know, honey," she said, softly.

"You know the woman I was with at the Farmer's Market?"

"I was so nervous I didn't look at her."

"That was Donna Mason; she's still my best friend."

"Donna Mason? That was Donna? My goodness."

"Yes, she loved you when we were children. She wants me to bring you up to her house now."

"Oh," she said, apprehensively, "I can't just move around freely, I shouldn't . . ."

"Mom, you don't get it. You're completely safe because tomorrow at noon, we agree to Mazzelli's demands."

"Well, maybe some other time, I'm tired and . . ."

"No, we'll just stay a few minutes. Please, Mom, for me?"

"Well, all right. I'd love to see Donna, but just for a short time," she said, putting her head back on the headrest, closing her eyes. I started the drive to Donna's house, elated.

Money was the liberator—I had money. I would buy my mother back from them. They had no idea I was in the picture. I woke her when we got to Donna's. She took out her compact, powdered her nose, fixed her hair, then we went in.

"Mrs. Stein, it's wonderful to see you," Donna said, when we walked in. She threw her arms around my mother.

"Donna, I never would have recognized you. You look beautiful. It's just so amazing that you and Elizabeth have remained close all these years," my mother said, kissing her. Donna led her to the couch, sat down with her.

"Leticia, bring some refreshments, please. I don't know if I would have recognized you either, Mrs. Stein."

"Call me Lorelei, honey."

"Lorelei. Now that I look at you, you do look very much like you used to," Donna said. I sat down in the chair across from them, astonished at how wonderful life was. My mother and I were visiting my best friend, just like people do all over the world. It would be an ordinary afternoon for anyone but me.

"I recognized her at once," I said.

"Yes, but you've been searching for her every day since she disappeared. When you're looking for something you find it," Donna observed. My mother looked at me lovingly. She valued my vigil. Leticia brought tea, coffee and cucumber sandwiches.

"May I smoke?" my mother asked.

"Of course," Donna said, handing her an ashtray and lighting a cigarette of her own. "My house may be the only place left in L.A. where you can smoke without breaking the law and encountering severe moral indignation."

"You're married, Elizabeth tells me. Are you happy, dear?" my mother asked.

"Relatively," Donna said. She then fixed her gaze on my mother as she always did whenever a true answer was required. She had always been mistress of the white lie. It served her well.

If she failed to meet me at the vending machines for coffee after class because a cute guy talked to her, the excuse was always that the professor kept her. If she needed to borrow money from me, it was always for an emergency, contact lenses, medicine.

The term "borrow" was used generously— I knew it wouldn't be repaid. Then she would secretly spend it on clothes or makeup, pretend she did otherwise.

I hate liars. Early on, I asked her to tell me the truth, whatever the consequences. I feel patronized by white lies. She said she would, but she never did. I just accepted her, tried not to let it matter. I judged Donna by a different set of standards than I did others.

"You know, Lorelei," she said, very seriously, so seriously that her weak left eye turned to the wall. She had a walleye. Several operations, which she had had as a small child, had failed to correct it. Whenever she felt strongly about something, her eye veered to the left. It was unnerving because you never knew whether to stare at her functioning eye or at her nose.

"Security is more important to me than to most people, because of what I went through with my parents," she said, slowly.

"Even though I wasn't wildly infatuated with Randall when I married him, I knew he was a good prospect. He has been so kind and generous that I have fallen in love with him," she said. This was shocking, but then, she never felt compelled to be completely truthful with me.

"Well, I'm just glad you're doing well," my mother said. She probably couldn't conceive of not being madly in love with your mate; she was with my father.

"Because of my support, he's now on the verge of a big deal, foreign money," Donna said. "I knew he could do it," she added, proudly.

"Do you have children?" my mother asked. Donna's face clouded.

"Yes, Lorelei, I have a son. He has so much potential but . . ." She paused. "There are problems." Then she shrugged her angular shoulders, clothed in a black cashmere sweater set, and changed the subject.

"But let's not talk about him. What happened with Mazzelli?" Donna asked, eagerly. My mother jumped involuntarily. Maybe she hadn't expected me to discuss it with Donna.

"Don't worry, she won't tell anyone," I said, rushing to reassure her. My mother gave Donna an apprehensive look.

"Our problems are over," I said.

"Now, Elizabeth, it's complicated," my mother cautioned.

"No, it isn't. It's as simple as writing a check for one million dollars. Or giving him a cashier's check if he prefers."

"A million bucks?" Donna asked, raising her black pencil-thin eyebrows into an unfriendly arch.

"Donna, you can't be against this. The money means nothing compared to my mother's life!"

"It's not that I'm against it, Elizabeth. But just follow my thought, if you give him the million, what's to prevent him from coming back, demanding another million?"

"Mazzelli doesn't even know I'm involved; he doesn't know I have any money. He probably thinks the million is my mother's money that she managed to take with her when she left the country. Or, he may think she still knows some of my father's wealthy friends."

"It's a lot of money," Donna said.

Why did I have to convince both my mother and Donna of the only correct decision? It was so obvious. "Look, I'm giving him the money, and that's that," I said.

My mother smiled gratefully. She was done protesting.

8

When I got home, I had an upsetting thought. Would Mazzelli make my mother hand the money personally to one of his associates? That would be far too dangerous for her. I couldn't do it either; I didn't want them to know about me.

Jane had a field trip, wouldn't be home till six. I had resisted the urge to make my mother move out of her apartment today, to bring her home and install her in the guest room permanently. But I decided to wait until after the phone call tomorrow.

She was jumpy. Maybe she couldn't quite grasp that her torture was coming to an end. She had lived in the shadows for so long as a nonperson.

It hurt me so, what she had endured, and all for me. She seemed to lack the vitality that I remembered. But, what could I really remember? After all, I had been nine. Then again, maybe my memory was correct, and she had just been diminished by fear over time.

I was surprised at her reaction to the news about my wealth. I didn't remember that she liked to travel. She seemed satisfied to be a homebody when I was little. She never wanted to accompany my father on his business trips to New York or Chicago.

Maybe it was the nature of those trips that she didn't want to be exposed to. Or, maybe because she had been forbidden to experience the world for nearly a quarter of a century, she now equated travel with life.

I walked into the bland guest room. Would my mother like it? Maybe she would prefer a guesthouse in the back. I hoped she would want to live with me. If not, I'd buy her her own house in the neighborhood. She always loved the English country look. I remembered our old home. Pine furniture and floral couches would perk up this room. I heard a knock, let Blue in.

"How did it go?"

"Perfectly," I answered, telling him what happened.

"Your priorities are completely in order, I admire that," he said.

"Thank you for saying that, Blue. I had to brook opposition from Donna and even my mother! I mean, it's the only choice. I can't imagine any rationale for not paying Mazzelli."

"It's just that a million dollars is a lot of money for most people. They think twice about spending it. You have so much that it's nothing to you."

"It's not that it's nothing, Blue. But money intrinsically has no value for me. It's a metaphor for security, freedom. If I only had a hundred dollars and Mazzelli asked for that, I'd give it to him. My mother's life is priceless; its value is far above any monetary amount."

"You're a good woman, Elizabeth," he said.

"That sounds like something someone would say to Sally Field in a movie. I'm just a daughter who loves her mother."

"OK, I know better than to argue with you. Want to do a few errands with me?"

"Sure, I don't feel like staying home. I'm in too good a mood."

This was the first time I had ridden with Blue in his van. It gave me a feeling of power to ride in such a large vehicle; it was a strange angle from which to look at L.A. I was used to closing out the sound environment, unfriendly music, unwelcome invitations; I never drove around with the windows open. This type of closure was unnecessary in the van. Blue put a tape in the tape deck.

"I've never heard this, but I like it," I said. For a moment, I was able just to enjoy myself, without being inhabited by sad memories and longings. After tomorrow I would have the life I've always wanted. I was not a daughter of the Mob who became an Italian heiress, whose self-defining moment was the day she had lost her mother. Now that had all changed. I had my mother, was part of a three-generation family. I was a single mother, living in L.A., dating an attractive man who found me desirable.

"Where are we going?" I asked, as we slowed down on a busy west L.A. street.

"Right there, but it looks crowded," he said as he pointed to a post office. There was a line of people all the way to the outside door.

"Do you ever go to the old Beverly Hills Post Office? It's like a huge historical landmark. It's gorgeous," I said. "Not that many people go there, it's never crowded. Just go east on Santa Monica Boulevard toward Beverly Hills."

"That's a post office?" he asked, amazed when he saw it. We went in. The huge brick building was ornate, murals were on the tops of the walls, the ceiling was domed. There was a plaque stating that the post office was built under the auspices of President Franklin Delano Roosevelt.

"Don't you think they should let the homeless in here at night or something? All this wasted space," I said.

"It would make a great shelter," Blue said drawn to the murals, especially one painting of a cloud. He studied it for a moment, then got in the short line to send a letter overnight mail. I waited in the empty, large, outer room, which contained all the post office boxes. The floor was marbled linoleum; it was shiny, clean, looked like real marble.

The edifice, because that was what it was, seemed like an anomaly in modern, multicultural, crime-ridden Los Angeles. I felt safe under its voluminous ceiling, inside its cavernous walls. The air had a strange cool quality to it, a quality I always associate with European museums.

I remembered coming here with my parents when I was a child, when a visit to a post office was fun, before it became a matter of avoiding the line leading up to the "disgruntled" postal worker.

Bored, I walked to the glass door to look at the trees outside. That was when I saw it, the silver car, with two men inside. It was too far away to see the license plate.

We were parked at the end parking meter, the car hovered at the exit driveway. Once we left, they could make a fast getaway, hide on the side street, then fall in behind us in traffic.

I stared at them as they watched the door. They couldn't see me. They were Italian. Their gestures, their look convinced me. Blue finished and approached me. I grabbed him, dragged him quickly off to a corner.

"The silver car is here," I said.

"Are you afraid? Give me my gun, I'll go and confront them. They're not after me," Blue said. I wasn't giving him his gun, didn't want him to get in trouble because of me.

"But what if I'm wrong?"

"What do you mean?"

"What if it is just a crazy coincidence, like there's no connection at all or they think I'm someone else?"

"Is that likely?"

"I don't know. But if you confront them, it's not like they'll admit it. Look, what can they do to me if I'm in the van with you? Let's test it.

"If they're following me, then maybe after I give the money to Mazzelli," I said, "I'll tell the police. I don't think they're connected to Mazzelli unless he knows about me, somehow." I started for the glass doors. Blue tried to stop me, but I eluded him. I was out the door in a second; he was right behind me.

As soon as they saw me, they zoomed out. We got into the van.

"Just start driving, I bet they follow. This time I'll have you as my witness," I said.

Blue turned right out of parking lot, it was the only way he could turn. The police station was right across the street. There was no sign of the silver car. We turned right again, still no sign of them. Then we turned onto Santa Monica Boulevard to go home; there they were, one car length behind us. I could see i clearly—it had no front license plate.

"I'm going to lead them on a chase," Blue said.

"Be careful, it's not worth it. They could be dangerous." But Blue's testosterone level was soaring. Before I could stop him he was heading down Avenue of the Stars toward Olympic Boulevard, where you could really fly.

Blue changed lanes like he was in the Indy 500. The silver car kept up with us, soon was forced to abandon its pretense of staying one car length behind. The driver seemed more intent on not losing me this time than previously. We almost grazed a Jeep.

"Blue, please, they already know where I live, let's not have an accident."

"Goddamn bullies," he said, heatedly, plowing through more traffic. He turned into the freeway lane.

"Blue, I don't want to get on the freeway with them, it would be easier for them to shoot at us, anything, even ram the van."

"Don't worry, I know what I'm doing," he said, as his speedometer climbed to its peak. Just as Blue reached the freeway ramp, he pulled off onto a shoulder. I was thrown against the side of the cab.

The silver car tried to do the same, but spun round, instead, and hit two cars, resulting in an awful bang. All three cars were smashed.

Blue picked that moment to peel out, but not before I saw shoulder holsters with guns beneath the jackets of the two men and heard them swearing and shouting in Italian. They had no rear license plate.

"Did you see what I did?" Blue asked.

"The guns?" I asked.

"No fucking kidding."

"They were speaking Italian, you know what that means."

"You've got to go to the police about this," Blue said, very concerned.

"I don't know. Let me do the Mazzelli transaction first. I can only worry about one thing at a time. Meanwhile, Jane and I will be very careful," I said, suddenly tired, with too much to worry about.

"Can you take me home? I don't have the energy left for any more errands. This is all getting me down," I said.

"I don't blame you," Blue said, kindly. He dropped me off, asked if he could come over after dinner. I agreed. I walked into the house, sat down, again questioned whether I should stay in L.A. My original goal was to relive my childhood with my mother, look for clues that would lead me to her. Now I had her.

If I took my mother and Jane to another city whom would I miss? Only Donna. And Blue

Would my mother care if we left L.A.? Prob ably not. Mazzelli had found her here. Jan and I could be in danger from him and fror the mysterious occupants of the silver car. I' discuss it with Donna. Maybe I was ove reacting from the recent events—they were terribly unsettling.

As soon as I thought of her, Donna called, as if she could read my mind. She reminded me that she and Randall were taking me to dinner tomorrow night.

"I don't know if I can. What if something happens with my mother? She might be upset."

"You could always bring her," Donna replied.

"Maybe."

"Good luck tomorrow, Elizabeth, we'll pick you up at 7 P.M."

I scrubbed the guest room so it was presentable for my mother. I hoped she'd like it. I'd have to hire a maid if she moved in; I never was a very good cleaner. I couldn't wait for her to meet Jane; children loved my mother.

She put them at ease immediately. When I was a child, I thought she had magical powers, sprinkled fairy dust on children wherever she went.

Jane came home later from her field trip, sat down, started to eat her snack.

"Honey, you're going to meet my mother soon. Your grandmother. She's just so excited," I said.

"I hope she likes me," Jane said.

"What?" I asked, laughing. "Of course she'll like you, you're her granddaughter."

"You mean for sure?"

"Anyone would love you," I said, gazing at her. How could they not? She was such an innocent, fresh, bright, little spirit. I could almost picture them planting purple tulips in the front yard together. Blue came over after I put Jane to bed.

"No silver car?" he asked, worriedly.

"No, and they'll probably be in a different car next time, after that accident," I said.

"Blue, you know what? This is the last night that I will have a different life than everyone else. Tomorrow, I join the human race, start again, with the life I should have had all along. I want to pretend that the past never happened," I said.

Blue sat down on a window ledge, upset. He stared outside, moodily, didn't speak.

"What's wrong?" I asked.

"Am I part of the past, when tomorrow begins?" he asked, hoarsely. His question surprised me. I hadn't included him in the equation. How could I answer? I moved to him, kissed him.

After tomorrow I was going to be let out of prison after a life sentence. I couldn't even promise to be the same person. My entire being might regenerate into someone new.

We went into the bedroom, didn't continue the discussion, made glorious love instead. After he fell asleep, I got up, paced around almost soundlessly. I didn't want to get back in bed; my demons wouldn't let me sleep.

Blue mumbled, opened his eyes. He got out of bed, put his arm around me, led me back to bed, put me in the spoon position at his back. Finally, hours later, or maybe minutes, I fell asleep.

I immediately began to have one of those vivid "you are there" nightmares that always terrify me. My dreams never seem like dreams, they seem real.

I was a small girl, lost. It was in Europe, maybe Switzerland. I was in a small village surrounded by snowcapped peaks. I was running up and down the streets looking into shops, trying to find my mother. Strangers tried to catch me, but I wouldn't stop running. I had to find her soon or I would lose her forever.

It started to rain, my search became urgent. The streets were narrow, I pushed past many people. Finally, I caught sight of her—she was getting into a car. I had to get to her fast. In a final burst of energy, just as she was closing the car door I grabbed her skirt.

"Elizabeth, thank goodness," she said. Her voice comforted me. Then I looked at her face. She was a stranger. She reached for me, I resisted. "You're not my mother!" I screamed.

"Of course I am; get in, honey," she said, as two men got out of her car and started pulling me in.

"No, you're not, help, save me, save me!" I

begged people on the street. I woke up, confused, chilled.

What did it mean? There was a thought in the back of my mind, lurking, demanding to be recognized. I shook my head to clear it out. Something in my gut questioned whether Lorelei was really my mother.

How could she not be? She had childhood pictures of me, pictures of my father, my mother's jewelry, the same memories of the past that I did. Besides, who else could she be?

Yet her hands seemed bigger than I recalled, her finger joints, larger. I remembered her fingers as longer, her skin, softer. But it had been over twenty-five years. The something that didn't feel right was probably just me, not being able to accept that I'd found her at last. There was a feeling of unreality about everything lately.

I dismissed my apprehension. The dream was about my past search for her, it had no relevance. I went back to sleep, hoping that disturbing dreams would not visit me again.

In the morning, Blue woke up at dawn, woke me. I was so nervous about the noon phone call that I didn't want to discuss it. He offered to accompany me, I refused.

"I'm going to stop by later this afternoon to see how you are," he said.

"That would be nice," I said. He left, looking worried.

When I walked into my mother's apartment,

she was incredibly composed. I thought that she would be as nervous as I was. The apartment was almost barren.

"It's so empty in here; I can't wait to move you to a better, homier place," I said.

"I do need a few more things, but I wouldn't want to live in as crowded a room as you did when you were growing up."

"What do you mean?"

"Don't you remember? You had so many toys that we had to take out one of the twin beds in your room. You loved those big stuffed animals, but you didn't like your dolls," she said. I had forgotten that they took that bed out. How did she remember a detail like that? Now that I thought about it, I could see that vacant side of the room gradually filling with more toys.

She picked up her sweater and her purse.

"Are you nervous?" I asked.

"No, I'm really not, Elizabeth. I'm in your hands, I trust you," she said.

"Thank you, Mother. I'm so glad you said that. It'll work out. I'll do whatever Mazzelli says. We'd better go before we lose our nerve." My mother nodded.

We parked a few feet away from the phone booth. I looked around to see if we were being followed. There was no one in the phone booth. My mother entered it a couple minutes before noon. The phone rang, she answered.

"Hello," she said, pausing, then, "this is Lorelei Stein, Mr. Mazzelli." She listened for a moment.

"Yes, I can get you the money. Today?" she looked at me. I nodded "yes."

"Yes, today. The park on Beverly Glen south of Sunset? At Comstock? No, I don't know it, but I'll find it. Right, go to the pay phone outside the playground, then wait for your call. A cashier's check for a million dollars made out to Trenton Corporation? You'll have to give me say . . ." She paused again, looked at me.

I held up two fingers.

"Two hours. I can have it there at 2 P.M.," she said, then paused.

"Yes, I understand if I deviate from the instructions I could lose my life," she said, softly. Then she just looked into the phone.

"He just hung up," she said, hanging up, too.

"That's fine, let's go. We've got to get to the bank," I said. "I notified them yesterday that I would need a million dollars in a hurry. They said they'd accommodate me.

"It's not like on TV or in the movies," I said, driving to the bank.

"What's not?" asked my mother.

"The money drop, of course, it's a different situation. We don't have to give them unmarked bills because they know we won't try to trace them. They know we're not going to the police."

"Oh, Elizabeth, I hope this is the right thing to do," my mother said, worried.

"It's the only thing to do. After this, you're free," I said, clasping her hand quickly. She smiled at me.

We walked into the bank. I asked for Christopher Matthews, the bank officer I had talked to. He came out of the back offices, a professional-looking middle-aged man. He ushered us into his cubicle.

"I'm Elizabeth Manganaro, I talked to you earlier about the million dollars?"

"Yes, how would you like that?" he inquired as if he did this every day. Maybe he did.

"In a cashier's check."

"No problem, do you have a withdrawal slip?" he asked. I handed him my checkbook, he filled it out, handed me the slip to sign. He pulled out a signature card, compared the signatures.

"I'm sorry, we have to be careful with large sums," he said.

"I appreciate that," I said.

"I'll be right back," he said, going into the back office. I looked around to see if anyone was following me, but I didn't see anyone. My mother and I stared at each other as the minutes ticked by.

It was 1 P.M. already. What if something went wrong? There was probably some way to expedite this process, but I didn't know what it was. My mother fingered her purse anxiously, looking like she'd like to run out of the bank.

"What's taking so long?" she whispered.

"I don't know, but the park is only ten minutes away. We'll make it," I answered, reassuringly. It was frightening to realize that my mother's very life depended on the next hour. We had no way to contact Mazzelli if there were an unavoidable delay. If we weren't on time, would he just hire someone to kill her, no second chances? Where was the banker?

At that moment Matthews came out, handed me the check. I put it in my purse.

"Do you want an escort to your car?" he asked.

"No, we'll be fine," I said, wondering immediately if we should take the escort. What if something else prevented our meeting and my mother died for it? I smiled at her with what I hoped was confidence.

We walked quickly to the car, practically jumped in and locked the doors.

"We're halfway there, Mom," I said.

"I know," she said, visibly shaking. I put a calming hand on hers, but she pulled it away.

"What's wrong?"

"I just realized something. Mazzelli can't know you exist—I don't want to endanger you."

"He doesn't, remember?"

"I know, but you can't be with me when I deliver the money. Whoever picks it up or is watching the phone booth could see you."

"I can't let you go there yourself. Anything could happen."

"Elizabeth, this is one thing I'm going to insist on. I've let you assume such a risk for me. Who knows whether he's had someone watching my apartment? He knows where I live. I thought about that this morning, too late. I should have met you at the bank. That way they would have thought I got the money out of my account."

"Mazzelli wants the money. He doesn't care where you get it. Even if his associate saw me, he wouldn't necessarily think it was me. Mazzelli hasn't seen me since I was nine. And he doesn't know I'm the widow of a very wealthy man," I said, turning off Wilshire in Beverly Hills, going up Beverly Glen toward the park.

"There's the phone booth, on that corner," I said pointing to it on a street bordering the children's park. The park was ringed by expensive cars and limousines; small children played in the sandbox and on the climbing equipment as their parents and nannies looked on. A little girl was pushed in a swing by two bodyguards. Their guns showed in their belts.

I looked around for the courier, but I didn't see anyone that looked out of place.

"I wonder if the person picking up the

money is here or if he'll call you with additional directions?" I asked.

"He didn't say. What time is it, honey?"

"Twenty to two; it turns out we're early."

"How long would it take you to drive home?"

"About ten minutes."

"I want you to go home now."

"What? What if he directs you to another location? You don't have a car."

"As soon as he calls, I'll call you."

"No, I'm staying, Mother."

"Elizabeth, I really don't want you to. Please show me some respect by at least doing this one thing for me. He's not going to kill me; he doesn't want to. He just wants the money.

"Let me end this nightmare alone. If you don't, I won't ever be able to relax, constantly worrying that he's going to go after you—or even Jane."

"I guess you're right. I wouldn't want to take a chance where Jane is concerned," I said, reluctantly.

"I'll wait for your phone call. If you need to go somewhere else, I'll come right back; if not, I'll pick you up immediately. Nothing can happen to you here. There'd be a dozen witnesses. It's a public place."

"Well, this will do it," my mother said quietly. "They would never think I could get my hands on any more money." I opened my purse, took out the check, handed it to her. She kissed me lightly on the cheek, got out.

"Call me as soon as you know. I'll be waiting by my phone," I said.

I drove away from the park with great difficulty. Why couldn't we have mailed the check? If only she would be safe, that's all I asked. I glanced at her as I turned the corner. She looked so small, so helpless. Would we ever escape the Mob noose that was constantly threatening our lives? Would this, really, be the end of it?

I rushed home. It was five to two when I walked in. It could be a while before she called. I made a pretense of cleaning the kitchen, anything to take my mind off the obvious. Ten after two, still no call from her. Should I rush back?

Two-fifteen. What was going on? I sat down, descending into sheer terror. The minutes ticked by, very slowly. Was she hurt? Did they have her? Was she even alive?

At two-thirty, the phone rang. I grabbed it. I jumped at the sound of her voice. She asked me to pick her up on a corner on Wilshire. I rushed out the door.

9

She was standing alone near a phone booth a few blocks away from the park. I was so relieved to see her. She quickly got into the car. I grabbed her, kissed her, started to cry.

"I'm sorry, I was just so worried," I said. Someone honked at me. I composed myself, pulled away from the curb.

"There, there, honey, it's going to be fine now," she said, almost in a monotone. How could she be so calm? Then again, she had a lot of experience living inside a repressive shell, blocking out feelings. It was her strategy for coping.

"I'm such a baby, I've just been so keyed up all day. Forgive me, Mother. Do you want to get something to eat? Jane's at school for a soccer meet."

"I feel like I haven't had any sleep for a week. I want to go back and rest."

"Mom, after you've recovered from this, would you consider moving in with me? You don't have to hide anymore now."

"Moving in with you?" she asked, surprised. I thought she would have already envisioned it. Why would she want to live alone?

"It would be wonderful for you to live in the same house with Jane. We're a family again. I have a room for you, but if you don't like it, we could move to a new house. I just want to stay near Fairburn School for Jane."

"It's a family tradition, that school, right?"

"Absolutely."

"That might be nice, to live with you, honey, if you really mean it," she said.

"Mean it? Of course, I mean it. I don't want to lose a moment with you."

"I wouldn't be invading your privacy?"

"I don't need privacy," I said, conflicted for an instant about Blue. Well, if we remained involved, we'd find privacy elsewhere. No one was as important as my mother.

"Let me think about it, Elizabeth. So many changes . . . so much has happened . . . nothing seems real, you don't know . . ."

"Yes I do, Mom, I feel the same way. Just rest today. Anybody would feel a little unstable after all we've been through," I said, pulling up to her apartment.

"Let me walk you in," I continued.

"No, dear, don't bother. I'm just going to lie down."

"Do you want to go to dinner with Donna and her husband and me tonight?"

"No, no, I'm exhausted."

"This is the end of the misery, Mom. We finally have each other. Tomorrow, it's a whole new world."

"I know. I'll call you when I get up tomorrow," she said, giving me a quick kiss as she got out. I watched her go in the front door. She moved slowly.

I felt let down, had somehow expected the two of us to be raucous and joyous now that we had prevailed. But we had been through too much for an energetic celebration. Separately, we had faced years of loss, grief, mourning, and now, together, reunion, danger and, finally, triumph. We earned our future.

I went home. Just as I got out of the car, Blue pulled up. He jumped out of his van.

"How did it go?" he asked.

"Not a hitch," I said, smiling with relief.

"That's great, just great," he said, with exuberance. He picked me up with those strong arms, twirled me around.

"Blue, put me down. The neighbors might see," I protested. He set me down.

"You care too much what people think. You don't even know the neighbors."

"Yes, I do. The Shapiros live on the left and Irene O'Connor, the television casting director, lives over there."

"All right, you know them, you've met

them, but you don't really know them."

"That's true," I said, walking into the house. Blue followed me. As soon as we shut the door, he grabbed me, kissed me. He stroked my hair gently.

"I was imagining all sorts of horrible things, that he grabbed you, didn't even want the million, that he was after you for some sort of revenge thing."

"You have a very active imagination. It was the money Mazzelli wanted. Now he has it, and I have my mother. It was a cheap price to pay," I said. He pulled me down on the couch, wrapped his legs around me, started kissing me passionately. The phone rang.

"Let it ring," he said, breathing heavily.

"I can't, it might be Jane," I said, extricating myself from his embrace, answering it. It was Donna, just checking to see if I was all right. She said Randall was running late, could my mother and I meet them at Chinois on Main Street in Santa Monica?

"My mother can't make it. She's just drained from this afternoon. But I know where the restaurant is. I'll be there," I said, hanging up.

"You have plans for tonight? I wanted to take you and Jane out—to celebrate," Blue said.

"That would have been great, but I promised Donna and Randall I'd go to dinner with them," I said. Blue looked disappointed. I thought of asking him to join us for a moment, then thought better of it. Donna would be scandalized if she knew I was sleeping with a house painter. That's how she would see him. She didn't care for penniless artists, or anyone penniless, for that matter.

"What about Jane?" he asked.

"Jane?"

"What will she do?"

"I have Mrs. Chapelle coming over, she used to baby-sit for Valentine when he was a child."

"Does Jane know her?"

"No, but there's never a problem with Jane."

"What about the silver car? Do you think you should leave her unguarded like that?"

"Maybe you're right, I'm not thinking straight. Donna suggested Mrs. Chapelle last week. You are right," I said, more convinced as I thought about it.

"I'll take her," I said.

"What about her homework?"

"We'll do it before we go, or after we get home."

"That's not necessary. I don't have anything to do tonight, I'll stay with her. She'd be bored with three adults for dinner."

"Are you sure, Blue?"

"Positive. I have to go home and do some stuff. I'll be back at six-thirty. You can cancel the baby-sitter," he said.

"It's too late for that, but it would be perfect if you were here, too," I said.

"Whatever makes you comfortable," he said, heading for the door. After he left, I had an anxiety attack. How could I even have thought of leaving Jane with an elderly baby-sitter? I was so preoccupied with my mother's danger that I forgot about the Italians following me. Or, maybe I wasn't as reliable as I thought.

When Jane came home from the soccer meet, she wanted to take a bath. I helped her fill the tub, and poured in her bubble bath. She got in.

"Want me to scrub your back?"

"Yes, use that rough sponge," she said. I took the loofah down and scrubbed her small back. It was so narrow. In just a few years she would be a woman. It went so fast. Could she already be ten?

"Jane," I said, "remember how I used to tell you in Italy that people we don't even know might want to harm you? Because of Daddy's family?"

"Uh-huh, I remember."

"Well, there could still be bad people out there, so I want you to be careful. Remember never to talk to strangers. All those rules still apply."

"Don't worry, Mom, I'll be fine."

"I know you will, honey," I said, kissing her. "I won't be late tonight. I told you Mrs.

Chapelle is staying with you. And Blue said he'd come over. He really likes you."

"I know. I like him, too."

Blue came to the house right on time.

"Let me have my gun back, Elizabeth, just in case," he said. I gave it to him. He had that leather satchel. He slipped it in. I paled.

"It'll be fine, Elizabeth. Better safe than sorry," he said. I nodded in agreement. Mrs. Chapelle arrived, and I introduced her to Blue. Jane came bounding down the stairs ready to get help on her homework from whoever volunteered. Blue did.

"I put the number for Chinois on the refrigerator," I said, kissing Jane good-bye.

I was unusually nervous on my way to Santa Monica. How could I have totally forgotten the Italians? I berated myself again. One situation had nothing to do with the other—my mother was now safe.

But what about Jane and me? Maybe I would talk to Randall about it tonight, as Donna suggested. I scanned every intersection carefully, kept glancing in my rearview mirror, but no vehicle appeared to be following me.

Chinois was full of interesting, prosperous-looking people. Such a change from the way L.A. looked by day, reflecting economic downturns and many homes for sale at rock bottom prices.

"Over here, Elizabeth," Randall yelled.

made my way to a table in the back. Randall and Donna looked as if they could decorate a magazine cover on a pocket of affluence in Los Angeles.

She was wearing a black linen dress; it looked terrific on her. She wore small diamond earrings and a diamond watch. Randall was in a gray Hugo Boss suit that fit him perfectly. Every time I saw him, he had on a thinner watch. He had a shock of dark blond hair that he brushed straight back.

"Your mother didn't come?" he asked, as I sat down. "Donna has told me part of her story. Boy has she been through it," he said.

"She's exhausted. The story is true. Thank God it turned out all right."

"Elizabeth never gave up hope," Donna said. "I could never understand how important it was to her. You know how I feel about my mother. I haven't heard from her in years, and I probably never will."

"Well, I love my mother," Randall said. "She made me everything I am after my father died. She saw to it that I did well in college, got into Wharton, even helped me get that first interview at Price Waterhouse through friends."

"Valentine was named for her—her name is Valentina," Donna said.

"I never knew that," I said. The waiter poured some white wine into my glass.

"This is one of Wolfgang Puck's restaurants," Donna said. "You like Chinese food, so I thought you'd like it. And I wanted a chance to take you out to dinner. I don't think we've all three been out to dinner since we visited you in Rome."

"That's right," I said.

"You know, I think you are Donna's only female friend from college," he said.

"No shit, Sherlock," Donna said. "I hated the rest of those girls."

"Well, you weren't exactly interested in getting to know them. As soon as you were fixed up with Randall, you were never around," I said.

"I guess I was pretty exciting riding my motorcycle from Beverly Hills to S.C. every day," he said, smiling at Donna. She smiled back. The waiter brought the menus.

"Can I order for all of us? I take clients to dinner here a lot," Randall said. We nodded. He seemed to order some of everything. Donna seemed happy, but tense.

"You OK?" I asked.

"Yes, it's just that we had a Valentine incident earlier, problems at his new school. There are only ten students in a class. I don't know how he could have gotten into an argument."

"Did you have a rough time, emotionally, in adolescence?" I asked Randall.

"No, it was just me and my mother. We got along pretty well."

"I just hope he's not unbalanced; I hope he

doesn't have a personality disorder. I swear my sister has one, she's never been normal," Donna said.

"Don't be ridiculous. No shrink has said that. He's just going through a lot," Randall said.

"The world is harsher than when we were adolescents, especially in California," I said. They nodded.

"What did you do today, Donna?" I asked, trying to lighten the conversation.

"Other than worry about you? Well, I looked at a house Randall and I are thinking of buying. It's in old Bel Air and looks like it was once part of an estate. It's Spanish, has a main house, a guesthouse, and wonderful grounds.

"It needs some fixing up, actually quite a lot, but I think we could do it, if we could swing the price. It's what I've always dreamt of," she said, gazing happily at Randall. He smiled at her, put his hand over hers. The waiter walked over with the food.

"I'm going to go to the ladies' room before we start eating," Donna said, rising with her usual grace, slipping away soundlessly.

As soon as she left, Randall tensed. Did I make him nervous? Or was he the type of man who was always nervous in a social situation without his wife? The waiter started putting the food on the table.

"Elizabeth, before Donna comes back, could I talk to you for a minute?"

"Of course."

"Can I trust you to keep what's between us, just between us. In other words, I don't want Donna to know what I'm about to tell you."

"It will be confidential, Randall," I said. What could it be?

"This is hard for me to say, but you know how much I love Donna, and I always have. I want to give her everything she wants, and I'm going to be able to."

"I know that, Randall. She said you were on the verge of a big deal."

"I am. But a few things have come up. I may need some money for a very short time to put the deal together. It's complicated, I could call you later and tell you the whole story . . ."

"You don't have to. If you need anything, just call me. Of course I'll lend it to you."

"Thank you, Elizabeth, oh, here comes Donna. So as I was saying, we want to go skiing in Telluride for Christmas vacation. Maybe you and Jane will come with us."

"That would be great. We'll talk about it when it gets closer to the holiday," I said, as Donna approached. Randall, always the gentleman, got up as Donna sat down. We started eating. Chinese food never tasted so good, but everything in my life was better now that I had my mother back.

I looked at Randall. Was he not all that he

seemed? I was uninformed as to financial deals, as Paolo handled his business without discussing it with me. Why did he need to borrow money? Maybe it was usual—extra costs at the end of a deal that one was not expecting. I hoped he wasn't involved in anything unethical, or even illegal.

"Elizabeth, tell Randall about the men following you," Donna said.

"What men?" Randall inquired.

"There have been two Italian men following me. They had a car accident recently pursuing me."

"Jesus, Elizabeth, that's not funny. Do you have any idea who it could be—or why?"

"She thinks they're Italian kidnappers after her because of Paolo's money," Donna added.

"Did you report it to the police?"

"I did. But there was just so much going on with my mother, then a woman being murdered in Venice with my gun . . . nothing seems to have been done."

"Donna told me about that. Let me ask a few people what the best way of dealing with the situation is," Randall said.

"Thanks, Randall," I said. Later, when I left, I noticed two men in a car across the street staring at me when the valet brought my car. It was probably just my imagination.

But when I turned east on Wilshire, going home, I saw the same two men in a green Cadillac behind me. Was it a coincidence? They continued trailing me all the way to Beverly Glen. When I turned right, they followed me.

Just as I got to my street, they turned off. I parked in front of my house, took a deep breath. Did they want to snatch me? Did they think I had Jane? I didn't even have Blue's gun. What if they had attacked me in front of my house? I forgot that Jane and I each needed protection when we weren't together. I was jangled.

Was I losing it? I had to be completely aware, acutely aware of any potential danger that Jane could face. There was no one but me to protect her. I was her only line of defense. Maybe this was a temporary lapse in judgment from stress. Hopefully, tomorrow I would regain confidence in my ability.

Mrs. Chapelle was watching television, Blue was reading. I didn't want to alarm Mrs. Chapelle, so I didn't mention the car trailing me until she left. When I told Blue, his face darkened.

"This is my fault, I shouldn't have let you leave the house without a gun," he said, jumping up, furious. He took a chair, banged it down on the floor, hard.

"Blue, stop it, it's not your fault. You'll wake Jane!"

"I forgot, you're right. I just freaked because I can't stand the thought of anything happening to you after . . . after . . ."

"Stop," I said, taking his hand. He was

probably thinking about his first wife Alex's disappearance. "I understand. I didn't think of it either. I told Donna's husband about it . . ."

"He's a cop?"

"No, no, he's a financier of some type, but he knows about cops. People like that that can advise me."

"You'll call him tomorrow?"

"I will," I said, putting my purse and coat down. Blue came over to me, circled my waist with his hand, slowly pulled me toward him.

He started to kiss me. It felt so good, so intimate, so familiar all of a sudden. But I didn't want to lose myself in the kiss, I had to keep a clear head so that I could set up a protective network around Jane in the next couple of days. I moved away from him.

"What's wrong?" he asked. "Jane's asleep."

"It's not that. I have to get a good night's sleep so I can deal with everything tomorrow."

"No problem, whatever you want," he said, kissing me quickly on the cheek.

"Jane's homework done?"

"She's a little angel. She was completely prepared."

"I know, I can't believe how focused she is. I wasn't that together at ten years old."

"Me neither. Call you tomorrow," he said, opening the door. "Oh wait," he said, taking his gun out of the pouch, handing it to me.

I made sure the house was locked, turned

on the alarm. I knew I should go right to sleep, but I wasn't tired. Should I call my mother? No, too late, didn't want to wake her.

I went into Jane's room to check on her. She was sleeping; moonlight illuminated her small face. I gently stroked her hair. She woke up.

"I'm sorry, honey, I didn't mean to wake you," I said.

"Hi, Mommy, you're home."

"Yes, honey, but it's late. Go to sleep."

"Yeah," she said, yawning. "Blue said I did really good on my homework."

"I know, he told me," I said, giving her a good night kiss.

"He said I reminded him of his little girl," Jane said.

"That's nice, honey, now go to sleep," I said, getting up.

I went into the kitchen, made some hot milk, drank it, hoping to get sleepy. Nothing worked, I finally got into bed. I stretched out on my back, pretended I was floating. Sometimes that cured my insomnia. I was starting to fall asleep when I jerked straight up.

Blue's little girl? Blue told me he had no children.

10

I spent a sleepless night. I was worried about the men following me, and I couldn't get the inconsistency about Blue out of my mind. The articles on Alexandra's disappearance didn't mention a child, but would they if the child was not also missing?

Why would he tell Jane he had a little girl? Did he have a child and not want me to know about it? Or did he not have a child and want to pretend to Jane that he did? Is it possible she misunderstood?

Why was I wasting time on this? I had my mother back! The clock said 7:00 A.M. I went downstairs, started Jane's breakfast. There was something so comforting about making oatmeal, the real kind, not instant.

I put coffee on, anxious to smell its rich caffeine odor. Was it too early to call my mother? Probably. By tonight, she would be living here, I was almost giddy with excitement.

I found myself wanting to hear cheerful music. I slipped a Bob Marley CD into the disc player, started dancing around the living room.

"Mom?" Jane said, in a quizzical tone.

"Just happy, honey, and I feel like dancing," I said, grabbing her hands and swaying with her. Her eyes opened wide. She wasn't used to seeing her sedate mother so happy.

"Mom, we'll be late for school," she protested.

"You're right, come eat," I said, dropping her hands and walking into the kitchen. I sang to the reggae beat as I spooned oatmeal into her bowl.

"Grandma Lorelei might be moving in with us."

"Doesn't she have her own home?"

"She does, but wouldn't it be wonderful to have her with us?" Jane nodded. I handed her an orange cut into four parts the way she liked. "Did you tell me last night that Blue said he had a daughter?" I asked.

"Uh-huh," she said, with a fourth of an orange in her mouth, her famous orange-rind smile. She took the rind out.

"He said that I remind him of his daughter when she was my age."

"Are you sure? Maybe he said you remind him of a friend's daughter."

"No, Mom, he didn't. You always tell me to

listen to what people say and I do. He even told me her name. Alison," she said.

I was so shocked that I bolted from the table to pour some coffee, so Jane wouldn't see my expression. The name Alison was close to Alexandra. Why did it matter anyway? It mattered if it was true because Blue had told me a lie. The phone rang.

It was Randall. He had already called people for me and wanted to know if he could come over around ten and discuss options. I was impressed with his efficiency; it hadn't even been twelve hours.

When I came home from walking Jane to school, I called my mother. She was out. Where did she go? She probably went to the coffee shop for breakfast. I called ten minutes later. She picked up.

"Mom, this is your first day of freedom."

"I know. It feels so strange, Elizabeth."

"I'm taking you to lunch. I'll pick you up at noon. Would you like that?"

"Of course, dear, I'll be ready."

I changed from my jogging outfit into a new black cotton sundress that I had bought in Beverly Hills. I felt free, such a load was lifted off me. I wanted to wear fewer clothes—I didn't need the usual protective layers.

Randall knocked, and I let him in. He was dressed as usual in a designer suit. This one looked like Armani. He wore a red-and-black Italian silk tie.

"Please sit down," I said, indicating my big comfy white couch.

"Thanks, this is nice," he said, making a motion encompassing the house, "but modest compared to what you could afford. Or has Donna exaggerated?" I was surprised by his comment. Did I dislike his crassness or Donna's indiscretion?

"Oh, I'm sorry, Elizabeth, you look upset. It's my L.A. thing. Everybody buys the biggest house they can afford, conspicuous consumption. You obviously don't need to live large."

"No, this is fine for Jane and me and even my mother."

"She's moving in?"

"I'm sure she will."

"Well, you've waited years for the privilege of living with her. You deserve it."

"Thank you, Randall. I feel as if my life is just starting."

"Which reminds me, I've got a couple terrific guys working for me, investment bankers, want to meet them?"

"You mean—professionally?"

"No, personally, dates."

"Oh," I said, caught off guard, "I don't know . . ."

"Well, when you're ready. Now I spoke to my friend. He's an ex-cop, now in the security business big time. He provides home security and bodyguards for celebrities. I think he does Arnold, Q . . ."

"Arnold? Q?"

"Oh, sorry, Arnold Schwarzenegger, Quincy Jones. Anyway, he says with L.A. so underpopulated with cops and all the urban problems, the chance of the cops getting these guys is virtually nil. Unless they actually commit a crime like murder or kidnapping, it's hard to get a restraining order since they haven't made a verbal threat."

"But they're stalking me."

"True, but hard to prove. Look, what I'm going to suggest is that you get a bodyguard . . ."

"I hate that. We had them in Italy, and they lived in the house."

"He doesn't have to live here. He can be in his car on the street all night long—and during the day if you want it. He can take you wherever you want to go. There's no charge."

"No charge?"

"Nah, the guy with the security business is a client of mine. He owes me big time. I'll just put you on the list. It's a drop in the bucket," he said, getting up. I forgot how tall he was, at least six-four.

"I'm going to have Ari start today. He'll be here to meet you at 8 P.M. If there's a problem, any personality conflict, you tell me."

"Ari?"

"The bodyguard. He was in the Israeli army. Everyone wants Israeli commandos, they're fearless. Talk to you later, I'm late," he said, glancing at his watch, racing to the door. I closed it behind him. It was finally time to go to my mother's. I couldn't wait to see her.

She was waiting outside her apartment building. Her dowdy dress reminded me I had to take her shopping.

"Mom, get in," I said, as I pulled up. She smiled sweetly, got in.

"Right after lunch, I'm taking you shopping."

"Oh, that's all right, dear, I've never been too fond of shopping. I have enough," she said. How could she say that? Maybe it had been so long since she had indulged herself, she had no desire left.

I pulled up before the Hamlet Gardens. It was an old standard in Westwood. It wasn't fancy, so it wouldn't make my mother nervous, but it was good.

We were seated in the big airy room. The restaurant was full, bustling. The waitress/actress, a beautiful, bored blonde handed us menus. She recited the specials without a single inflection. We both ordered the rosemary chicken.

"How did you sleep?" I asked.

"Oh, well, all right, no better than that."

"I thought you would have slept well, no more danger."

"I did, I did, but remember I'm old."

"You are not! Our life together is just beginning. I need you, Jane needs you," I said, squeezing her arm. "Now let's discuss when you are moving in with me, tonight or tomorrow?"

"Oh dear, I don't know, I'm not sure . . ."

"Why wouldn't you?" I asked.

"I just don't know if I have the energy, honey, I feel all worn-out. Jane is a child, she'll have so much energy."

"She does, but that won't affect you. You'll come over after lunch and meet her."

"All right. I saw the house that morning. It's lovely, honey."

"If the layout isn't right for you, we can move. Look Mom, I'll put you on a monthly income from my inheritance. There's plenty of money."

She looked around apprehensively. She still appeared frightened. It would take a long time for her to heal. I wanted to be part of her recovery.

"Mom, I have an idea. Why don't we all go away for the weekend?"

"The weekend?"

"This one, the next one, it doesn't matter."

"Gee, honey, if you want to . . . let's talk about it," she said. The waitress brought our chicken. My mother ate slowly. I felt let down. Somehow, I thought that if I ever found her, we would be together forever.

Just because we didn't share the same vision of the future didn't mean I loved her less. I couldn't judge her. My childish view of our relationship was based on when I was nine. I was a grown woman, and the time we lost couldn't be relived now.

She was right, I was wrong. She looked so tentative eating her meal. She still glanced around every few minutes in apprehension. I had to put her at ease.

"Mom, I didn't mean to stress you out," I said. She smiled.

"It's just that I almost feel like today started a new century for me. Of course, I want to be with you and Jane, honey, but let's just take it one day at a time."

"Sure. Whatever you want. Do you still want to meet Jane later?"

"Maybe I should wait a couple of days until I feel a little more solid," she said. I turned away, blinking back tears of disappointment. It was so selfish of me, I had waited all this time. I could wait a little longer to bring Jane and my mother together.

"Is anything wrong, dear?" she asked.

"No, just my allergies. The pollution today is terrible."

I watched her eat her fresh berries for dessert. Once I would have given my life just to have one day with her, now I was demanding her whole life. I was obsessed, completely out of line. I felt so ashamed.

"Is there anything I can do for you after lunch, Mother?"

"No, I can't think of anything, everything

seems to give me anxiety except being alone. I feel like I'm living in a dream."

"You don't still fear Mazzelli, do you?"

"I do, always will, even if it's not rational. It's just not so easy to undo a lifetime of fear," she said. I nodded. We drank our coffee in silence, each lost in her own thoughts. I don't know what she was thinking of, but I knew now that I could never give her her life back. She was shut down, still in prison.

I drove her home. Before she got out, I handed her five hundred dollars. She was surprised.

"What's this for?"

"For whatever," I said. She seemed conflicted about taking it, but finally put it in her coat pocket.

"Thank you, dear," she said, kissing me on the cheek.

"Will you think about going away for a weekend?" I asked.

"Of course, honey," she said.

As I drove home, I knew she would never want to go away for that weekend.

11

I dropped by Donna's house on my way home. Her car wasn't there. Leticia let me in, said Donna would be back in fifteen minutes.

I sat down in the living room, looked through some real estate brochures for magnificent homes. Valentine thumped down the stairs, dressed in black, earphones in his ears.

"Hi, Val," I said.

"Oh, hi, Elizabeth. I got my nipples pierced down on the promenade, underground, want to see?" he asked, pulling up his black tee shirt before I could answer. Tiny gold rings hung on each nipple. He flipped his shirt down.

"I guess body piercings are big, right?"

"Yeah, gotta have 'em. Heightens the sensation, I like to run my hands over them," he said, loping into the kitchen, returning with a Coke. He sat down, projected his usual anger, not at me, just in general.

"I heard about you finding your mother. She was like, in another galaxy, for years, right?"

"Absolutely. The galaxy of South America."

"Yeah, well, I gotta jam. There's a way cool Japanese video toy store in Beverly Hills. Say, do you know my dad well, from like before?"

"Not really. He and your mom were fixed up when we were at UCLA, but I was pretty involved with Paolo and Randall went to S.C."

"Well, was he like a stud animal?"

"I don't think so. Handsome, a fraternity guy, but he seemed pretty crazy about Donna from the beginning. Why?"

"Because I think he's buggin', and I think he's fooling around." The words stunned me.

"Why do you say that?"

"I've seen things."

"I don't know anything about that, but if this is bothering you, you should talk to him about it. He's your father."

"He's bogus. Well, I better go, say 'hi' to Jane for me," he said, leaving. I felt bad for him. He was in torment, had a constant strange look in his eyes. Was it a biochemical problem? Was he just drugged all the time? Drugs aren't the cause, they're just a symptom.

Was Randall a fraud? First, the money problems, and now the possible infidelity. I wished I could talk to Donna about it, but Randall swore me to secrecy concerning his financial problems and Valentine's allegations of infidelity could be a delusion.

Donna came in with the groceries.

"Hi, Elizabeth, I saw your car," she said, putting down bags of groceries on the table.

"I hope you don't mind, I just dropped over."

"Oh right, I really mind. Leticia, can you put the groceries away?" Leticia came in, got the groceries.

"I'm exhausted, this house hunting sucks. Every time I find one, it's not quite right for Randall. I don't know what that man wants. Is Val still home?"

"No, he went out. I think he's really troubled, Donna."

"I know. I've taken him to every shrink in town. I just don't know what to do at this point. Please don't make me talk about it, it'll bring me down even farther."

"Sorry. I just had lunch with my mother. She's wonderful, but I think I expected too much of her. I somehow thought she'd be as interested in me as when I was nine."

"Isn't she?"

"I don't know, but that's not the issue. The issue is I have to find ways of relating to her now, after her holocaust life, that she's comfortable with. She doesn't want to move in with us."

"No?" she asked.

"No. The intensity would be too much fo

her. She's led an isolated, fragmented life for so long."

"Maybe she feels she's still a Mob target; maybe she doesn't want to put you and Jane in danger."

"That's possible. I suggested we go away, the three of us for a weekend, maybe just to break the ice. She won't be able to help but love Jane."

"What did she say?"

"She was ambivalent. I gave her five hundred dollars, I want to open a bank account for her and give her a big check so she can be independent, but I can't seem to find the right words to bring it up.

"I thought maybe if we went on a vacation, she'd relax. I have a horrible feeling that if she's not in my house, something bad will happen to her, and I'll lose her again."

"That's ridiculous, twice in a lifetime?"

"I know it's crazy but that's the way I feel."

"That's very nice of you to give her money, Elizabeth. You always were generous," Donna said.

"It's hers anyway, in my mind."

"Leticia, bring us some iced tea. You want some?"

"Sure."

"So Randall told me he offered to fix you up with a couple guys at dinner the other night, and you declined?"

"Yeah—for now."

"Elizabeth, tell me you're not sleeping with the house painter," she said, fixing me with that one-eyed stare, her walleye flickered toward the left. There was a long silence.

"I can't, Donna."

"What can you be thinking of, Elizabeth? Since when do you like slumming? It's not bad enough that he's nothing but a blue-collar hunk. He killed his wife!"

"Donna, I don't expect you to approve, but don't chastise me."

"I'm just worried about you," she said, picking up a glass of iced tea when Leticia brought it in.

"I know, it's just something I fell into, for the comfort, whatever. There's no way he killed his wife."

"You want to believe that."

"Maybe, but I'm sure. And he's not a blue-collar hunk. He's an artist."

"It's just that you could do better. Have some iced tea," she said. I squeezed some lemon into the tall glass, took a sip.

"Randall got me a bodyguard, and he's paying for it," I said.

"I know. Now I won't have to worry about you. Talk about a hunk, wait till you meet Ari. But he's only twenty-five."

"Really, Donna, that's not who I am. Well, I better go pick up Jane," I said, giving her one of our usual air kisses. She turned her cheek toward me to receive it.

"Good luck with your mother, sweetheart," she said.

"Thank you, Donna." I drove quickly to Jane's school, picked her up. I tried to concentrate on Jane's spirited rendition of her school day, but my heart was heavy.

The closeness I desired with my mother might not be possible. Well, any relationship with her was better than nothing, certainly better than not having her at all.

At exactly 8:00 P.M., Ari showed up. He was a tall blond Israeli with dual citizenship. He spoke English, but his verbal skills were on the low side either from a lack of intelligence or a difficulty with the language.

"I was born in Israel, then we moved here to L.A. when I was eight. After I graduated from high school, I went back home and joined the Israeli army, I was a paratrooper," he said, exuberantly.

"That's exciting. Well, Ari, I kind of feel guilty about you sitting in front of my house all the time."

"That's my job, to protect you and the little one," he said, smiling at Jane, who was eating chips, watching TV in the living room.

"Just let me know if you have to go anywhere that requires a suit or whatever. My shift is from now till 6 A.M. If you leave your back door open once you go to sleep, then I can come in and go to the bathroom, get some water."

"Fine, and maybe after a while, I'll feel comfortable with you in the house."

"No problem." The doorbell rang. Ari turned toward it, on alert.

"It's just my friend, Blue," I said, letting him in. Blue looked at Ari, gave me a questioning glance.

"Blue, this is Ari Golanis, my bodyguard. Ari, this is Blue Calloway."

"Hey, man," Blue said, friendly, shaking his hand. Ari shook hands coldly, then walked outside. The phone rang. Now what?

"Hello?"

"Elizabeth, it's Mother. I've been thinking about going away with you and Jane. Could we do it this weekend?"

12

She wanted to go! I put down the phone, exhilarated.

"What?" Blue asked, seeing my expression.

"My mother wants to go away for the weekend with us. She's feeling better," I said.

"That's great. Where will you go?"

"I don't know, let's see it's Thursday night. We could fly to Cabo San Lucas, that's a short flight tomorrow, and stay till Monday. It wouldn't hurt Jane to miss a couple days of school."

"Have you been there?"

"Yes, when I was at UCLA, with Paolo. We stayed at the most romantic hotel. The water was so blue and warm. There's such a festive atmosphere there. Jane can swim or ride on a jet ski. She used to love the water on the Italian coast. Have you been there?"

"No, my Mexico vacations have been

cheaper, driving down to Mazatlán, sleeping
on the beach, painting the sunrises."

"Honey," I said, interrupting Jane's TV
viewing, "we're going on a vacation this
weekend, to Mexico, and Grandma Lorelei is
coming." She smiled. Before we went away, I
needed to clear up the question of whether
Blue had a daughter or not.

"Blue, could I ask you something?" I asked.

"Anything."

"Can you come into the kitchen for a moment?" He nodded, followed me into the
kitchen, then started kissing me.

"I missed you today," he said. I wanted to
pull away but was full of desire for him. I
hugged him for a moment, then backed away.

"I missed you, too. But I have to ask you
something. Did you tell Jane that she reminded you of your daughter Alison? I'm certain you told me that you didn't have
children," I said. He was surprised.

"Are you calling me a liar?" he asked,
shouting. I was taken aback.

"Please lower your voice, Jane is in the next
room!"

"Fine, I'm a liar. Next, you'll say I killed my
wife. Don't do me any favors, Elizabeth!" he
yelled as he rushed out of the kitchen and
stormed out. Jane got up from the TV.

"What happened?"

"He forgot something. He had to hurry
home."

"Oh," she said, apparently satisfied, sitting back down. I finished the dishes, still shaken by Blue's outburst. He didn't deny having a child, but he was angry at me for asking. What an odd reaction. Was it just defensive tactics, so I wouldn't press the question?

Well, I had no time to think about it. There were more important matters on my mind. Tomorrow morning, first thing, I had to make a reservation for Mexico.

I woke up the next morning, anxious to be there already. There were a couple of dirty glasses in the sink; Ari must have come in for a drink last night. He was gone now. I rushed to the travel agent, took care of everything. Then I went home, called Donna, told her the good news.

"When are you leaving?"

"Tomorrow. I'm going to my lawyer now to make out a new will. If I die, half of everything goes to my mother, the other half to Jane, just in case I drown in the surf."

"God, are you morbid! You're just going away for three days. Have you told Lorelei where she's going?"

"No. After I get back from the lawyer, I'll tell her."

The lawyer was shocked when he heard the story about my mother. He was a recent acquaintance. I drew up my new will.

"Is it legal now, as soon as I sign it?"

"Yes, but we'll draw it up professionally

and have you sign the final copy when it comes in, in a couple of weeks."

I stopped at GAP KIDS in Beverly Hills, bought Jane a new bathing suit. She really wasn't a shopper—she was usually happy with whatever I picked out.

At the cash register, I noticed three generations, a grandmother, a mother and her daughter. You could see the resemblance, all blondes, maybe Nordic ancestry. Would that be my mother, Jane and me soon? We would be a train that couldn't be separated, three beings connected forever.

I decided to drive over to my mother's apartment to tell her the good news. I found a parking place right in front of her building, pressed her intercom button. No answer. She must be on a walk, or maybe getting groceries.

I waited around fifteen minutes. I had her key in my purse—she had given it to me with the key to her safety deposit box. But I didn't want to just let myself in her apartment without permission.

I walked outside. Just as I was getting into my car, I saw a car pull out a few spaces behind me. It was the Italians!

They were in a green Cadillac, the one I had seen before. They backed up quickly, turned the corner, not realizing that I had seen them. I was shaking. Did they know my mother lived here? Had they followed me here before? I couldn't think straight.

I waited five minutes, then I headed toward Wilshire, through alleys crowded with garbage cans. There was no sign of them on Wilshire, so I took it home. I hurried into my house, called Randall.

"They're back. I'm terrified. Can you get me a bodyguard in an hour to pick up Jane with me?"

"I'll send Ari back today, he's had a few hours' sleep, and I'll get you another one tomorrow. They'll work split shifts. I think you'd better report this to the police, whether they do anything or not."

"I'll do it when I get back from Mexico. We're leaving in twenty-four hours. I've got too much to do to take the time now. Besides, they can't get near me, or Jane, if Ari is with us."

I put the house alarm on, made sure all the doors were locked, paced. I called Donna, but she was out. I called my mother again. She still wasn't home. Where could she be?

Ari knocked. What a relief. I let him in. He checked the doors and windows.

"I want you to understand, Ari, that these men have never approached me. I don't know what they're waiting for. Maybe they'll just follow me forever."

"If they try anything, I'll take care of them," Ari said, pulling back his jacket, showing a shoulder holster with a gun in it. He lifted his pant leg—there was another gun on his ankle.

"Just don't let Jane see the guns. She'd be frightened."

"*Kane.*"

"What's *kane?*"

"That means 'yes' in Hebrew. Sometimes I forget and speak Hebrew. Sorry."

He drove his car, it was high-tech, with unusual equipment in the front.

"I'll just introduce you as a friend. We had bodyguards in Italy, men going everywhere with us, Jane is used to it."

"*Beseder.*"

"*Beseder?*"

"Sorry, that means all right."

My heart was racing. What if they grabbed Jane before we could get to her? But why would they try now if they hadn't tried before? I was uneasy because I couldn't reach my mother, that was the underlying problem.

Jane waited inside of the gate within sight of the crossing guard as usual. Ari and I got out of the car. She saw us, ran to us.

"Hi, Mommy."

"Honey, this is a friend of mine, Ari. Let's get into the car." We got in, I gave Ari the address of my mother's apartment. It would be safe to stop over there with him. I couldn't wait any longer to introduce her to Jane.

In the car, Ari was taut, like a rock. His reflexes, no doubt, were lightning quick. I felt secure.

I buzzed my mother's intercom. Still no answer. I considered entering her apartment, leaving her a note, but discarded that idea; it was invasive. But where was she? It had been a couple hours. Maybe she had come back and gone out again.

I asked Ari to cruise the neighborhood. I went into a couple of coffee shops, a hardware store, a secondhand bookstore. My mother wasn't there. I even walked through a large grocery store, hoping I would see her buying tomatoes. No luck. I finally decided to open her door, leave her a note.

I told Ari to wait in the car with Jane. I buzzed the manager's intercom, talked him into letting me in, saying I was worried about my mother.

I went up to my mother's apartment, knocked. Could her intercom be out of order? I called, "Mother, Mother," a couple times. Still no answer.

I stuck the key she had given me in the envelope in the door and tried to turn it. Nothing. How odd. I checked to see that I had the right key. I did. Maybe she had it made at a cheap key place, and they had screwed it up. I went back outside.

After we got home, and Jane was in her room, I told Ari about the key. He said he could knock the door down if I wanted. That was the last thing I wanted. It was probably silly of me to worry. Maybe she had gone shopping with the money I gave her.

The important thing was that she was going away for a vacation with us. Besides, it was only four-thirty, it wasn't even night yet. There was no reason she had to stay in her apartment all day. She was no longer imperiled.

"Ari, please stay in the house with us. Don't go back out to the car. I'm still nervous. Will you eat dinner with us?" I asked.

"Sure. I'll watch TV in the living room."

I started to prepare dinner, chicken and rice, a green salad. It was basic. Jane would eat it, and I'm sure Ari would. It seemed disconcerting not to have Blue around. I hadn't heard from him since he ran out of here yesterday. I tried not to think about him. I had more important things on my mind.

While we ate dinner I kept hoping the phone would ring, that it would be my mother. Now it was beginning to seem odd and a little scary that I couldn't reach her.

"What's wrong, Mommy?" Jane asked.

"Nothing. Why, honey?"

"You seem weird—you've hardly said anything and you didn't make me eat my salad."

"I'm just tired," I said, starting to clear the plates.

"Jane, want to play cards? Fish?" Ari asked.

"Yeah," Jane said, running to get the cards in the living room. I gave Ari a grateful smile as he followed her. I finished doing the dishes, it was 8 P.M. Now, I was really worried. I called my mother again, no answer. I called Donna, told her what was going on.

"Could I ask you a big favor? Could I bring Jane up for a couple hours?"

"Now?"

"Yes, if it gets late, just let her sleep there and I'll pick her up tomorrow. I have to get Ari to take me over to my mother's and have the manager let me into her apartment."

"Elizabeth, she's a grown woman. Maybe she went to the movie. You're completely overreacting, but sure, bring her up."

"Thanks, we'll be there by eight-thirty."

"But why do I have to go to Donna's, Mommy?" Jane asked again, when we got there. I had explained it a half dozen times.

"I told you, Ari and I have an appointment. You'll have fun, and I'll be back for you soon," I said. Donna's porch light was on. She answered the doorbell as soon as I rang it.

"Thank you so much, Donna," I said.

"No problem. Come on in, honey. Just be careful, Elizabeth. Remember, you're my best friend."

We got to my mother's apartment at nine. I buzzed the intercom, hoping against hope that she would answer. But she didn't.

"I'll buzz the manager to let me in the building," I said to Ari. I buzzed and yelled, "Can you hear me? This is Lorelei Stein's daughter, I need to get in the building." He said nothing, but the door clicked. Ari and I took the stairs to the second floor.

I knocked on the door, still thinking maybe her intercom was broken. No answer. We walked up another flight to the manager's door. I knocked.

"Whazzit?" he yelled.

"Hi, I'm Elizabeth Manganaro. Could you let me into my mother's unit? I've been trying to reach her all day. Have you seen her today?"

"She went out this morning, I saw her come back in," he shouted again, through the door.

"When was that?"

"I don't know, lady, I'm sleeping."

"Well, can you let me into her unit? She might be ill."

"No, I'm sleeping, go away," he shouted, now slurring his words. I turned to Ari in exasperation. Ari shook his head and motioned for me to follow him back downstairs. I did.

We stood in front of my mother's unit. Ari knocked loudly. No answer. Now I was really worried.

Terrifying thoughts returned to me. What if she had been murdered, was lying dead somewhere? What if Mazzelli had kidnapped her. I had to go to the police. I asked Ari to take me home.

I called Detective Karowisc, the homicide detective I had met when my gun was stolen. He was still there but was just leaving. I told him the entire story about my mother, the past, Mazzelli, the ransom. I could tell he thought it was a strange story and didn't entirely believe it.

"How long has she been missing?" he asked.

"Since this morning. Or, actually, I don't know. She called me last night. That's the last time I talked to her."

"We can't even file a missing persons report for forty-eight hours. If she doesn't turn up, call me," he said.

"But what if Mazzelli is holding her? He could kill her in that time," I said.

"I'm sorry, my hands are tied for forty-eight hours. We have regulations," he said. I hung up disheartened. I knew something was wrong; she had been gone too long. I asked Ari to take me back over to her apartment. I buzzed the manager again.

He didn't answer the intercom, he just buzzed me in. We knocked on her door. No response.

"Do you want me to break in?" Ari asked.

"Yes." It had come to this. He examined the lock, then took out a thin-bladed knife, began working on it.

"Soon," he said, working the blade. I tried to think of acceptable scenarios. Maybe my mother would come out of the elevator any minute, maybe she had gone out for dinner. I finally heard a distinct click. Ari stood up.

"After you," he said. I hesitated. The elevator opened, I jumped. It was an old man. He shuffled down the hall. Ari looked puzzled.

"Will not turn?" he asked, indicating the doorknob.

"No, no it's fine," I said. As I was about to turn the knob, there was a horrible scream. Ari and I looked at each other. The scream ended in a meow. It was a cat screeching.

I took a deep breath, and turned the doorknob. I pushed open the door. The room was dark, a chair was in a corner, there was a dress thrown over it. The shades were drawn, I felt for a light switch on the wall, nothing.

I stumbled into the room, over to a small lamp on an end table. I reached under the stiff lampshade, almost knocking the lamp over. I felt a small chain hanging down, I pulled it.

The room was suddenly illuminated by a dull yellow light. It took my eyes a second to adjust, then I saw her.

My mother was on the bed. She was dead.

13

I screamed, ran to her, took her in my arms.

"Mother, please wake up, breathe, I love you, did you hear me? I love you," I said, shaking her, trying to shake life into her. Ari ran to me, tried to tear me away from my mother's corpse.

"Mrs. Manganaro, she's dead, leave her, leave her," he said, breaking my grasp.

"NO!" I screamed. It was too horrible to be true, she couldn't be dead!

"Mazzelli murdered her, he got to her, call the police! HE MURDERED HER!" I shouted, and then my whole world collapsed. I no longer wanted to live. I let go, completely let go. That's the last thing I remember.

When I regained consciousness Donna cradled my head in her arms. She was washing my face with a cold cloth. I jerked out of her embrace and rushed toward my mother. A sheet covered her body.

I fell to my knees at her bedside, and started crying, wailing. It was too cruel to be true. She couldn't be dead. I hadn't even had her for a week. She couldn't be dead! No, I needed twenty more years with her. I needed twenty years to make up to her what she had given up for me, twenty years to laugh and love, twenty years to be a family.

Ari and Randall lifted me to my feet, looked to Donna for help as to what to do with me. Donna rushed over, guided me to a chair, pushed me into it.

"It's horrible, I'm so sorry. I can't believe it, either," Donna said, tears in her eyes.

"What happened, Mazzelli must have killed her. He must have . . ."

"Your mother . . . committed suicide," Randall said, gently, handing me a note. I looked at the note, unable at first to make sense of it.

"Elizabeth," she wrote, "please understand, I am so tired. I can be of no use to you and Jane. I don't want to cost you more money or pain. I will always love you, Mother."

"Oh my God, no! No! No!"

"Elizabeth, calm down, calm down. We can't bring her back. Stay calm, get ahold of yourself," Donna begged me.

"She didn't kill herself, I know it. Mazzelli killed her. He made it look like suicide, he made her write that note."

"There's the pill vial," Randall said, pointing to an empty bottle.

"She wouldn't do something like this. She wasn't tired of living, just tired of being afraid of Mazzelli. She was looking forward to her freedom. Get someone to do an autopsy."

"They will automatically conduct an autopsy. The police are already on their way," Randall said.

"The police?" I asked.

"Honey, you have to call the police in cases of suicide," Donna said. Randall looked at me, hesitated, then spoke.

"I don't know how to ask this, Elizabeth, but what should I tell them about a funeral home? Whom do I call? There's already someone buried in her family crypt, Donna tells me."

Maybe the autopsy would show she had been killed. But what difference did it make? She was still dead. That wouldn't change. I put my head in my hands. What to do about burying her? Wait, I remembered that she wrote me a note, just in case something happened to her the day we gave Mazzelli the money. I'd never read it. I reached for my purse, took it out, unfolded it.

Dear Elizabeth,

Here are the keys to my apartment and safety deposit box. The box contains some of the jewelry your father gave me and some legal papers. It's at the Bank of America, the branch at Wilshire and Fairfax. If something should happen to me, I wish to be cremated.

I love you,
Mother

I finished reading, started to sob.

"She wants to be cremated," I said. Randall nodded.

"Elizabeth, let's go home. I don't want you here when the police pick up her body," Donna said.

"I'm not leaving her alone."

"All right, then you stay, I'll go home to Jane. . . ."

"You left Jane at your house alone?"

"No, no, of course not, she's with Leticia, and Valentine . . ."

"What if my mother was murdered and they're after Jane?" I asked, jumping off the bed.

"Why don't you and Donna go home with Ari," Randall said. "I'll wait here for the police. There's nothing you can do for your mother now."

"But her things . . . I want her things."

"I'll pack up her things, I'll get it all,"

Randall said. Donna put her arm around me, started to lead me to the door.

I broke out of her grip, ran to my mother. I pulled down the sheet, leaned down and gently kissed her cool cheek.

"Good-bye, dear Mother. I love you more than life itself," I said, gazing at her beautiful face one last time. I squeezed her fragile hand, twice, then I covered her up. The world went mute.

On the way home, I saw Donna talking to me, but I didn't hear her. Then she was talking to Ari, I heard nothing. Horns probably honked, life went on outside our car. I was untouched. All of a sudden, Donna was shaking me, her mouth moving again. We were at her house.

I got out of the car, moved silently to the front door. Leticia opened it. I shook Donna's hand off my shoulder, rushed upstairs. I opened the door to the guest room, rushed in.

My darling Jane was asleep in the big white fluffy double bed. Tears ran down my face in relief. I touched her rose-petal cheek gently so as not to wake her, then slipped out of her room.

"Come on, honey, I've made up the couch for you," Donna said, kindly. I nodded, too drained to respond. I climbed into the plaid flannel bedding, closed my eyes. I heard Donna close the door, knew she had shut off the lights.

I opened my eyes, afraid to go to sleep. What if she had killed herself? How could she have left me again? It was my fault. First, I paid Mazzelli the million dollars, then I told her I wanted her to move in, be part of us forever. I pushed her over the edge. She couldn't bear intimacy and all its demands after being solitary for so long.

Tears poured out of my eyes. Her ashes. What if they threw out her ashes? I bolted up, got out of bed, ran into Donna's bedroom. She was in bed, reading.

"Donna!" I shouted. She jumped.

"My God, Elizabeth, what?"

"Quick, call Randall, call Randall."

"Why, what's wrong, what is it?" Donna asked, getting out of bed.

"My mother's ashes. They can't throw away my mother's ashes. I want them, call. Quick, before it's too late."

"Elizabeth, they haven't even done the autopsy yet. As soon as they do it and fingerprint her, they'll release the body. Please go back to bed," she said. "They won't throw away your mother's ashes, we told them to return them to you. Randall will select a nice urn. That way you can keep her with you forever."

"An urn?"

"That's how it's done, honey."

"Oh, I see. Thanks, Donna," I said, walking out of her room. I crawled back into bed, my last bit of energy seeped out of my pores. I fell asleep.

The nightmare began. I was on a cookie sheet, cut in the shape of a gingerbread man. I was thin, one-dimensional. Someone was decorating me with blue frosting buttons. Every glob hurt. I felt like I couldn't breathe.

I'm in here I tried to yell, but I had a red frosting smile that pasted my lips together. Some of my foot was cut off by a knife to make room for another gingerbread man. It hurt so much. I wanted to cry, but white frosting was spread over my eyes, sealing them shut.

Suddenly, I was nauseous. I was being bounced around as the cookie sheet slid into the oven. The oven door snapped shut. It was hot then, stifling hot. So hot I couldn't breathe, so hot I was dying!

Then I disappeared and it was my mother on the cookie sheet. She started to burn. I smelled her singed flesh. "No, no, no," I yelled. I woke up as Donna rushed into my room, turned on the light.

"Elizabeth, Elizabeth, you'll wake the kids. What is it?"

"They're burning her now, she's in excruciating pain. Stop them, stop them!" I sobbed.

"She's dead, she doesn't feel anything, Elizabeth. Stop it," Donna said, shaking me. It took a minute for the truth of her words to sink in. I closed my eyes in sadness and total defeat, went back to a fitful sleep.

"What's wrong with Mommy?" Jane asked Donna the next morning during breakfast. The sound shattered me. I hadn't heard anything all morning, but I heard my daughter's words.

"Honey, her mother, your grandmother Lorelei died last night. Your mother is very upset," Donna said. I looked around the table. Once again people's lips were moving. I went in and out of the realm of sound. Everyone at the breakfast table was looking at me.

Randall was talking to Donna. I heard the word "psychiatrist." Valentine stared at me like I was from a different planet.

Jane looked at me. She was tense, sad. Ari was expressionless. Leticia was jumpy when she brought in the coffee and tea.

"I never even got to meet your mother," Jane said. That saddest fact brought me back to reality.

"Oh, honey, I know," I said, bursting into tears and running to hug her. She clung to me, comforting me, attempting to mother me, she, the child. I had to deal with my grief in a way that would not harm Jane.

"I'll be all right. In fact, I'm feeling much better," I said, lying, but determined not to undermine Jane's faith in me.

"Don't worry about me, Donna, Randall, I'm much better, really," I said, sitting back down, putting cream in my coffee. They exchanged worried glances, but I smiled at them, reassuringly.

"Well, that family crisis is over. I'm outta here," Valentine said.

"Where are you going?" Donna asked.

"Video store," he said, almost out the door.

"Be home by dinner," Randall said.

"Yeah, like I take orders from you, loser," Valentine said, slamming the door. Randall shook his head in aggravation. Donna rolled her eyes.

"I better get to my meeting. I packed all your mother's things in that suitcase over there. I'm so sorry, Elizabeth," Randall said, pointing to a small suitcase.

"Thanks so much," I said, trying to sound normal. Donna and Randall exchanged a skeptical look. They would see no more outward evidences of my inner despair—no one would. I'd keep going as long as Jane needed me and only for her, because life held no joy for me now, or ever. My mother was dead.

"Elizabeth, I just heard, Ari told me. Oh my God, I am so sorry!" Blue said, as Jane and I got out of our car. I angled my head toward Jane to indicate I didn't want to discuss it in front of her. Blue nodded.

We walked into the house. I carried my mother's suitcase, put it in the closet. I couldn't deal with it now. Somehow, Blue was still with us. Hadn't he rushed out in a rage, was it yesterday or last week? What was the argument about? I couldn't remember. What did it matter?

"Honey, why don't you go upstairs and take a shower?" I said to Jane.

"All right," she said, as she skipped up the stairs. Ari carried a Coke out of the kitchen.

"I'll be in the car out front if you need me," he said, giving Blue what looked like a suspicious glance. Or did he give everyone suspicious glances as part of his nature? He slammed the front door.

I staggered to the couch, fell on it rather than sat in it. Blue sat down beside me.

"Elizabeth, I am so sorry. How awful," he said, as he stroked my hair in gentle sweeps. I said nothing. Words couldn't bring her back, so what good were they?

"What can I do to make it better? Nothing can make it better, I know, but can I be any comfort?" he pleaded, rubbing my hand between his two big paws as if to make sure that the blood circulated in my lifeless limbs.

"You don't have to answer, you don't have to talk. Just let me be with you, that's all I ask," he said. I was glad for his presence, it was a boundary enforcer. He would save me from doing anything irrational in my despair.

I struggled to sit up—my spine was syrup, my body a bean bag without definition. Any movement was a Herculean effort. My depression made the air seem like lead, and it was hard to move through it. I stood up, wobbled a bit. Blue jumped up, put his arm around me.

"Steady, what do you need?"

"I have to take a shower myself, get in some clean clothes."

"And then?" he asked.

"Then what?" I responded dully.

"Is there anything you need to do today? Should I get some groceries?"

"That would be good. No ... wait, I'm not thinking. Is there anywhere we could take Jane today? Someplace she would enjoy? This has all been very traumatic for her. I have to get her mind off it, distract her."

"Sure, let me think. How about Olvera Street downtown, they have all those Latino handicrafts and stores? And food, musicians, you know."

"That's perfect, just let me change."

"Elizabeth, I don't know if you're up to it. You just lost your mother."

"That's why I have to do it. I can't drag Jane down with me. Will you tell Ari where we're going?"

"Why?"

"He goes where we go, just in case."

"I'm not enough protection, Elizabeth? By the way, where's my gun? I better take it, in case that car does show up." I handed him my purse. He took the gun out, put it in an inside pocket in his leather jacket.

"You don't need that, Ari carries guns."

"I don't need Ari to protect me," he said,

angrily. I shrugged. What difference did it make if he had attitude? What difference did anything make? Everything was futile—my mother was dead. I just had to go though the motions of life for Jane.

Blue drove us in his truck, Ari followed. He had country western music on. Jane sang along with him. I opened my purse, took out the letter my mother had given me.

"Blue, Blue, I need to stop at the Bank of America for a minute," I said.

"Now?"

"Yes, now."

"You need an ATM?"

"No, no, my mother left me her safety deposit box key. I want to open it."

"But it's Saturday. They'll be closed. Shouldn't you wait and do that when you're stronger?"

"No, I want to find it now." Maybe she had left me a message about who killed her. "It's the branch at Wilshire and Fairfax," I said.

"I don't remember seeing a branch there," Blue said.

"Well, maybe it's small or new. Just go by it, we're on Wilshire anyway."

"No problem," he said. When we got to Fairfax, he pulled over to a curb. We looked at all four corners, no bank. Then he drove all around the area, Ari following us.

"I don't see a Bank of America," he said.

"But it's right here in black-and-white," I said, checking the letter again.

"She must have gotten mixed-up, meant another branch, maybe Wilshire and Robertson. When you get home, you can call," he said, heading downtown again to Olvera Street.

If my mother meant Wilshire and Robertson, why didn't she write that? It didn't make sense. Nothing made sense anymore.

Jane loved the joyfulness and color of Olvera Street. I pushed myself to pretend I was enjoying it. My heart was a stone, my feet were in concrete.

It was just an ordinary day, but people thronged through the handicraft and clothing shops. Ari walked in front of us; there was no love lost between him and Blue.

I looked from face to face. All these people were alive, breathing the air, people with pasts and futures. My mother was dead. I blinked back tears. I couldn't start crying again. I owed some control to Jane.

"Mom, can I have a burrito?" Jane asked.

"Sure, honey," I said, getting out my wallet at the burrito stand.

"You want one, Blue?" I asked.

"No, but I see a sweater over there I want to look at," he said, diving through the crowds and disappearing.

"Ari, how about you?"

"Sure, thanks," he said. He put his arm

around Jane to keep her out of the way of a group of teenagers.

"Two burritos," I said to the man making them.

"Don't you want one, Mommy?" Jane asked.

"No, honey. I'm not hungry." I said. The man wrapped the burritos, handed them to me. I handed one to Jane and the other to Ari. I took cash out of my wallet.

Suddenly, I heard a loud noise, Ari pushed Jane and me to the ground, fell on top of us.

"Stay down, stay down, that was a shot," Ari said, drawing his gun. People scattered all around us, screaming. Jane was trembling, I held her firm. Ari crouched now, scanning the area. He started to get up; my leg was so cramped I couldn't move it. I started to rise, too.

"Stay down," he said, loudly, pushing my head down. Jane started to cry.

"It's OK, honey, he's just protecting us," I said. Ari got up, looked around. People started to move around again. He turned toward the burrito stand, stared at something.

"The bullet, here, right where you were standing," he said, pointing to where it was lodged in the wall. Jane and I stood up, hovered close to him.

"You can't think someone was shooting at me?" I asked, incredulous. "It was just some kid shooting off a gun, or something."

"We go home now," Ari said, pushing Jane and me toward the curb.

"Don't be ridiculous, Ari."

"We go!" Ari shouted, grabbing Jane's hand.

"Wait," I said, "I can't go without Blue. Where is he?"

"He'll come," Ari said, pushing us ahead of him. On the way to Ari's car, I caught sight of Blue's blond hair a few feet behind us.

"Hey, where are you going? There's a lot more to see," he said, rushing to us.

"There was an accident. Someone shot a gun near us," I said, apologetically. Ari was practically making us run. Blue kept up.

"Right at her but missed, the bullet over her head," Ari said, grimly.

"You mean someone shot at you?" Blue was confused.

"No, I don't think so," I said.

"You didn't see the Cadillac on the way over, did you?" Blue asked.

"No," I said, as if I would notice anything except the absence of my mother's presence on the earth.

"We can always bring Jane back another day," Blue said. We got to the cars. Blue opened the door of his truck.

"You go with me!" Ari yelled, grabbing my hand and pushing Jane into his car.

"I'll meet you at home," Blue said, with an angry glance at Ari. All the way home, Ari tried to convince me that I had been the bullet's target. I didn't think so.

Once home, Jane decided to take a nap. Blue left, saying he would come back and cook us dinner. He agreed with me that it was probably a stray bullet.

"Elizabeth, you need to call Randall," Ari said, as soon as Blue slammed the door.

"Ari, please. If it was the Italians, they'd kidnap either Jane or me, they wouldn't kill me. If they killed me, I couldn't pay the ransom."

"Call Randall or I will," Ari said forcefully, picking up the phone, handing it to me. I dialed, reluctantly. What was the point? The bullet didn't have my name on it. I related the event to Randall.

"Report the car that is following you to the police, just in case there is a connection. Why not, Elizabeth?"

"I'm just not up to these hysterics, Randall. I guarantee no one shot at me. Besides, no one bothers with the police in Italy, and I'm sure it's the same here. I asked them to help with my mother, and they didn't. Now she's dead! I couldn't have better protection than Ari," I said, closing the subject.

"Is there any news about my mother's autopsy?" I asked.

"No, I'll call you when they call me," he said. Soon Ari's replacement arrived. Elon

Basch was to wait in his car in front of the house unless I needed him.

Jane asked if her friend Carrie could come for dinner. I said "yes." I wanted to make things as normal as possible for her.

I called the Bank of America branch at Wilshire and Robertson. They didn't give out information about the owners of safety deposit box without proper documentation.

I called my attorney, told him what happened. He was upset to hear about my mother. I didn't know how to reply when he said he was sorry. (Was the coroner cutting her apart at this very minute?) He said he'd take care of the bank process.

There was a knock at the door; it was Blue. I opened it, nodded at Elon.

"Eggplant Parmesan?" Blue asked, bringing in a bag of groceries.

"Sounds wonderful," I said, in a monotone. He walked into the kitchen, started putting things away.

"Blue," I said, "I want you to know you don't have to stick around. I probably won't have much emotion to give for quite a while." His long blond hair swept around as he turned to look me in the face.

"Elizabeth, don't you think I know how you feel?" he asked, taking both my hands in his.

"Let me do for you and Jane, if you don't want company at any time, just tell me."

"Jane is having a friend come over."

"So it will be dinner for four, ma'am?" he asked, his blue eyes twinkling. I nodded.

"You look wasted, why don't you rest? I'll call you when dinner is ready," he said, kindly. Grateful to be able to be alone for a while, I went into my bedroom.

I was afraid to close my eyes. What if terrible images filled my head? Were they examining the contents of my mother's stomach now? When would they render a verdict? When would her body become ashes?

I had a sickening thought. What if they gave me the wrong ashes? How would I ever know? I deserved her ashes!

I was becoming irrational. I had to get a grip on my emotions. The phone rang, it was Randall. He asked if he could come over.

"Randall, you don't have to come over. You need the money, right?"

"Yes, Elizabeth. I want to explain the entire situation to you."

"Donna is my best friend, whatever you need is yours. I'll have Ari or Elon bring me to your house after I drop Jane off at school tomorrow. Or will Donna be there then?"

"No, she'll be having breakfast with a friend. I'll be waiting for you, Elizabeth—and thanks."

What did it matter whether he wanted a thousand dollars or a hundred thousand? My mother was still dead. I put my head down on the pillow, fell asleep. I awoke to Blue stroking my head.

"Feel like some dinner? Jane and Carrie are ready to eat."

"I'll be right down, just let me clean up. Why don't you start?"

I walked into a sweet domestic scene when I went downstairs. Blue, Jane and Carrie were eating their salad, carrying on an animated discussion. There were tall white candles illuminating the meal. It was the way life should be, and my mother never would be a participant. I could hardly muster the spirit to join in.

Blue could tell my energy was low, so he took up the slack. He served the eggplant with a flourish; it looked fabulous.

"Mom, this is the best meal we've had since we got here from Italy," Jane said, chewing happily.

"You're right, honey," I said. Blue said he'd run Carrie home and help Jane with her homework. I took him up on his offer, went back upstairs.

I thought I'd just rest for an hour before I went in to see if Jane needed anything. I slept for hours and woke up sobbing.

14

"*There, there, I've* got you," Blue said, kissing away my tears. Light was coming in through the curtains. At first, I just felt skin on skin, his face against mine, my grief was too deep even to figure out who he was. Sorrow shrouded me tightly. I sighed.

"Just let it all out, then there'll be less of it in," Blue said. I continued crying, but softly so as not to wake Jane. I woke up later in the morning frantic. Had I missed getting Jane up for school? At that moment, Blue walked in carrying breakfast.

"Don't worry, I got her up and fed, she's getting dressed," he said, putting a tray full of cold cereal, fruit, and coffee on my bed.

I sighed again, tried to eat a few bites of strawberries, took a gulp of coffee. Everything tasted of ashes; my mother was ashes. I had to find the strength to get up, out of bed. I put my feet over the edge, didn't have the energy to walk.

"Why don't I have the bodyguard drive Jane to school? It's only one day," Blue said.

"Fine, tell her I don't feel well. But, Blue, I have to get up. I have to see Randall."

"I'll take care of Jane, then I'll come back, get you ready," he said, walking out. It occurred to me that I was probably in a clinical depression. Should I see a therapist? But, why? It wouldn't bring my mother back.

Once again, I tried getting up. I managed to stagger into the bathroom. My face looked ghostly, ghastly. As I took a shower, I reflected that the water had never seemed to run with such force. It almost knocked me over. Maybe I was just weak.

Suddenly, Blue's hand pulled back the beveled glass shower door. I jumped in fright; my heart started palpitating rapidly. He was holding a fluffy white towel.

"Sorry, I didn't mean to startle you. I wanted to make sure you didn't drown. Come on, let me dry you off," he said, turning off the water, wrapping me in warmth. He took a separate pink towel and wiped my face very gently, then rubbed me down like I was a child.

"Jane's already gone to school, don't worry about her. Can you get dressed by yourself? Then I can clean up the kitchen."

"Yes, thanks, I'll be down soon," I said. I

watched him as he left. How could someone so big, move so small when he touched me? He was unbelievable. How could I be so lucky? Why was he so wonderful? I couldn't reciprocate now, might never be able to reciprocate.

Should I offer to pay him for helping me the next few days? I had to find clothes that matched, shoes that matched them. Things that I did before by instinct, now required careful thought. I went downstairs, Ari was ready to take me to Randall.

"Here's my phone number, and my address, just in case," Blue said, pressing a paper into my hand. I looked around for my purse, found it, walked slowly over and put the piece of paper in an inside flap. I didn't trust myself to locate anything that I just left around.

"Call me if you need me. If not, I'll be over later. I'm off to paint," he said.

When we arrived at Donna's house, only Randall's car was in their driveway. I went in; Ari remained outside.

"Elizabeth, I appreciate," he began, then stopped and looked at me, "God, you look terrible."

"It's depression . . . don't worry, I'll be fine. How much do you need?"

"Do you want to sit down, you look faint."

"I'm fine, Randall. Grief takes its toll. But I am tired, how much do you need?"

"I hate to ask, Elizabeth, but I need $100,000

for about two weeks, I want to explain . . ." he started to say. I put my hand up to stop him.

"Just let me write the check, I'm not worried." I quickly wrote the check, handed it to him. He looked at it, crossed to give me a hug.

A side door opened, Valentine peered at us angrily. He slammed the door.

"What was that?" Randall asked, breaking the embrace.

"Valentine," I answered, "I've got to go home, Randall, I'm exhausted."

"Elizabeth," Randall said, "there's one other thing." He started to say something, faltered, stopped, started again.

"The police called. There was no evidence of foul play. Your mother's death has been ruled a suicide. I'm sorry."

His words thudded in my heart. So, her death was my fault! Randall looked at me, worried, as he took me out to Ari's car.

"When will I get her ashes?" I asked him. He said he'd call the mortuary. Would I feel any different if I had her ashes in my home? Nothing would bring her back. I had to remember that.

Once home, I knew I had many things to do but couldn't remember any of them. I started to fantasize about being with my mother in her apartment; a surreal feeling came over me. I felt strangely happy.

Could I pretend she was alive for the rest of my life? I'd only emerge from my fantasy when I had to take care of Jane. I liked that idea. Yes, that was the best option.

The knocking sounded very far away. Gradually it got closer, penetrated my consciousness.

"Elizabeth! Elizabeth! Open up before I have Ari break in!" Donna shouted. I looked at the clock, I had almost missed picking up Jane!

"Donna, I'm late, I have to go get Jane," I said, as she rushed in. She was dressed in a stylish short linen black suit, with a black-and-white-striped silk blouse.

"Randall was right, you look terrible. Ari, go get Jane; Elizabeth isn't up to it," she ordered.

"Now you listen to me," she said. "You cannot die from sorrow. Your mother's death is a tragedy, but you have Jane. I've made an appointment with a psychiatrist in Beverly Hills. Now get a jacket, it's cool outside," she said.

"What good will it do to talk to a psychiatrist?"

"Forget talking. I want you on medication. You've completely fallen apart. People are on antidepressants over a lot less terrible things.

"You've got to feel better any way you can. I know you've never considered psychiatric medication, but you've got to, you're losing it," she said, pushing me toward the closet.

"I'll go," I said, feeling incredibly lethargic, "but I don't want to talk. You tell him that my mother died, and I'm severely depressed."

"Fine, whatever, let's go," she said. "Everyone I know is on Prozac or Zoloft or Paxil. He'll find something for you."

"I have to wait for Ari to get back so he can go with us," I said.

"Why? Jane is with him."

"But what if that car starts following us?"

"I'll protect you. I'll yell," she said, dragging me out the door.

The psychiatrist was compassionate, wanted to help, wanted to heal. But there could be no help, no healing, there could only be death. All else was incidental. He gladly wrote the prescription.

"It takes a couple weeks to build up in your bloodstream, you might feel tired initially, find yourself yawning. I'll want to hear from you. Call me in a couple days so I know you're not having any adverse effects. We have to monitor the medication," he said.

"I will. Thank you, Doctor."

"If you don't feel better in a couple weeks, we'll try something else. Your depression is situational, we can help you," he said, as we left. Situational, true, but the situation would never change. Donna got the prescription filled.

"You'll be able to function this way until the pain starts to go away," she said. I hated her for saying that. The pain would never go away, could never go away, must not go away.

We pulled up to my house, Ari was listening to the radio in his car, parked next to Blue's big truck.

"Whose truck is that?" Donna asked, waving at Ari.

"Blue's."

"Elizabeth, the man killed his wife!" Donna shouted. A moment later, Blue came out of the house.

"That's him? What's the matter, he can't afford a haircut?" she asked. Blue opened my car door, gave me a kiss on the cheek. Donna stared, aghast.

"Blue, this is my best friend Donna Mason Scott. Donna, this is Blue Calloway," I said, softly, hoping Donna would not erupt.

"Happy to meet you," Blue said. Donna nodded briefly, gave him one of her walleyed stares, which she then transferred to me where it became a glare that said, "You're sleeping with him!"

"I'll call you tomorrow," Donna said to me pointedly, starting her car. I knew what that conversation would be about, already dreaded it. I walked with Blue into the house. Jane was eating a snack that he had prepared.

It was such a comfort having Blue here. Ari could guard Jane's physical safety, but who could keep her spirits up if I floundered? Blue provided emotional support that she could count on. After she went to her room, I turned to him.

"Blue, the coroner said my mother killed herself," I said, my eyes filled with tears. "It was my fault." He shook his head, "no." I went on. "I don't want to insult you, but can I ask you something?"

"What?"

"Would it be possible to hire you for a couple hours a day to come over and be with Jane after school?" I said, slowly. I couldn't even find the breath for a strong sentence.

"She's so fond of you, it would give me such a feeling of security to know she'd be around a loving, feeling adult," I said. Blue looked angry for a moment.

"It is insulting, Elizabeth, but I know you don't mean it. You're desperate, you want to be sure Jane is going to be taken care of. That's your priority, right?"

"That's exactly how I'm feeling."

"I understand," he said, pulling up a chair across from me. "I don't need to be paid for what I'm happy doing. I enjoy the time spent with you and Jane. If we remain lovers, that would be wonderful, but if not, I'll just be your friend. I'm here whenever you need me."

"Thank you, Blue, thank you so much," I said, tears running down my face. "Would you mind if I went upstairs now? I'll be happy to take us all out for pizza later."

"Good idea," he said. When I got to my room, I took the antidepressant. I felt anxious about a minute later, then yawned. I decided to take a nap, took off my clothes, put on my white silk nightgown. Was white the color of death? Or was that black?

I didn't wake until morning. When I woke up I was in Blue's arms, again.

"You slept well, darling," he said.

15

Donna called at ten that morning.

"Come over right now. I don't have to leave for a luncheon until noon. How long before you can get dressed?" she asked. How did she know that I was still in my nightgown? The time dimension had changed. I lost huge blocks of it without noticing.

"I'll be there soon," I said. Donna always got what she wanted, there was no way I could avoid her. If I pleaded illness, she'd come to me. I knew what she wanted to talk about—Blue.

He said he wouldn't be back until later, but he could drop in anytime. I didn't want her to run into him again. Elon drove me to her house.

Donna was perfectly attired for her lunch in a short Donna Karan suit. She was reading a biography of Mary, Queen of Scots, her favorite historical character, and puffing on her cigarette when I walked in. She took an especially long puff when she saw me. She wasn't looking forward to this conversation.

"Elizabeth, please sit down. Leticia, bring her some tea," she said. "Honey, you really look pale."

"I'm depressed. Please don't start."

"I'm sorry, Elizabeth," she said, shrilly, slamming her book closed. "I'm just so frustrated, I don't want this whole mother thing to have such a devastating effect on you. And now you're involved with a man who murdered his wife."

"He didn't murder his wife. He has told me things I can't share with you."

"Oh, I'm sure he did, come on! What's wrong with your judgment? You've got *paisanos* stalking you, maybe trying to get Jane, your mother just killed herself, and you turn to Ted Bundy for comfort? Are you crazy?"

"Donna, I know you're concerned, and I thank you. I'm going to feel better as soon as the medication kicks in. But don't worry about my involvement with Blue, he's innocent."

"What? He killed her for the money, that's what I read in the paper."

"He didn't kill her, and he didn't get the money. He didn't even know she had made out her will in his favor. He wouldn't kill for money; it doesn't matter to him."

"Well, then maybe he kills for the thrill of

it. Maybe he's a sex murderer, hates women, something like that."

"Donna, he's not a killer. I don't care what you think!"

"You don't care what I think? Thank you, Elizabeth. We've been best friends all this time, and now I find out you don't care what I think," she said, angrily.

"I'm sorry. I didn't mean that."

"Elizabeth," she said, moving closer, "I just want you to be all right. Things are going so well for me right now. Randall pulled off that deal. He's going to buy me the house. I want us both to be happy."

"I'm happy for you, Donna. That's the best I can do. Now that my mother is dead, I just want to get through the days as painlessly as possible," I said.

Didn't she realize that I could never be happy again? Leticia brought us some mint iced tea. I took a very cool sip. The door swung open, Valentine walked in.

"Hi, Val," I said. He glared at me as he walked past.

"Valentine, don't you say hello to Elizabeth?" Donna asked.

"No, I don't," Val said defiantly, rushing out of the room. Donna threw up her arms in exasperation.

"I'm sorry. We're sending him away to boarding school, that's what we've decided. His blood is just constantly boiling."

"I feel bad he's angry at me now. Should I go talk to him?"

"No," she said, getting up. "It won't do any good. I've got to go. Nancy Kendall is taking me to lunch. I've been trying to be friends with her for years."

"Look," she said, suddenly animated, "I have an idea. Why don't you and I and Jane and Randall go away this weekend?"

"Away?" My mother and I were supposed to go away! "Well, Jane would enjoy it, but I'd want Blue to come." I couldn't manage it without Blue, I knew it. Donna looked upset.

"Fine, bring Blue. I'll have Randall make a reservation somewhere, maybe Laguna Beach. It's close, but it feels far away. I want to stay near L.A. because of the house situation."

"Anywhere is fine. I'd better go," I said, getting up, then I paused. "You know I appreciate your friendship, I do, Donna, it's just a rough time for me. I can't promise I'll ever be the way I used to be." I gave her a kiss on the cheek; she hugged me.

I went back to the car. Even ten minutes of conversation thoroughly exhausted me. On the way home I wondered if Randall had pulled off the deal he talked about or if he was lying. I would never tell Donna that Randall came to me for money. I hoped he was all that Donna wanted him to be. I was so lucky to have her as a friend, and especially at this time, when I wasn't easy to be around.

I could understand her distrust of Blue. She was protective of me and figured "where there's smoke, there's fire." But once she got to know him, she'd know there was no way he could murder anyone, not Blue.

I was becoming more dependent on him than I wanted to admit. But why not? He was a gift, and demanded nothing in return.

Once home, I invited Elon in for some coffee, but he wanted to stay in the car and listen to a sports event on the radio. I went in; every step I took felt like pushing a boulder up a hill. There was so much to do, yet nothing really mattered. The only thing I cared about was getting the contents of my mother's safety deposit box. I called my attorney.

"I've had my assistant call every Bank of America in the area. None of them have a record of your mother renting a box," he said.

"But how can that be? She said it was the Bank of America, she enclosed a key."

"It seems odd. Maybe in her confusion, she got the name of the bank wrong. Shall I try all the banks in the Los Angeles area that rent safety deposit boxes?"

"Please. I just can't figure it out. Check under her maiden name, Lorelei Ewald, at the Bank of Americas, too. I don't know why she wouldn't rent it under Lorelei Stein, but check anyway, just in case."

I put down the phone, disappointed. I had to resist the temptation to go back to bed. It was only eleven-thirty in the morning. What could hold my interest? Nothing.

Well, I'd just have to pretend that something did. I'd make oatmeal cookies for Jane, she loves them. Maybe going through the motions of motherhood would reassure me that I could feel something again.

I went into the kitchen, took out the ingredients, the oatmeal, the sugar, the rest of it, started mixing them. I would have to warm the butter, it was cold. I turned on the oven, then I heard a sound. It was a car starting, it sounded very close. Was Elon leaving? I looked out the front window, he was still parked.

Where was the sound coming from? It sounded like it was coming from my garage. My car was in there. It couldn't start up by itself. I went to the side door that led to the garage, opened it. My car was running.

How? Someone could have gotten in the garage from the outside; I had the alarm off. But why would anyone start my car? What if the thief who stole my purse in Malibu came to steal my car?

He could have walked around the side of the neighboring house, eluding Elon, slipped into the garage. Then something scared him, and he left, abandoning his plans. I looked inside the garage, there was no one there. I would have to report the theft of my purse to the police after all. And I'd tell Elon to look around the neighborhood. I had to turn off the car.

I got my keys, walked toward the garage. I went down the steps, and suddenly lost my balance. I started to fall. That's the last thing I remember.

"Elizabeth, Elizabeth, wake up, wake up!" I opened my eyes and stared into Blue's face. He looked upset. What was I doing on Blue's lap in my living room? Who was that standing in back of him? Oh, it was Elon. I closed my eyes again, the back of my head hurt.

"Wake up, wake up, keep your eyes open, what happened?" Blue asked, shaking me gently, pulling me into an upright position.

"Happened? I, I don't know, oh wait. I was going into the garage when I fell, I must have hit my head."

"Thank God I dropped by. That car was on, you could have expired from carbon monoxide."

"What?"

"Your kitchen door was ajar but it could have blown shut. C'mon, get up, we're going to the emergency room."

"But I feel fine, it's just my head."

"We have to check it out. C'mon, Elon, help me get her into my truck."

"But Jane . . ."

"Elon, pick Jane up and stay here with her until we get home," Blue said. They bundled me into the car. Blue said not to talk, just rest until we saw a doctor.

The emergency room at UCLA was packed with victims of car accidents, random shootings, sports injuries, and people with unexplained pain. I sat with my eyes closed. The back of my head was beginning to hurt more. We finally saw a doctor.

"It's not a concussion, just a bad bruise where you landed," he said. "Luckily, you weren't in there long enough for the carbon monoxide to harm you. I'm going to give you some pain medication, take it easy for a couple days."

"Report this to the police tomorrow, in case the thief comes back," Blue said. He put me to bed when I got home and fixed Jane's dinner. My head was throbbing, I took a pain pill, went to sleep.

I woke up later, when Blue brought me dinner on a bed tray.

"Jane's coming up to see you. Eat something first so you don't look so weak," he said. He filled a fork with mashed potatoes and fed me. I chewed slowly. I needed sustenance to build strength.

"You look a little better, I'm going to tell her it's OK now," he said, sitting down on the bed. "Don't spend too much time with her. I have to talk to you about something important." Jane bounded into the room, ran to me and kissed me.

"You fell, Mommy?"

"That's right, honey, I tripped, but it was nothing," I said. I hoped Blue hadn't told her about the stalking car. It would only worry her.

"Have you done your homework?" I asked.

"Almost, I have a little more," she said.

"You go do it, honey and I'll be up to walk you to school in the morning."

"For sure?" she asked. She was beginning to doubt my word. I appeared weak. I took the tray off my bed and crossed my legs, tried to appear vibrant.

"Absolutely, it's just been a bad spell. I'm changing all that tomorrow. How about a movie after school?"

"Which one?"

"We'll find a good one, any one you want to see." She kissed me again, clung to me just a little longer than usual before she ran off. The phone rang—Donna. She had heard the story.

"And I told you not to report the theft of your purse to the police. I feel like this is my fault," she wailed.

"Don't be silly; it did seem like a reach that they'd try to steal my car. Don't blame yourself. He never could have gotten into the garage if I hadn't turned the alarm off because of Ari—sometimes he comes in."

"Well, start keeping that alarm on. Is your head all right?"

"Fine."

"You still want to go to Laguna for the weekend?"

"Sure, and I'll ask Blue; make the reservations," I said. As soon as I hung up, Blue walked in, sat down on the bed.

"I have to talk to you," he said, upset.

"And I want to talk to you," I said. "Me first." He didn't smile.

"I want you to go away with Donna and Randall and Jane and me this weekend—to a fabulous hotel in Laguna Beach. Would you like that? It would be nice to get away."

"If you want me to go, of course I will," he said, still grim.

"You met Donna, remember? She can be a little harsh, but she's very nice, once you get to know her. And her husband is very congenial. Have you been to Laguna before?"

"I've been there, I'm happy to go," he said, as if he was doing me a favor. He moved closer, took my hand.

"Elizabeth, listen to me. I went into the garage to look around. You know that step you tripped on?"

"Yes?"

"Well, somebody deliberately removed a brick from the stairway."

"What?" Did I hear him correctly?

"I was in the garage a couple days ago storing some paint there; that step was fine. If it hadn't been, I would have tripped. Someone purposely removed one of the bricks. Come with me, I want to show you."

I followed him into the garage. It had been an addition to the house, the stairs were four deep composed of oversize red bricks with painted green flowers on them. One was missing. There was no way it could have fallen out. It was removed. "But why would anyone do this?" I asked.

"I don't know. They wanted you to have an accident."

"But how did they know it would be me that would trip? It could have been Jane, anyone."

"I don't know that either, but you have to report the incident to the police tomorrow."

"All right, all right," I said, suddenly fatigued beyond belief. It must be the painkiller. Or maybe the antidepressants.

I don't remember even going back up to my room, or saying good night, I just fell asleep, my thoughts confused and cascading into one another. Was someone trying to harm me? But why?

Blue roused me in the morning. I got up and walked Jane to school, with Ari accompanying us. The neighborhood was peaceful, comforting. After I got back, Ari took me to the police station to see Detective Karowisc. He was surprised to me.

"Is this about your mother? Hasn't she

turned up yet?" he asked, as if we were talking about a teenage runaway.

"She . . . she's dead. She committed suicide," I said. The words stuck in my throat, fell on each other and made a barrier. I couldn't swallow. I started coughing.

"I'm sorry for your loss," he said, giving me a confused look. "Do you want some water?"

"No, I'm all right. I'm here about another matter," I said. "I think the thief that stole my purse came to my house to steal my car," I said, recounting the incident.

"And someone took a brick out of the staircase so that I would trip and fall on the cement floor. Also, I feel silly even mentioning this, but a shot was fired near my head on Olvera Street."

"Olvera Street?"

"There are a lot of gangs down there, right?"

"Well, it's not exactly the killing fields. Did you get the license plate on that car following you?"

"No," I said, explaining why. He took notes while I talked to him. Then he looked up, just stared at me as if to ask, any more fantastic stories?

"I know it must sound confusing. So much has happened. Maybe these incidents are unrelated. Maybe it wasn't the thief who came into my garage. But who else?" I said. He still said nothing, had no opinion or didn't care enough to express one.

"I'm on antidepressants so maybe I didn't relate the incidents as clearly as I should have. I'm a little foggy," I said. He nodded, still not smiling.

"I shouldn't have bothered you," I said, feeling like I had to apologize.

"You can just forget the whole thing if you want to," I added. What did I care if someone wanted to kill me? My mother was dead.

16

"*The garage incident* could be under the jurisdiction of the West L.A. Division," Detective Karowisc said, "but I'll do it, in case it's related to the homicide in Venice. "Can my partner and I come out in about an hour?" he asked. I nodded.

I was tired when Ari took me home. What did I used to do during the day? My interests were as flattened as my affect. Ari wanted to make some phone calls from his car. This time I put the alarm on, but I gave him the code so he could come and go. Why hadn't I done that before?

It was only eleven. I daydreamed about my mother until the detectives came. They spent a long time in the garage, asked me several questions that I couldn't answer, left and said they'd be in touch.

Again, I had time to fill until Jane came

home. There was only one thing I wanted to do, look through my mother's suitcase. I knew I should wait until I felt better, but the lure of being able to handle her possessions was too much to resist. I gave in, took the suitcase into my bedroom.

I opened it, and it was as if a light emanated from the clothes. I was dazzled momentarily by the heat from them. There were so few of her things. It was amazing that she had nothing at the end of her life.

I took out the dress that she wore to the lunch at the Hamlet Gardens. I ran it over my cheek. The fabric was so soft, it smelled like her perfume. I looked at her shoes, couldn't bear to touch them. They still had the shape of her feet in them. I looked away.

There was the album of pictures she kept of our family when I was a child. There was her purse. I opened it. There was hardly anything in it. The few pieces of jewelry that my dad had given her were in a tiny jewelry case. As I was putting the last dress back, I felt something hard.

What was that? Something was sewn into the hem of her black skirt. It felt like a small book. I grabbed a scissors, tore open the hem. A passport fell out. I picked it up, opened it.

There was my mother's picture. I read the information. "Anna McClusky." Who was Anna McClusky? Why had she used a phony name?

It had been recently issued, there were no stamps in it. She listed the address of her apartment. Her other passport must have expired, did she get this one in case she had to flee the country again? But wait, her birthday was wrong.

Why would she get a passport with a phony identity? Did she use a different name to elude the Mob? Who would know what was required for a passport?

Blue, Blue would know. I couldn't wait until he came tonight to find out. Where was that piece of paper with his name and address on it? I found it in my purse, called him. No answer, no machine? I waited fifteen minutes, tried again. Nothing.

I decided to go over to Blue's, asked Ari to take me. We found the address in the elegant Gold Coast section of Santa Monica immediately, on Georgina Street. He had a guesthouse behind a beautiful pink Spanish mansion. Brilliantly colored flowers decorated the front yard. There was a side gate to the guesthouse.

The gate was open. I walked up the stone path. Between the guesthouse and the main home was a pool surrounded by natural rocks. I knocked on the door. I peeked through the windows in the door, saw several huge canvases inside, paintings of flowers.

He wasn't home, unless he was in another room. I knocked again. Still, no answer. I turned the doorknob, walked in. Disappointed, I found a piece of paper, started to write him a note.

"Who are you?" someone shouted at me. I jerked around, put down the pen. A teenage girl around fifteen stood in the doorway. She was tall and thin, messy blond hair hung in her eyes, her clothes were deliberately baggy.

"I'm a friend of Blue's, Elizabeth Manganaro."

"What are you doing here?"

"I came to see Blue. I couldn't call him, he doesn't have an answering machine."

"He's not coming back till five," she said, walking in and putting a large envelope down on his desk. She turned to go. Was she a delivery person? But why wouldn't she leave the envelope outside the door? How would she know when he was coming back?

"Wait a minute. How do you know Blue?" I asked.

"I'm Alison, his daughter," she said, as she left. His daughter! So he did have a daughter, just as Jane said. Why wouldn't he tell me? What was going on? What was Blue's agenda? What possible reason would he have to lie about Alison?

I grabbed the piece of paper, crumpled it. I no longer wanted to leave him a note. Did it matter that my mother had a false passport? Nothing would bring her back.

I walked out the door. At that very moment Blue walked across the yard.

"Elizabeth, Elizabeth," he yelled, as I rushed toward the car. "Wait." I turned around. He looked so wholesome, so honest, in his work shirt and jeans and mustard-colored hiking boots. Who was he?

"Wait a minute."

"I have to get back," I said, continuing toward the car. He grabbed my arm.

"Please don't," I said, jerking away.

"Elizabeth, what is it? Why did you come over?"

"I came over to ask you something, but I don't want to anymore."

"Why?"

"Because I don't even know who you are, or why you didn't tell me you have a daughter," I said. He looked surprised.

"While I was waiting for you, Alison stopped by. I met her," I said. He looked down, then away. "I met her, Blue," I repeated.

"Come on in, I'll tell you about it," he said. I didn't want to, but I did. We walked in silence to his guesthouse. He ushered me in, offered me a seat. He sighed, sitting down.

"It's not what you think, whatever you think. Alison was Alexandra's daughter, she had her when she was nineteen. She was a single mother when I met her.

"Alison was about four when I came into her life. She never knew her father. She knew I wasn't her real father, but she thought of me as him. When she was five, Alex and I started living together so I practically raised her.

"When Alex disappeared, her family took Alison. I wanted to keep her, but I had no legal rights. I even hired an attorney. Alison wanted to stay with me. Her family said I just wanted Alison for her trust fund. It's always about money with them."

"Is this true?" I asked. I couldn't take any more confusion.

"Of course. She's not allowed to see me, but she sneaks over, brings me her drawings," he said, as he opened the envelope. There were drawings of faces.

"When she's eighteen we'll be able to have a family relationship again. I didn't want to tell you because it's painful to be without her. And I thought you'd read something sinister into the fact that I'm not allowed to see her. You might think I did something to her," he said.

Did something to her? Like what? Molest her? Oh God, he had been alone with Jane! Maybe he had molested Alison and Alexandra found out so he killed her.

No, my imagination was running away with me. This was Blue, I knew Blue.

"You believe me, don't you?" he asked, as if it meant the world to him.

"Yes, of course." Did I? "I'm sorry. I'm just so upset with everything that has happened."

"Come here," he said, pulling me toward

him. He kissed me tenderly. I wanted to believe him. I did believe him. He took my face in his hands.

"Why did you come over?"

"I . . . I wanted to see you," I said, opening my purse and handing him my mother's passport. He opened it, looked at it.

"Wrong name."

"I know, but why? How could she have done it?"

"I don't know 'why,' but 'how' probably isn't so difficult. They sell false passports all the time. I read that former intelligence agents in some countries specialize in it, I think mainly American and Israeli."

"She must have bought it in case she had to leave the country again," I said.

"This is so sad. She had to worry every minute, all the time," he said. He was right. I didn't feel any better. Why did I think sharing it with Blue would help?

"I better get back, will you be over later?" I asked.

"If you want me, I'm there," he said, squeezing my shoulders and walking me to the car. Going home, I asked Ari about the phony passport business.

"Very complicated, but I have friends, you want one?"

"No, I just wondered how they do it."

"They find someone who died, then they get his birth certificate. They make how you say, an identity for him. They get other identity papers based on the birth certificate.

"Then, they use them to get the false passport. The birth certificate of the dead person has to have a birth date that is around the same age as the person getting the passport, so no one will notice," he said.

"Is it expensive?"

"*Kane*, very expensive." How did my mother pay for it? I would never know the answer to that. That answer, like my spirit, died with my mother. When we got home, Donna was just parking in front of the house.

"Elizabeth, I've got to talk to you," she said. She was flushed and breathing heavily, something must have happened. Had Randall told her about his financial difficulties? Were there improprieties?

We walked into the kitchen. Donna sat down, pulled out a cigarette, lit it, inhaled. A red lipstick stain immediately appeared on the white stalk when she took it out of her mouth.

"Sit," she ordered. I sat down.

"What's wrong?" I asked.

"Randall just told me that Blue discovered you in the garage when you fell."

"That's right. He saved my life. What if the door had blown shut? I would have died from carbon monoxide poisoning." Donna took an especially long drag.

"Elizabeth, listen to me. You're not functioning at top level. Don't you think it's a coincidence that Blue found you and rescued you?"

"Why?"

"Follow my thought here. He wants you to think of him as your rescuer. So he breaks into the garage, hot-wires the car, starts it. He loosens the step before he goes out through the garage door. Then he waits until you fall down the step."

"But how would he know when I fell down the step or even if I did? How would he know if I went into the garage? I used the house entrance."

"Easy. He went around the back of the house. There's no way Elon would have seen him. After he did his dirty work in the garage, he watched the living room through that back window, then knew when to make his move."

"But why?"

"I told you. He sets up an accident, then rescues you. You'll feel he's your protector now." I said nothing. She gave me an exasperated look.

"If he's going to try to kill you, you have to completely trust him," she said.

"Trying to kill me? Donna, you're hysterical. It's just not what's happening."

"Oh yeah?" she asked. "When I was talking to Ari about this, he let it slip that Blue was not with you on Olvera Street."

"Blue came to Olvera Street with us."

"Yes, but Ari said he was nowhere to be

seen when that shot was fired. And you told me he loaned you his gun, so I know he has one. Did you have it that day or did he?" I had to think.

"I think he had it."

"Exactly," she said, triumphantly. "He was already setting up his plan, making you think someone was trying to kill you."

"But I don't think that shot was intended for me."

"He thought you would think it was. He thought you scared easier."

"I suppose he's also the Italian or the two Italians that are tailing me."

"Don't be ridiculous, Elizabeth," she snapped. "That's a separate issue."

"Donna, there's no way Blue did any of this."

"Elizabeth, you're falling in love with him. He could be a killer!"

"He's not. I'm not at risk from Blue," I said, with as much energy as I could muster. Could she leave now? This was insane. My mother was dead! That was all that mattered. Donna stood up.

"I think you're making a mistake on this, Elizabeth," she said, disapprovingly. "I've got to go over to that Realtor's. The owners of that house still haven't responded to our offer.

"Oh, by the way, to add to my problems, Leticia quit. So I have to bring Valentine with us this weekend. But don't worry, he'll have his own room, he won't bother us."

"I welcome him coming, but he's fourteen. I'm sure he'd be fine if you wanted to leave him."

"Are you kidding? If I left him at home, the house wouldn't be standing when we got back," she said. Then she hugged me a little tighter than usual.

"Just be careful, Elizabeth."

17

It was impossible not to obsess on every detail of my time with my mother when I was alone. Was there anything that could have predicted her tragic act? I called the mortuary, I still couldn't get her ashes.

I couldn't resolve the issue of the missing brick. Would Blue do such a thing? I already trusted him. He had opportunity, but no motive. It made more sense that the thief did it, but why? Was the thief connected to the Italians?

I felt tired thinking about it. My strength ebbed so quickly now. I had always been a good judge of character, and I trusted Blue. I wanted to forget about the whole thing. If the police turned up anything, they'd call me. There was no reason for anyone to try to kill me.

Friday morning, it was time to go to Laguna

Beach. What was the purpose of the trip? It seemed so long ago that Donna suggested it might relax me. Since Blue had a gun, I decided I didn't want Ari to come. Jane deserved a vacation without a bodyguard. If we ran into any trouble, saw anyone following us, it would be easy enough to beep Ari.

The doorbell rang. I hardly recognized Blue. He had cut his hair so that it barely covered his ears. He wore a nice pair of khakis and a sport coat.

"Blue! You didn't have to do that; Laguna is full of artists."

"It's for your friends. I want them to like me."

"They'd like you anyway, and if they didn't, I wouldn't care. Donna judges people by different standards than I do. I'm not that close to her husband, and their son is stoned all the time watching television, oblivious," I said.

"So why are we going?" he asked. I smiled. I don't think I'd smiled since my mother died.

"That's a good question. Donna's like a sister to me; she thought I might feel better if I got away. By the way, this is my treat to you. I had Donna put your room with mine on my credit card."

"I want to pay for myself, Elizabeth. I wish I could afford to pay for you and Jane, too."

"Don't be silly, I want to do this, Blue. You've been so lovely," I said. Jane ran into the room already wearing her beach clothes.

We had to go. We had arranged to meet Donna and Randall at the hotel for lunch. I put the house alarm on. We were on our way.

Anyone looking at us would think we were a nuclear family on an outing. Jane and Blue kept up an animated conversation about Rollerblades over the sounds of reggae on the radio.

Blue looked so different since he changed his appearance. I hardly recognized him. Who was he? Who were the three of us together? If only the past could lose its strangulating hold, then our lives could start fresh whenever we wanted them to. How could Blue desire someone whose soul was drenched in tears? He'd had enough unhappiness. Why would he want to share mine?

I felt lighter in spirit as we drove along the ocean. It was as if some of my pain blended with the omnipresent smog over the L.A. basin, congealed and stayed there, while I moved beyond it. I looked at the clear blue sky and felt cleansed.

Donna had already checked in. All four rooms were on the same floor of the elegant hotel. We took the elevator to our floor. Blue got us settled in our room; his was next door.

I heard a knock on the connecting door when Jane and I were unpacking.

"Want to open it?" Blue said through the door. I opened it.

"Oh, it's all one big room," Jane said, delighted. She went into Blue's room to look around. The phone rang. It was Donna. She was standing on ceremony, calling rather than bursting through the door because Blue was here. She asked me if we were ready to eat, they were waiting for us. Valentine was starved.

As we walked into the dining room, Donna gave Blue a frosty smile. I began to dread the weekend, and it was just beginning.

"Donna, you've met Blue. Blue this is Randall Scott and Valentine Scott," I said. Valentine had earphones in his ears, heard nothing. When Jane entered his visual field he gave her a high sign. Blue shook Randall's hand.

"Traffic OK?" Randall asked.

"No problem," Blue replied. He looked so earnest, waiting for more interrogation, determined to perform well for me. Randall was obviously far more gracious than Donna, who was in a terrible humor. I knew it was because of Blue, hoped he thought it was her usual personality. Donna took credit for my marriage to Paolo even though she had nothing to do with it.

From the time we were teenagers, she stressed marrying for money, or at least not without it. All I cared about was love. When we found out that Paolo's family was wealthy, she was more excited about it than I was.

She considered my romance with Blue a personal affront; it was beneath her vision of me. I hoped she had enough respect for me not to be outright rude to him.

"Blue's from the Bay Area," I said, hoping to break the ice.

"How nice," Donna replied.

"San Francisco?" Randall asked. "I have clients in Pacific Heights. Do you know that area?"

"I'm not from San Francisco. I'm from a suburb, but I've been to Pacific Heights. It's lovely. I like the Victorian homes and the old Russian-style houses," Blue replied.

"And what is the name of the suburb you're from?" Donna asked. Randall signaled the strolling waiter and had our glasses filled with champagne. Valentine looked briefly interested in the possibility of alcohol but was passed over by the waiter. A waitress followed, handed us menus.

"Foster City. It's dull," Blue said, giving her an irresistible smile. She resisted, her lips were on a downward path.

"And your parents are still there?" Donna asked.

"No, they're dead," Blue said.

"I'm sorry," Donna said, insincerely. I gave her a disappointed look; she had the grace to look down. Since Blue didn't know her, maybe she just seemed preoccupied with other things, someone who wasn't capable of more than superficial conversation. Valentine ripped off his earphones.

"Where's the food?" he asked. "I have a program to watch in twenty minutes."

"We won't have eaten in twenty minutes, Val. It takes longer than that," Donna said. Valentine abruptly pushed away from the table, got up.

"I'm ordering room service then," he said. He started to walk out of the dining room, then came back. All eyes were on him. He leaned down to me and whispered in my ear, "I know." The whisper was unfriendly. He walked quickly away.

"What did he say?" Donna asked.

"I couldn't hear him," I lied. What did he mean?

"Is he upset again?" Jane asked.

"Yes, honey," I said. Randall shrugged in annoyance, Donna quickly changed the subject.

"Elizabeth, the owners of that house accepted our offer. It's ours!" she said, excitedly.

"Well, pending loan approval, but that won't be a problem," Randall said.

"That's terrific," Blue said in his congenial way. He raised his glass in a toast. Randall looked anxious. Did he need more money to swing the house? He seemed to read my thoughts, launched into a discussion of who his biggest clients were. Who was he trying to impress? Blue wasn't interested in finance. I smiled politely.

Randall dominated the conversation, explaining to Blue exactly what he did for a living, how he had started out and what his future prospects were. It all sounded too rosy. Blue was unfailingly polite. Donna lightened up. Somehow, we got through lunch.

"Elizabeth, shall we play tennis later this afternoon?" Donna asked.

"I'm not that energetic. I think I'll take a sauna later."

"Can we go to the beach now, Mom?" Jane asked.

"Of course, honey," I said.

It was a sparkling day, the water glistened. Jane and Blue started building a sand castle. I looked at my body, I was stunned at how thin I was. Hadn't I been eating? Blue had a very healthy girth compared to me.

I watched Blue and Jane playing in the sand. Blue decorated the front of the castle with shells. I was lulled into a drowsy state. I was almost asleep when something jarred me.

Hadn't Blue told me he was calling his mother for her birthday when we first met? But he said she was dead? Why had he told Donna that? Had he lied to Donna? But what for? Or had he lied to me?

Once again, what for? Was there some acceptable explanation? About half an hour later, Jane tired of building sand castles and ran into the surf to go swimming. Blue stretched out next to me. He took a handful of warm sand, dripped it over my arm slowly. It felt so sensual. I smelled Blue's Coppertone; it coated the shiny blond tufts of hair on his chest.

I wished I could just enjoy the moment, but too much was at stake. What was the story with his mother? He dribbled some Coppertone on his hand and rubbed it on my back in big oily circles. He smoothed it down my arm and started to massage my hand, repeating the circular motions in my palm with his thumb. I melted into the delicious sensation when I remembered what I had to ask him. I started to sit up.

"Don't worry, I have my eyes on Jane, she's fine," he said, pushing me back down. Did he do it a bit roughly? I struggled to sit up again, now resting on my elbow.

"I know, I've been watching her, too. Blue, I'm concerned about something you said."

"What?"

"You said your mother was dead."

"That's right."

"Is she?"

"Yes, why?"

"When I first met you, you said you had called her to wish her a happy birthday," I said. He looked down angrily, said nothing.

"Well, did she die last week?"

"No," he said. He turned away from me and stared into the ocean. Case closed?

"So is she alive?" I asked.

"Yes," he said, very softly. It was almost inaudible.

"Why did you say she was dead?"

"It's rough," he said.

"What's rough?"

"The truth," he said, with a distant look in his eyes. I sat all the way up, touched his shoulder and turned him gently toward me.

"What is the truth, Blue?"

"It's hard to talk about."

"Look what you've been through with me. I had a hard time telling you everything."

"She's a schizophrenic."

"What?"

"It happened when I was ten. They found her roaming by the side of the freeway eating paper. She had been missing three days. They called my dad. He brought her home. The next day he had her committed. It's hopeless."

"There's nothing . . . ?"

"They're always trying new medications. She's better some of the time but never well enough to live by herself, out of the hospital. She hears voices, has delusions."

"How sad for her, Blue, and for your entire family. They know so little about that illness."

"There's still a stigma even though it's biochemical or genetic," he said. "All the kids in the neighborhood said my mother was a 'crazy lady.' They'd stare at her when we brought her home for the day."

"Do you have a relationship with her?"

"Of course. I take care of her since Dad died. I go up and visit her once a month to make sure they're treating her right. She's very bright when she's lucid. She has some general health problems though now, and she's not that good at managing them, so it's a constant worry."

"But why do you tell people she's dead?" I asked. He looked embarrassed.

"I know it's wrong of me. It just cuts off a lot of questions. Before I started saying she was dead, people used to ask me if I had the illness, if I was violent, if I heard voices. Mental illness is still misunderstood."

"But why would they think you—" I started to ask. He shook his head in disgust, interrupting me.

"It can run in families, it's true, but those questions just seem so insensitive. They ask me if I was an abused child. You can't imagine what people ask. Sure, my mother was violent with me a few times, but I weathered her storms.

"Please don't make me talk about it," he said, pulling away from me and flipping over on his back.

He had been abused? Yet, he was so gentle. How little I knew about the man I was sleeping with. I had been so consumed with my mother.

Jane ran out of the surf, she was dripping. I bundled her in a towel, started to dry her off.

"I'd like to take a sauna, Blue, will you join me? The men's and women's are probably in the same areas."

"Nah, I don't like saunas, too hot. I'll stay here, sleep in the sun."

"Can I stay with Blue?" Jane asked.

"Sure. Blue, can you bring her back to the room about five so we can get ready for dinner?"

"We'll be there," he said. I gave her a kiss good-bye. Her cheek tasted like the salt water. Just as I got to the building, I turned around and looked at them. Why was I anxious? I shook it off.

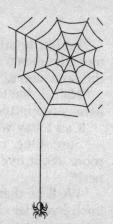

18

The uneasiness persisted when I got back to my room. I changed into a cotton dress to go to the sauna. There was a knock on the door.

"Yes?"

"It's Valentine." I opened the door, Valentine walked in, slammed the door shut. He sat down on the bed.

"Val," I said quietly, sitting down across from him, "what is it? What's wrong?"

"You are so lame."

"What are you talking about?"

"You pretend to be my mom's best friend, and you're fucking my dad!"

"What?" I couldn't believe he had said that. What was going on? "I assure you I am not having an affair with your father. I can't imagine where you got that idea. It's dead wrong."

"I saw you sneaking in to see him last week."

"Val, I came up to see your dad on a business matter. Why don't you ask him?"

"Oh, yeah, like he'd tell me. Do I look like a fool?" he yelled. He got up and stormed out of the room, slamming the door in my face. I was openmouthed. What was wrong with him? What had Randall done in the past? I'd talk to Randall after dinner, have him straighten Valentine out with respect to our relationship.

I wasn't looking forward to dinner with Donna and Randall. Maybe she would ease up on Blue. I wanted to keep busy. After the sauna I'd take a massage. I couldn't let myself fantasize about my mother. It would ruin Jane's vacation.

I walked out of the room, toward the sauna. I followed the arrows down the path of the spa. The sauna was a small wood building with an outside entrance. Two women came out the door wrapped in robes, and turbans, faces flushed. There were two Jacuzzis nearby; they headed for those.

I walked into a small waiting room, could smell the hot wood already, I inhaled deeply. It was warm and dry in my lungs. I took off my clothes, put my hair in a towel, washed my face. I wanted to rest in the sauna, I hoped the other women weren't chatty.

I opened the thick wood door, walked into the sauna, climbed onto a bench, stretched out. I extended my arms as far as they would go, it felt good. I was somewhat drowsy already from the medicine and the sun, I had to be careful not to fall asleep.

It seemed to be getting hotter all of a sudden, was it my imagination? I took in a deep, dry breath of air, there seemed to be less oxygen. When the next woman came in, I'd ask her if it seemed too hot. I looked around for the temperature gauge, it was nowhere, probably outside.

I used to love saunas, the medication must be making me more sensitive to heat. If I relaxed, my body temperature would adjust. My chest was dripping, I never remembered sweating so profusely.

I closed my eyes just for a moment, sweat was pouring into them. I really was drowsy. Maybe I should get out. I started to get up, then I felt like passing out. I began to panic, I couldn't pass out. I had to get control, or I could die. I started to get up, then slumped over, unconscious.

I woke up, where was I? In the sauna, I felt nauseous, it was stifling. I couldn't breathe, I had to get out! I sat up, tried to take a step off the bench. My feet collapsed under me, I crumpled to the ground. I tried to get a breath, I couldn't! Oh my God, I was going to die!

If only I could get a breath. I was conscious of my desperate need for air. I started to crawl toward the door. If I could just get into the main room. My limbs were so heavy, I dragged myself toward the door feeling the splinters from the wood floor pierce my flesh.

The door was only another foot away, I had to stay awake. It was as if my blood had been sucked out—I had no energy.

If I couldn't make it out the door, maybe I could push the door open. I could hardly think. Would it stay open with a shove? Then I could get a good breath. I pushed the left side of my body ahead, inching up until I could touch the wood door. I gave it a push, nothing.

I had to push harder. I had one more moment of consciousness in me. I inched up close and then coiled my body for power. Then, with all my might, I fell against the door, it opened! I lay on the floor, the door resting against me.

Waves of weakness tumbled over me. It would be so easy just to go to sleep, but I couldn't. Somehow, I had to get out of the building. A terrible attack of nausea hit me. I threw up. I rolled away from the vomit. It gave me an idea. Maybe I could roll toward the door, over and over again if only I didn't get dizzier. It looked like I would have to roll around a table and some benches, but maybe I could do it. *I had to do it.*

The room was spinning before my eyes as I started to roll. No, rolling wouldn't work. I was getting too dizzy. I'd have to crawl again. I stretched out my arms, tried to grasp the floor with my palms and pull myself toward the door. I couldn't get any traction in my palms, that was a bust.

Could I scrunch up my legs and push off? No, it was as if my separate body parts could not be coordinated because of a lack of strength. Nothing worked. I just was too debilitated.

I couldn't give up; I had to make it. Then my mind lost its resolve as my body completely collapsed. I knew I was lost. I began to lose consciousness. My last thought was for Jane, my darling Jane.

"Oh my God! What's wrong with her?" I dimly heard someone say. The next thing I remembered was someone shaking me, two women pushing and pulling at me until I was placed on a bench. I let go.

I woke up in my room; a doctor was sitting on my bed. Donna, Blue and Jane were staring at me.

"You had a close call, but you're going to be all right," the doctor said, smiling at me. Blue smiled at me, then took Jane's hand and led her out of the bedroom. I felt too nauseous to talk. The doctor got up, put his stethoscope in his bag.

"You have my number," he said to Donna. "Call if you need me, but I think she'll continue to feel better. Keep her in bed for a few hours, let her regain her strength."

"Thank you very much," Donna said, as he

walked toward the door and left. She sat down on my bed.

"How do you feel, sweetie?"

"Weak," I managed to squeak out.

"Are you too weak to listen carefully?" she asked, very upset. I shook my head "no." Then I got dizzy again.

"Can't it wait?" I asked.

"No," she said, adamantly. She leaned down. I could smell her smoker's breath.

"Blue," she yelled, "can you take Jane down and get her something to eat?"

"Sure can," Blue said.

"Bye, Mommy," Jane said, before I heard the door slam. Donna waited a moment, then looked over her shoulder, making sure they weren't coming back into the room.

"Listen to me, Elizabeth. You didn't just faint. Someone turned up the controls on that sauna. The spa manager checked; they were turned up way past the average temperature."

"What?"

"Elizabeth, you've got to believe me. Blue is trying to kill you."

"But . . . why?"

"He's a serial killer, first his wife, you're next," she said.

"I don't know his motive. Maybe he just kills for the fun of it. I'm no shrink. But I know one thing. You've got to get away from him before this relationship is fatal!"

19

It couldn't be true. How could it be true? But the garage incident and this close call couldn't both be coincidences.

"Donna . . . I don't know . . . I . . ."

"Just rest now. When Blue comes back with Jane, I'll lock your door and sleep here with the two of you. He's not going to come after you if I'm in the room," she said.

I knew I should think about this, but it required a clear mind. My mind wasn't clear, it didn't even feel like my mind, anymore. I fell asleep.

Donna woke me the next morning when room service arrived. Jane was already dressed, Donna was in her robe. The waiter rolled in the silver tray with the rosebud in a slim silver vase.

I sat up in bed. He brought me a bed tray with hot oatmeal, toast and a cup of coffee. He

poured steaming hot milk over my cereal.
Donna always ordered room service perfectly.
She and Jane pulled chairs up to the table and
started eating as the waiter left.

"Can I go swimming with Blue?" Jane
asked.

"Honey, Blue had to leave this morning. I'll
take you swimming," Donna said. I wondered
what she said to him to make him leave. When
Jane went to the bathroom, I asked her.

"Don't worry, I didn't tell him I thought he
was trying to kill you. I said that I wanted you
to have complete quiet and that he wouldn't
be able to see you. I told him we'd be leaving
today."

"He must know you suspect him," I said.

"So what? He's not trying to kill me. Randall called Ari, he's on his way. When we get
back to L.A. I want you to report this to the
police. You can never see Blue again," she
said, her lips pursed to make her point.

"You have to get a restraining order against
him. The manager of the hotel called the police
last night, but they didn't find anything. The
sauna controls were wiped clean of fingerprints.

"The manager hopes it was an accident,
some employee who turned the controls the
wrong way. Like right! They said they'd conduct an internal investigation, but believe me
it was Blue!

"The police here in Laguna want to talk to

you, but my advice is to forget them, just talk to the police in L.A. We have to get you back there today," she said, rubbing my forearm protectively. Could it really be Blue? My brain was on half throttle. How could I figure this out? Jane came out of the bathroom.

"I'll take Jane down to the beach while you rest," she said. "I want you to lock your door when we leave."

"Why? Who would come in?" Jane inquired.

"Oh, just the maid, honey. It's so I can sleep," I reassured her.

"We'll come back and have lunch with you, then we'll go home," Donna said, as they walked out the door. I shut it and locked it, as instructed.

I climbed back in bed and pulled the covers over my head. What was happening? How could all these things happen to me? Could Blue be trying to kill me? Was he crazy?

An odd thought occurred to me. Maybe it was Valentine. Was he that disturbed? He did have fantasies of killing Randall. Was that fixation transferred to me? If he believed I was romantically involved with his father, he could have flipped and become homicidal.

He couldn't have been responsible for the step in the garage, but he could have done this. Wait a minute. He had been in my house before the garage incident. What was I thinking? He was only a kid!

But what about Randall? Is there any reason he would want me dead? I couldn't think of one. His financial problems didn't impact on me. It was a stretch to think he would kill me so he wouldn't have to pay back the $100,000.

How could I know for sure? Would the police find out? Would they find evidence against Blue? The thought was too horrible. I closed my eyes and thought of my mother's beautiful face so it would be the last thing I saw before I fell asleep.

I don't know if Donna and Jane came back and tried to rouse me for lunch. The next thing I remember was around 2 P.M. when Donna woke me and started packing my things. There was a beautiful bouquet of roses in my room. I read the card aloud.

So sorry about your accident. Your room and expenses are complimentary, it is our pleasure.

Sincerely,
The Laguna Beach Hotel

"They don't want a lawsuit," Donna said. "All right, you're completely packed. Put some clothes on. We're leaving."

When we got to Ari's car, she put me in the backseat, then whispered before Jane got in, "Rest, then call the police when you get home. I'll call you tonight."

Ari's driving was so smooth that Jane and I slept on the way home. I woke up with difficulty when Jane shook me.

"Mom, get up, we're almost home," she said. I felt like I had been drugged as I struggled to fully wake up. Just as we turned off Wilshire, I saw the green Cadillac parked a block from our house.

"Ari, there's the car. Get the license plate, the green Cadillac!" I shouted. He turned around in the middle of the street, started to drive toward it, just as they saw us and pulled away from the curb.

"Who's in it?" Jane asked, upset.

"I don't know, honey, but we have to get the license plate number. Nothing can happen to us, we're with Ari," I said, as he gave chase. Jane held on to my hand very tightly. But the car was too far ahead of us. By the time we got to Wilshire, it was long gone.

"Why are we chasing a car?" Jane demanded, as Ari swore, gave up and headed home.

"Someone has been following us, honey. Remember we always feared that in Italy?"

She nodded. She had had many lectures from Paolo about what to do in case of kidnapping. She looked weary. She'd been through a lot for a ten-year-old. The death of her father, coming to L.A., my depression over my mother's death and now, my dazed medicated demeanor and "accidents." How vulnerable she must feel.

Next, I'd have to explain to her why she wouldn't be seeing her friend Blue anymore. That would have to wait. Why did we ever move back to America? Was it worth the few slim days I had with my mother?

There was no thought of Ari's staying outside now, he would be glued to us forever. We all walked in. Jane went to her room.

"You call the police now," Ari dictated. The thought of dealing with Detective Karowisc was exhausting. How was I going to explain this? Did these events have a connection?

"It's Saturday. He probably won't be there. I'm going to take a nap, then I'll call and leave word for him," I said. Ari didn't look pleased. What difference would a couple of hours make?

I looked in on Jane; she was playing video games. I went into my room and fell asleep. When I woke up, I felt drugged again. My slumber seemed so heavy. It was already dark. The clock said 6:00 P.M.

I went downstairs; there was nothing for dinner. I asked Ari to order a large pizza for the three of us. He called it in, added salad and soda to the order. I went in the kitchen to fix some coffee. The light was flashing on my answering machine. I pressed "MESSAGE."

"Elizabeth, it's noon. You're probably still in Laguna. I know both you and Donna think I'm trying to kill you. I swear to God, I'm not! I love you, Elizabeth, I would never hurt you. But the shadow of suspicion will always be with me because of my wife's disappearance.

"I'm leaving town tonight, going back to the Bay Area to look after my mother. I've brought you bad luck, I'm sorry, I'll always love you."

Oh, Blue! He sounded so desolate. He had called before I got home; I never check my messages. He was leaving town? He was leaving because I suspected him of trying to kill me!

But did I? Or was it just Donna's idea based on no evidence. Oh God, I hoped I wasn't making a big mistake, the biggest mistake of my life.

Blue couldn't hurt me, he loved me. He had had so many opportunities. He had been alone with Jane. If he wanted to destroy me, he could have hurt her. I wanted to believe he was innocent!

He had probably already left. I started weeping. I thought of Blue, so kind, so gentle. I hated to admit it, but I had fallen in love with him. And now I could never see him again. Had I fallen in love with a murderer?

I remembered his soft touch, his smell of paint and turpentine, how strong his arms were. He was understanding, compassionate. I had to dry my tears. Jane would be coming to eat any moment.

The phone rang again. Could it be Blue? I

couldn't answer it. I was weak, in love. If I talked to him, he might convince me to see him. My heart raced with every ring. The machine finally picked up. I hungered for Blue's voice. But it wasn't Blue.

"This is the Coroner's Office. We are calling to inform you of the results of the fingerprinting done on a woman you identified as Lorelei Stein. The suicide victim is Anna McClusky. If you need any more information, call us Monday."

I stood there, too stunned to pick up the phone. What? What were they talking about? Anna McClusky? That was the name on the passport. I quickly called back the Coroner's Office. Closed. They wouldn't reopen until Monday. I must have just missed them.

Monday! I couldn't wait till Monday! What should I do? I called Donna. Not home. I was frantic. What did this mean? Was my mother somehow not dead? But how could that be? I saw her. Who could figure it out?

Blue. I had to see him, no matter what the danger! What if he had already left? I called him. Nothing, no answer, no machine. I had to go to him, I'd take Ari. But I couldn't take Jane. I called Elon.

"Elon, it's Elizabeth. Ari is here, and we have to leave. Would it be possible for you to come over in half an hour to stay with Jane?" I asked. He agreed.

The doorbell rang; it startled me. It was the

pizza. Ari brought it in, cheese and pepperoni. I cut it into three sections, dished the salad out, called Jane.

"Let's hurry and eat, Jane. I have to go somewhere for a little while." I wanted to at least eat with her, bad enough she'd be left again, this time with Elon. Ari stopped in mid-bite when I said I was going somewhere. He was puzzled. We finished the pizza in record time. Jane went to do her homework.

"Ari, Elon will be here in five minutes to stay with Jane. I need you to drive me to Blue's. I don't know if he's there. He may have already left."

"What?" Ari shouted. "But Mr. Scott said he is the killer, I am to protect you from him!"

"You're my bodyguard. You have to go where I go. That's your job. I'm going to get dressed now, and then we're leaving."

"I'm not going to take you there. I'll call Mr. Scott," he threatened.

"Mr. Scott is not home right now, I tried earlier. If you don't come with me, I'll go anyway. You'll have to shoot me to stop me. Now, are you taking me or am I going alone?"

"I take you," he said, glaring at me.

"Good," I said, handing him the piece of paper with Blue's telephone number and address on it.

"Please give this to Elon, tell him to call us at Blue's if there's any problem." Ari's face was still set in a grimace. The doorbell rang again, Ari let Elon in. I went upstairs to get dressed, knowing they were talking about me. I didn't care. Ari hardly spoke to me on the drive over to Blue's. He was furious, sure I was walking into a certain death.

"Is not too late, we can turn back," Ari said, gruffly, when we got to Santa Monica.

"It's going to be fine. Besides, you'll be with me when I talk to him. He knows you're armed. He wouldn't even be able to reach for his gun without you shooting him," I said.

I didn't know if that was true, I didn't know anything anymore. Who was Anna McClusky?

We parked in front of Blue's van.

"I go first, you behind me," Ari said.

"No, Ari, I don't want to humiliate him. I just want to ask him something. We'll walk together." Ari glared at me as we got out of the car.

We went through the side gate and up the path that led to Blue's cottage. There were two entrances, we walked to the one nearest us. I could see the outlines of cartons inside. He was still here!

I peered in through a window, the cottage was almost empty, a few open cartons remained. It was dark, shadowed by leafy trees. It looked like no one was there—the lights were off, it was lit by one thin candle.

Wait, there he was, stacking his canvases!

Warmth flowed through my body, just the sight of him jump-started me alive. Oh Blue, Blue. As soon as I saw him, I knew that I couldn't live without him. I opened the door.

20

"Blue?" I *said*, softly. He jumped, then turned toward me.

"Elizabeth?" He rushed toward me, then he saw Ari, he stopped. Ari walked toward him.

"Give me your gun," Ari ordered. Blue pointed to his leather pouch on a desk. Ari picked it up, opened it, took the gun out, pocketed it. Blue walked to me until he faced me, only a few inches separated us. Ari stepped between us, jabbed his finger in Blue's chest.

"Stop there," he said. There was hurt in Blue's eyes.

"Ari, if you could stand just a few feet away, I'm sure Blue's not going to hurt me," I said. Ari gave Blue a belligerent look. He walked about a foot away. Blue looked so sad. I felt so bad for him. I took his hand.

"Blue, I can't stay long, Jane is with Elon, I

have to get back. But something happened . . . it's about my mother—"

"Elizabeth," he interrupted, "don't you know I would never hurt you? I'd kill anyone that tried to hurt you." Was he telling the truth?

"You'd never suspect me if my wife hadn't disappeared," he continued, agony in his voice. "But I had nothing to do with that either."

"Blue, don't leave L.A. The police are going to find out who's trying to kill me. They'll clear you," I said." I wanted to say that it might be Valentine, Randall, or the Italians, but I couldn't in front of Ari.

"It's torture for me to be in the same city as you and not be able to see you. I've got to leave."

"Well, then, give me your phone number up north, and once you're cleared, I'll call you," I said. He looked doubtful.

"Blue, I've got to ask you something." Even my own life meant less to me than finding out the truth about my mother.

"The Coroner's Office just called. The fingerprints showed that the identity of my mother was Anna McClusky."

"What?" he asked. Had I said it wrong?

"They said that my mother was Anna McClusky, that was the identity of the dead body. But I saw her. It was my mother!"

"And Anna McClusky was the name on her

passport. Maybe she legally changed her name to Anna McClusky," he said.

"But she couldn't change her fingerprints."

"I don't know what to make of this," Blue said, sitting down.

"I had to come here and ask you. Her maiden name wasn't McClusky. I just can't figure this out," I said. I wanted to throw myself into Blue's arms, lock my mouth on his and be strengthened by desire.

"Ari, could you wait in the car?" I said.

"What? But he could kill you!" he shouted. Blue gasped, hearing the accusation was almost too much for him. He took a deep breath to keep from exploding.

"He has no weapons, the house is almost empty. I don't think Blue is trying to harm me, anyway. Please wait outside in the car. If I need you, I'll scream. Please, Ari," I said.

Ari scowled, gave Blue a murderous glance and stalked out. Blue and I stared at each other, listening to the echo of his footsteps on the stone path. As they got fainter, Blue grabbed me and kissed me.

"Elizabeth, Elizabeth," he said, crying, "I love you, I would never hurt you, never!" His tears fell on my cheeks as he consumed me with his wet kisses. He was hugging me so tightly I could hardly breathe, I pulled away.

"Blue, don't move away; it's so extreme. Just stay here until this is cleared up."

"But it would be torture; it could take

months. If they don't eliminate me quickly, I won't be able to see you, and the police will hound me like they did when Alexandra disappeared. You have no idea how terrifying it is to have the police follow you everywhere," he said. He rested his long frame on his desk.

I went to him, folded myself into his chest. We just breathed together, not moving, every part of our bodies touching. There was a scent of gardenias in the cottage. I looked around, saw a cut crystal vase filled with soft white gardenias. I put my head on his shoulder.

"Blue, my mother . . . ?"

"It's completely mystifying," Blue said, shaking his tousled head. I missed his long hair. His short-haired clean-cut look had signified what he thought would be the start of our official friend-sanctioned romance. I was introducing him to Donna and Randall. His hopes had been dashed abysmally—so had mine.

"I'd better get on the road," he said suddenly, the pain evident in his eyes.

"Oh, Blue, don't go," I said, then circled his neck with my arms and kissed him.

"I have to. The police will try to get me for this, because of Alexandra. Sometimes, I still think I see policemen following me. They say some cops never give up. It would be a nasty repeat; I can't go through it again."

"I don't suspect you anymore. I don't care what anyone says. I'll be with you every day,"

I begged. I couldn't lose him! I couldn't! He peeled me off him, held my wrists together as you would with a child.

"It's just a matter of time until you begin to have doubts. They creep in. I'll be making love to you one night, there'll be a full moon outside our window and a slight breeze rustling through our bedroom.

"Our bodies will reach for each other. I'll be ready to burst with love inside of you, and then I'll see the fear in your eyes. I can't do it, Elizabeth," he said, with a catch in his throat.

I hated to admit it, but he was right. I had to let him go for now, even though the thought was wrenching. My abandonment anxieties pulsated through me. "The worst part is that I won't be here to protect you. Promise me you'll take no chances," he said.

"I promise," I said. I wanted to keep him with me, but it wouldn't be right. It could destroy him. I'd lost my mother, now Blue. I had only Jane and Donna left.

"Can I have your phone number in the Bay Area?"

"Right," he said, rummaging around in a carton. "My address book must be in my truck. I'll be right back." After he left, I leaned against the wall. I pictured his arty chaotic cottage the way it had looked. I already missed it. How would I survive without Blue?

Was any of this real? I was beginning to think I was just crazy. Maybe I'd imagined my mother. No, others had seen her. Maybe I was lying in a hospital bed, comatose, and this was all a dream. But when did the coma start? Before I saw my mother in the Farmer's Market? Maybe I had been in a plane crash coming here from Italy.

Was it possible I never got to L.A.? But if that was true, what happened to Jane? I looked around as my fantasy evaporated. No, this was all too real. In about two minutes I would kiss my lover good-bye, maybe forever.

Would he let me keep a memento? I looked around, the paintings were already rolled. I couldn't just ask him to pick one, it would be too crass. What about a small drawing? He probably had hundreds.

Maybe I could find one in the cartons. I rummaged around in the first one, just art supplies, wait was that a sketch book? I pulled it out, opened it. It was empty.

I opened the flaps of another carton, it contained odds and ends. Wait, what was that, a painting on a brick? I dug it out. It was a red brick with green flowers on it. Where had I seen it before?

Oh no! It was the missing brick . . . from my garage. It couldn't be! It was. This meant that Blue was trying to . . . trying to . . . kill me! I panicked. He was probably getting a weapon out of his truck right now.

Should I scream for Ari or make a run for it? I heard the sound of leaves crunching. He was coming. I blew the candle out.

The crunching stopped for a moment. Should I scream now? But he could shoot me before I got out the door. It was very dim. I started to creep along the wall; I had to get out.

I heard a door open, I had forgotten about the door in the back of the cottage. I started to run, I reached out to push the door open. That's the last thing I remember.

I was dreaming. It was a dark clear night, Blue and I entered a lush green forest. Was it the monkey forest in Bali? I think it was. I had visited Indonesia with Paolo.

Yes, there were the small furry monkeys in the trees. The leaves in the treetops blanketed out the sky, sheltered the chattering creatures. Blue picked a flat straw basket off the ground; he took some seeds out of his pocket and put them on the basket. Then he held it up. Two monkeys, one with an infant hanging on her, flew down from the trees and landed on Blue.

He smiled as they grabbed handfuls of seeds and happily ate. Three other monkeys came near us, hanging back in the trees waiting their turn. Blue put the plate on the ground, took my hand.

"I want to show you the castle," he said. We continued walking, lizards scampered in front of us. We came to a clearing. There was a small castle made out of gray stone. It had shrines on the terraces, tall thick candles surrounded a moat. Tall spires held spicy incense sticks which made the air fragrant.

He led me across a wood bridge; a servant opened the stone door. Blue took me up a flight of stone steps. There were several doors on the second floor. He opened one. The room inside had purple rugs, and a huge bed with a gold brocade canopy.

"Come with me into the bedroom," Blue said. I started to follow him, then I stopped. Had he really said, "Come with me into the dead room"? I started screaming, but no one heard me.

My dream faded as I woke up. Where was I? Everything was dark. Then I realized I was blindfolded. I tried to scream, no sound came out, my mouth was gagged. I was lying on my side. I tried to push myself up but my hands were tied.

I started to remember. I was at Blue's. He was on his way to kill me, I was running, I was almost out the door. That's when he must have knocked me out. I smelled gardenias, I must still be at Blue's. How long had I been out? Where was Ari? Surely he would come any minute to rescue me.

Was I lying where I had fallen? Or had he put me in a closet? I couldn't tell. Pain radiated down my shoulders, my back. I twisted my head in an attempt to alleviate it. My neck was stiff, but I could shake my head gently from side to side.

Suddenly, I heard shoes on the floor. I felt a shove. Then another one. If only I could talk, maybe I could talk him out of this. I felt something cold and metallic in my back. It was a gun! This was it, he was going to kill me. Jane, Jane, Jane, can you ever forgive me?

I took a deep breath. Was it going to be painful? I hoped I wouldn't suffer. I could feel tears in my eyes behind the blindfold. Could I just hold Jane in my arms one more time and tell her I loved her? I wanted to die picturing her face, keep her with me for eternity.

Why didn't he shoot me? He removed the gun. A door opened, then the gun was back, he prodded me with it. What did he want? I rolled over. He roughly jerked me up so I was on my knees.

What was he trying to do? He pushed me again, I fell over. He jerked me up again, pushed me with the gun.

Did he want me to move forward on my knees? I started to try to inch forward, but he jerked me to a standing position. He prodded me again with the gun, I walked forward. He was going to take me outside to kill me. There were a few more seconds before my death. Hurry, Ari, hurry!

He kept the gun in my back, guiding me with it. Cold air whipped into my face. What if I tried to run? But I couldn't see. He'd shoot me in the back.

He kept tapping me forward with the gun,

then he grabbed my hair so that I would stop. He placed the gun on my upper right arm and prodded me. I turned to the right. He prodded my back, I walked straight ahead.

He pulled my hair again, I stopped. I heard a door being opened, it creaked heavily, it was his truck. Ari was parked right behind his truck! Where was he? Why didn't he stop Blue? What was going on?

Why didn't Blue kill me in his cottage? Too many neighbors? Was he going to drive me somewhere, shoot me there? Why wasn't he talking to me? I was going to die in silence. I'd never know why he was doing this to me.

The thick steel muzzle of the gun was in my back, he prodded me again. I took a step forward, my shin hit the truck. I gasped. "Shhhh," he hissed. He shoved me toward the truck. I couldn't feel for the doorframe since my hands were tied. He grabbed the back of my sweater, gave me a push up to the truck. I tried clumsily to climb in.

My foot slipped. I fell, hit my chin on the car. I crouched on the ground, waiting, but nothing happened. I got up, started to climb in again. He gave me a boost. I made it. He slammed the door shut.

I felt the seat bounce as he got in, he slammed the door. He shoved me down so I fell into the space in front of the seat. I was lying on the floor. He threw something over me, maybe a blanket. Then he started the car.

He was taking me somewhere, I'd be alive a few moments longer. Was there a way out of this quagmire? Should I scream, would someone hear me before he shot me? No, too chancy.

How did he expect to get away with this? The police would find evidence to convict him, wouldn't they? Of course, they'd never find the body, just like what happened with his wife.

But people knew I came to his house tonight. Donna had been convinced of his guilt from the beginning. Why didn't I listen to her? Ari would tell the police I came here tonight.

Where was Ari? Oh my God, he must have killed Ari!! But Elon knew I was going to Blue's. Jane! What if he killed Elon and Jane once he finished with me? Could Elon kill him before he got to Jane? He was a trained bodyguard. Why did I tell him I left Elon with Jane? He might not have thought of her. They knew I was coming to see him; they would link him to my murder.

He shook my shoulder roughly. I continued squirming, he shoved the muzzle of the gun in my temple. I froze. This was the end.

21

He shoved the gun harder into my temple. It hurt horribly. Then he pulled it away. If only he would take my gag off before he shot me, I could plead for Jane's life.

But he didn't shoot me. Now there was nothing but the sound of the truck. There weren't even sounds of other cars. Were we on an isolated road? Where were we going? It seemed that we were going uphill. My head kept hitting what must be the bottom of the glove compartment. He was speeding; the truck swayed erratically from side to side.

He was taking me to the same place he killed his wife. It worked once, why not again? My body would languish at the bottom of a canyon somewhere for years. Was he a serial killer with a multiple personality disorder? Did the personality I knew as Blue even know his alter ego was about to murder me?

None of this had to happen! I should never have moved back to America. I should have never acted on my impulse and had an affair with a man I barely knew. I was warned. I made excuses for him. I deserved what I was about to get. But Jane. you do not deserve death, and you do not deserve to be an orphan. Oh, Jane, Jane, Jane!

All of a sudden I was slammed into the glove compartment, hard. The truck stopped. What now? He opened his door, slammed it. Silence. Was he digging my grave?

Had he planned to kill me tonight? Or did he just decide to do it when I came over? Would he have come to my house? Why had I gone to his cottage?

I heard noises, a swishing, a rustling, what was that? Now it sounded like groaning, someone in pain. It seemed to be coming from inside the truck. Was someone else in the truck, in the back? Had he knocked Ari out and thrown him in? Maybe there was hope. If only there was some way to let him know I was in the car.

There was a searing pain in the back of my head. I was starting to feel nauseous. Was it from the pain? How could I throw up with the gag? I'd suffocate. Dare I make a sound?

Wait. My blood froze. What if it was Jane? Was he going to kill us together? Would he kill Jane? Maybe that was the key—Jane, Alison. Did he kill the mothers so he could have the daughters?

But for what? Sex? There had been no allegations of that nature against him in the newspaper articles on his wife's disappearance. He had never acted improperly with Jane.

Was it Jane? How could I know? Now there was a lot of thrashing, more groaning, the voice was low.

"What's happening . . . where am I?" someone said. The voice was Blue's! What? What was going on? Blue was in the back? How could that be? Blue was trying to kill me. Wasn't he? If he wasn't, then who was?

"Hello . . . hello . . ." he whimpered. Was he bound, too? Maybe he was blindfolded and couldn't tell where he was. Should I try to make a sound? Would he know it was me?

A door opened, then I heard a loud thud. Blue cried out in pain, groaned again, then was silent. The killer must have knocked him out.

The killer wasn't Blue! He did love me. He had been telling the truth. He didn't kill Alexandra, and he wasn't going to kill me. Blue, how could I have suspected you?

But then who? Who was the killer? Valentine could never do all this? Randall, but why?

It must be the Italians. A vendetta against Paolo's family. Revenge. They killed Ari, knocked Blue out in his own truck when he was looking for his address book, all just to kill me. Blue was going to die because he loved me. I was deadly.

Or was it the Mob and Mazzelli? Maybe he did kill my mother. She couldn't have committed suicide. They must fear a lawsuit over my father's will. Or did they think that we knew something that would incriminate them? Again, Blue was an innocent victim. Would they kill Jane? The killer opened my door, jerked me out of the truck. I fell onto the ground. Gravel cut my cheek. A sharp pain pierced my shoulder. I must have fallen on a rock. The killer slammed the door shut, put that gun in my back again and shoved.

I was trained. I stood up. The killer prodded my left arm, and I turned to the left. I was cooperating in my own death. I was following his lead for the privilege of living a few seconds more, instead of making him shoot me now.

He prodded me forward. The death march had begun. Would it be far? I was almost too weak to walk, but I kept going. If I fell, I would be shot immediately, like a horse that couldn't work anymore.

How much time had elapsed since I left my house for Blue's? It wasn't that long. It had only been a few minutes before I was knocked out. But how long had I been unconscious there? My sense of time was skewed. Estimating that I was unconscious ten minutes, I'd probably only been gone about an hour and a half.

Would Elon be alarmed? Would he call Blue's number or page Ari? If he got no answer, then what? He couldn't leave Jane alone. Would he put her in the car and drive to Blue's? What if there were more murderers, either the Italians or Mazzelli's gang waiting there.

I couldn't go over more possibilities. My head was now splitting. I had to concentrate on taking one careful step at a time, praying I didn't trip or fall.

He walked behind me. I heard the steady clump of his boots. He set a brisk pace. If I slowed down a bit, he prodded me forward. He was on a timetable. Then, without warning he jerked my hair, I stopped.

"Don't take a step, you're on the edge of a cliff," a voice said. A voice that sounded like . . . sounded like . . . it couldn't be! I must be imagining this, there was no way . . . it couldn't be true!!! I must already be dead and dreaming, because this had to be a delusion.

"I want to tell you why I have to kill you. It's the only way," the voice said. "It became clear to me this summer, then everything just fell into place. It was so easy it was like a sign from God that I had made the right decision."

I started to sob, made agonizing sounds with the gag in my mouth.

"I might as well take that gag off; no one

could hear you if you screamed anyway, and you'll be dead soon," Donna said.

How could Donna kill me? Donna, my best friend, closer than a sister could ever be! This was just wrong. It couldn't be happening. What was she talking about? What was going on?

She ripped the gag out of my mouth. I couldn't swallow, I coughed. My throat was parched.

"Here," she said, pushing a bottle of water into my mouth and holding it   me. I drank it all, took a deep breath.

"Donna, why, why?" I gasped. I wished I could see her, see the look in her eyes.

"Money, Elizabeth, money."

"Money? You'd kill me for money?"

"What else? It's the only thing that's ever been important to me. You've always had it, first your wealthy parents, then your trust fund, and then Paolo. You never had to worry, want or do without. You just had."

"But I took care of you," I said, sobbing, still in disbelief. Donna! It couldn't be Donna! "I shared with you," I said. "I never denied you anything. If you asked me for something, I gave it to you. The money never meant anything to me."

"That last fact I find loathsome," she said. Then there was silence. Was she just going to shoot me? No, I heard her lighting a cigarette, inhaling. How close was I to the cliff? If I could only get rid of this blindfold.

"Donna, I love you, whatever you need . . ."

"It's too late for that. I'm thirty-five. I thought I was going to have it all with Randall, then I found out he's a fraud," she said, seething with anger.

"Once you're gone and I become Jane's trustee, I can buy my own house, get Randall out of trouble for now to save face, then divorce him later. I'll be independently wealthy. Who needs him?"

"But Donna, we've been best friends our whole lives, we love each other. . . ."

"Love? I don't know about that, Elizabeth. I'm fond of you, it's true, but I never would have hung around if you hadn't been rich. I figured you deserved the money because you were orphaned at nine, the one made up for the other.

"But when you married Paolo, that was too much for me. Why was that luck given to you? You already had money. But I just thought I'd hate you for your good fortune for the rest of my life," she said. I imagined her looking very grim. Maybe that walleye was fixated on a place over my left shoulder as she talked.

"Everything is based on money—respect, popularity, power, status," she said, the lust for such things evident in her tone.

"All those girls who wouldn't talk to me at UCLA, all those women who don't want to be my friend now because they have better homes or cars, or richer husbands, will be begging me for some time now. You had the money, Elizabeth, and you never threw it around. You're such a fool!"

"You've been planning to kill me all along?" I asked, still not believing what I was hearing.

"Just before Paolo died, Randall told me the extent of his financial disaster. What an asshole! We were even going to lose our house.

"When you came back to L.A., I formulated my first plan. But it didn't work," she said.

"What plan?"

"I stole your purse at Pacifica and shot a homeless woman in Venice with your gun. My luck, you had an alibi. I didn't know you'd stay late to talk to Jane's teacher that day. It was sloppy thinking on my part.

"But if you were sent to prison, I'd be Jane's trustee and start siphoning off money in the name of her health and welfare," she said.

"And when that didn't work, you thought of something else?" She had killed that homeless woman; she was insane. The woman didn't matter to her. She showed no remorse. She could kill me in a second.

"Oh, did I ever! It was so easy, like it was preordained. It happened when I ran into your mother; she had just arrived from Buenos Aires."

"You mean when we were at the Farmer's Market?"

"Oh, no. A week before, at a car wash. It

was fated. She just walked up to me and said, 'Excuse me, you're not Donna Mason by any chance, are you?' I don't know how she ever recognized me."

"What? She never mentioned that she ran into you," I said, mystified. A bird screamed. I jumped, then shivered. How close was I to the edge of the cliff? "Donna, please take this blindfold off."

"No, absolutely not. And don't worry Elizabeth, Jane will be fine. I'll treat her as if she were my own daughter," she said, then giggled.

"I wonder how long it takes to probate a will? Well, it can't take long," she said. I had to keep her talking. Maybe I could talk her out of this.

"After you ran into my mother, what happened?"

"Well, at first I was shocked. She asked me for my phone number. About two days later she called. She asked if we could meet. She was very secretive," she said. Donna had faked such surprise at the Farmer's Market. So had my mother. Why?

"She asked me to meet her at a small restaurant, a greasy spoon in the middle of Koreatown. I knew she wanted to ask me about you. When we were there, she gave me her phone number so that I could tell her when you arrived. That's when I got the idea," she said, proudly.

"The idea? The idea to kill me?" Did I hear a sound somewhere in the distance or was I imagining it? How far away was Blue in the truck? Had she killed him or just knocked him out? He wasn't gagged before. Was he now? Was he tied up? Could he rescue me?

"I didn't plan to kill you, initially, Elizabeth," she said, angrily. "That came much later. I just wanted to get a million dollars."

"What are you saying, that my mother co-operated with you in defrauding me?" I couldn't believe it. My mother wouldn't do that. Donna was lying.

"Not your mother. You're such a moron. Do you really think your mother would have helped me steal money from you?"

I couldn't believe she called me a moron. Well, I was one for ever thinking she was my friend. She was so right. "No, I don't think my mother would help you steal from me."

"Don't think of it as theft, Elizabeth. I earned it for putting up with you for all those years," she said. I was a pawn to her to be manipulated for her own purposes; her pathology was frightening. She had no respect for human life.

"Anyway," she continued, after a couple puffs, "it was easy to convince Aunt Anna to impersonate your mother. She needed the dough. She was around the same age, I knew her quite well. She was my mother's sister and lived in Seattle."

Impersonate my mother? Anna, Anna McClusky? Oh my God, that wasn't my mother? But she knew so much, had pictures. Wait, where was my mother? Had Donna killed her?"

"So that wasn't wasn't"—my voice shook so I could barely talk—"my mother."

"No, but your mother cooperated beautifully. All we had to tell her was that if she didn't, we'd kill you. She told us your childhood stories, gave us her jewelry and pictures, told us about Mazzelli."

"Is my mother, is my mother . . . dead?" I could barely get the question out.

"Of course. Take no prisoners," she bragged, triumphantly. A sob came out of my chest. I was surprised by the force of it.

"Elizabeth, let's not get sentimental. I always hated that about you, your soft and gentle side. Can you keep it together for a couple more minutes so I can finish the story?"

"Yes," I said, softly. All was blank. I could barely hear her; as soon as I heard my mother was dead, a soft buzzing started in my head.

"I never meant to kill you, honestly, Elizabeth. I didn't need to, to get the money. Who wanted to waste the energy? Your mother told me the Mazzelli story, and I made up the extortion threat. You fell for the whole thing from the setup at Farmer's Market, hook, line and sinker. My aunt and I had a good laugh when she handed me the check that day in the park.

"I was going to give Aunt Anna her cut, one hundred thousand dollars, and that was going to be it. She would disappear, as soon as you dropped her off. Obviously she didn't want to spend any more time with you than she had to; she was afraid she would slip up."

Maybe I was hallucinating, but I was sure I heard a sound in the distance now. Was it a car? Did Donna hear it?

"Anyway," she continued, enthusiasm in her voice, exhilarated by the recitation of her crime, "then you called me and said you were going to change your will and leave half your money outright to your mother. I had gotten Aunt Anna's phony ID made up, and by then you had told people that she was your mother.

"Why should I settle for nine hundred thousand dollars when I could get so much more? It was just a little jump to kill you. If I killed you and got the money as Jane's trustee, it was going to be so complicated.

"But I'll do it now, now that I have to. And I'll do it well," she said, with arrogance. I couldn't contain myself anymore. I started to cry.

"Shut up, shut up," Donna yelled, hitting me across the face with her gun. My bottom lip split. Was it sliced in half? I tasted salty blood in my mouth. I collapsed. She was going to shoot me now.

22

"*If you shut* the fuck up, you have another few minutes to live. If not, you're dead!" she shouted. Another few minutes to live, another few minutes to be Jane's mother.

"I'll be quiet," I said, weakly. Then I took a breath. I had just strength left for one final desperate bid for life.

"Donna, could you just undo the blindfold so I can see? It's so tight, my eyes hurt so much that I can't concentrate on what you're saying."

"Oh all right, Elizabeth, you're just so much trouble! Since I'm going to get all your money, and I'm going to value it, I'll do this one final thing for you. But don't look at me when I shoot you. I want you facing the other way. Agreed?"

"Agreed," I whispered. If only I could make eye contact, maybe it would empower me, help me think of some way to stay alive. She struggled with the knot of the blindfold. I panicked, what if it didn't come off easily? She wouldn't persevere.

"Christ! I tied some knot," she said, releasing the material. I was stunned for a moment, the tight band of pain that it caused around my head had become me. I felt strange without it. My eyes felt permanently sealed; my eyelashes were stuck to my eyeballs. I opened my eyes.

Donna held the gun on me. She sneered. She was dressed in clothes I had never seen, jeans, hiking boots, a windbreaker. She wore gloves. I looked at her, then at the gun. It was Blue's gun. I did a double take.

"That's right, Elizabeth, it's Blue's gun. See what I mean about luck being on my side?" Blue's gun, Ari took Blue's gun, then Ari must be . . . dead.

"But I'll get to that," she said. She looked at her watch. Where were we? In the wilderness, I glanced in back of me. There was that cliff. I couldn't see the truck. We were on a trail somewhere near L.A. I didn't recognize the environs but then why would I? Did the police patrol these areas?

"Did you kill your aunt?"

"She deserved it. We had a deal. She was to impersonate your mother for one hundred thousand dollars. Then when she found out you changed your will, I asked her to stick around and go away with you for the weekend, just to make sure you didn't have second thoughts.

"She wanted half the take. She was greedy. I offered her another hundred, but she refused."

"So you held a gun to her head and made her swallow the pills?"

"Right. I guess she preferred a calm death, not like you, Elizabeth?"

"Do I have a choice?"

"No. This time I won't miss. My first attempt to kill you on Olvera Street failed. I'm not a very good shot."

"How did you know I was going to Olvera Street?"

"Ari and Elon were instructed to call me every time you left the house, for your own safety. Even though I missed you on Olvera Street, it cast suspicion on Blue. Do you know how perfect it was that you fell in love with a wife killer?"

"He didn't kill his wife," I whispered.

"Whatever. Well, he's going to kill you, at least that's what everyone will think. He tried to kill you in the garage and in the sauna, remember? No one knows it was me."

"Is Ari dead?"

"Yes. When he called me and said you were going to Blue's, I saw the perfect setup. The police will think Blue killed him because his gun did. He killed him when he knocked you out and brought you up here."

"Would you have killed me tonight if I hadn't gone to Blue's?"

"Maybe not tonight, but very soon. I made one major mistake, so I had to do it soon."

"What?"

"I didn't realize they fingerprinted suicides. You found out that Anna's fingerprints weren't your mother's, right? Is that why you came to Blue's tonight?"

"Yes." My heart sank to the ground. The story was over. Could I stall? I had to.

"So you'll shoot Blue and . . . ?" I asked. Had she shot him already?

"Elizabeth, please," she said, sanctimoniously.

"You won't shoot him?"

"Why would I shoot him? He's supposed to have shot you. After I shoot you, and you fall over the cliff, I'll drive the truck here with him in it and simply release the emergency brake.

"It'll be one of those famous murdersuicides. You, Blue and Blue's gun will all be at the bottom of the canyon until they find you.

"So what do you think. Clever, aren't I?" she asked me. She wanted praise.

"Very clever," I said so softly it was almost a breath. Would it be the last thing I ever said?

"Well, it's that old one last request time, Elizabeth."

"Donna," I said, so softly, so hopelessly, that she had to strain to hear me, "is there any way you would let us live if I gave you all the money outright? If you spare our lives, I'll leave the country with Jane, turn Paolo's entire fortune over to you. Did Blue see you knock him out?''

"No, I was in back of him—both times."

"Then there would be no witnesses. You could leave Blue's gun with him here. He'd be arrested for Ari's murder. Why kill him?"

"Elizabeth, I'm not following you. What's the upside?"

"You don't have to murder us to get my money. And you don't have to raise Jane."

"Oh, I like kids. That's no problem," she said. A chill ran through me.

"Donna, I'll give you everything, just let me live—for Jane's sake."

"I can't let you live, I don't trust you. Turn around, Elizabeth." Tears tumbled out of my eyes. Oh, Jane, Jane, Jane!

"Donna . . ."

"Turn around, Elizabeth."

"Just one last thing."

"What?"

"Please tell Jane how much I loved her."

"Of course I will, Elizabeth. Face the cliff." I did as she asked, then closed my eyes.

Jane, Jane, know that I love you more than life itself. I took a deep breath.

Suddenly, I heard someone running! I started to turn around as the shot exploded. I cried out.

23

I felt nothing. Was I dead?

"I got her, she's down, she's down," a man with an accent yelled. Then I heard police cars. I turned around, Donna was shot. She was on the ground, not moving. One of the Italians who had been following me was standing over her with a gun. Detective Karowisc and two other policemen ran out of the forest. I passed out.

Donna died instantly. It's odd how the unconscious mind works. She tried to murder me, yet I still experienced her death as a loss. Sometimes, I miss her, or I miss the camaraderie I thought we shared. I'm an expert at experiencing loss. Anger, betrayal, these emotions are less familiar to me.

I should hate her for trying to kill me, but I don't. But I hated her for killing my mother.

She died before I could ask her where the body was.

I prefer to think the financial pressures of this year drove Donna over the edge, drove her insane. If she was always crazy, what does that say about me for being her best friend? Or maybe it's hard for me to admit that she never really loved me. I counted on her love.

It's ironic. I trusted Donna, and she wanted to kill me. I feared the Italians, and they were hired by Paolo's father, Papa Luca, to protect me and saved my life.

Detective Karowisc checked out the Italians when I first told him about the silver car following me. Since it didn't impact on his Venice homicide, he agreed to Papa Luca's request to keep their identity secret. Papa Luca knew I would never agree to their presence.

Again, the irony. I allowed Donna and Randall to hire bodyguards to protect me against the Italians. Because of Donna's connection to Ari and Elon, I was always in danger when they were around.

Blue and I are closer than ever. He'd been living at my house for about two months since the day I was almost killed. Donna planted the suspicion about him so well that when I discovered that brick in his cottage, I jumped to conclusions. But he had simply bought another brick and painted the same design on it, planning to surprise me and replace it.

My main concern is for Jane. She's a resilient kid but she's had so many traumas. I hope these past few months won't have a lasting negative effect on her life.

The day the phone rang, I was expecting Blue to call to say what time he would be home for dinner.

"Mrs. Manganaro?"

"Yes?"

"My name is Linda," said a young woman who sounded like a teenager.

"Is this the Mrs. Manganaro that was almost killed and was in all the newspapers?" she asked. I had to remember to get an unlisted number.

"What is it you want?" What could she want, she was a thrill seeker.

"Well, this is going to sound really weird. I just took a chance that you would be in the phone book, and you were the only Manganaro in west L.A.," she continued. Should I just hang up, then take the phone off the hook?

"Anyway" she continued, "well, don't think I'm nuts for calling but see, I work in a homeless shelter for extra credit at my high school . . ."

"I give to many charities, thank you anyway . . ."

"No, no, it's not that. Well see, there's this one lady here. Someone brought her in; it looked like she had been tied up outside somewhere, maybe to a tree. It was really sad, she had rope burns on her wrists where she wiggled out of them.

"She was cold and hungry. She never speaks; they say she has amnesia. She wanders around outside during the day and always comes back here at night.

"The other day I was reading an old newspaper and it was the article about you. And your picture was in it?" It had made the Metro section, probably because I was Paolo's wife.

"Anyway, this lady all of a sudden just grabbed the paper and stared at your picture. Then she started crying, saying, 'Elizabeth, Elizabeth.' She hasn't left the shelter since. She just stares at the paper all day."

"Where are you located, Linda?" I asked. Was it too fantastic? I had only Donna's word that my mother was dead. My heart started to beat very fast; it even skipped a couple beats. I was shaking as I drove to the shelter.

I found the small house and rushed in. Every one of the dozen beds was occupied. I walked down the center of the room staring at the hopeless, tortured faces. The woman in the last bed was resting, facing the wall. I couldn't see her face. But I knew her shape, the sway of her back, the delicate ankles.

I walked to the bed and said, "Mother?" Her body went rigid, then she turned her face toward mine.

"Elizabeth," she said, as if it was a prayer. I grabbed her and hugged her and we both started sobbing. I took her hand and squeezed it. She squeezed back; she did it twice.